D1636445

FIRE MOUNTAIN AND OTHER SURVIVAL STORIES

FIRE MOUNTAIN AND OTHER SURVIVAL STORIES

A FIVE STAR QUARTET

by Award-Winning Authors

MICHAEL ZIMMER
JOHNNY D. BOGGS
LARRY D. SWEAZY
MATTHEW P. MAYO

EDITED BY HAZEL RUMNEY

WITH A FOREWORD BY *New York Times* BESTSELLING AUTHOR DAVID MORRELL

FIVE STAR
A part of Gale, a Cengage Company

GALE
A Cengage Company

LIBRARY OF CONGRESS CIP DATA ON FILE.
CATALOGUING IN PUBLICATION FOR THIS BOOK
IS AVAILABLE FROM THE LIBRARY OF CONGRESS.

ISBN-13: 978-1-4328-7358-5 (hardcover alk. paper)

First Edition. First Printing: June 2021
Find us on Facebook—https://www.facebook.com/FiveStarCengage
Visit our website—http://www.gale.cengage.com/fivestar
Contact Five Star Publishing at FiveStar@cengage.com

Printed in Mexico
Print Number: 01   Print Year: 2021

TABLE OF CONTENTS

FOREWORD
BY *NEW YORK TIMES*
BESTSELLING AUTHOR DAVID MORRELL

This compelling group of frontier survival stories demonstrates the vastness of the Western genre. One of the authors here, Johnny D. Boggs, edits *Roundup Magazine* for Western Writers of America. When he asks publishers to send him books on a frontier topic, the publishers are sometimes surprised if the books he requests don't include cattle drives, cowboys, gunfights, and saloon brawls. Those elements are certainly part of the American frontier, representing an era that lasted from 1866 to 1881 as Texas ranchers herded cattle north to railroad towns in Kansas. But the frontier had many later phases and earlier ones also, going back to when colonists arrived in New England and Virginia in the early 1600s and when the Spanish reached what is now Mexico, Florida, and all of the southern United States a century before. The collision of those different cultures with each other and with the continent's original inhabitants is a dominant theme in frontier literature.

For New England and Virginia, the frontier was at first a hundred miles of forest, then another hundred miles of forest, then the wilderness beyond the Appalachian Mountains, then the expanse between the Ohio and Mississippi Rivers (the original Northwest Territory), then the vast lands of the Louisiana Purchase, then the trails to Oregon and California, and finally the transcontinental railroad, which linked it all.

From the start, there was a sense (often mournful) of how swiftly things changed. America's first great frontier novelist,

James Fenimore Cooper (1789-1851), wrote five novels about trail scout Natty Bumppo—also known as Hawkeye, Leatherstocking, the Deerslayer, and the Pathfinder. Writing *The Last of the Mohicans* in 1826, Cooper looked back almost three quarters of a century to 1757 and the wilderness of the upper New York region during the French and Indian War with Great Britain. Cooper's Pathfinder feels sympathetic both to the English settlers he guides and the Indians they displace. Indeed his closest friend is a Mohican, Chingachgook, whose son Uncas dies in the climax of the novel, thus making Chingachgook the end of his tribe.

Cooper's *The Prairie* (published in 1827, set earlier in 1805) takes the aging trail scout from the now settled New York region all the way to the frontier beyond the Mississippi. But the Pathfinder says he traveled even farther—to the Pacific Ocean— and complains that he can't find a place where there aren't any people. That scene was written sixty-three years before the U.S. government announced the end of the frontier in 1890 on the basis that nearly every state and territory contained at least a million people.

The four frontier survival stories in this anthology dramatize a comparable westward movement. The first—Larry D. Sweazy's "The Buffalo Trace"—takes place in Indiana in 1807, when its governor established The Indiana Territorial Rangers, a militia of men and woman who, for eight years, rode the route known as the Buffalo Trace, protecting settlers. As a character notes, the buffalo for which the road is named have long since been pushed westward. Similar changes are on the way. "A squirrel can go from treetop to treetop all the way from the Mississippi to the ocean," the character says. "It won't be like that forever. Every time someone moves in, they fell trees and plant a plot of corn. More people come, the less trees there will be. Less trees, less [animals]."

The main characters of Johnny D. Boggs's "Two Old Comanches" know about westward settlement too well. Set later in 1875, the story depicts the dark, brave humor with which two old Indians respond to having been forcibly removed from their western home and placed in the alien landscape of Florida in order to make room for newcomers. Imprisoned by the military, dreaming of their tribe, occasionally allowed to bathe in the impossibly huge pond of the Atlantic Ocean, they escape and begin a westward trek, which replicates that of the settlers who displaced them.

Set farther west than their Great Plains destination, Michael Zimmer's "Fire Mountain" takes us to the mining country of Idaho a few years later in 1878. The first thing Buck McCready notices when he rides into bustling Pineview Creek is how much the town has changed from having been "little more than a raw settlement scratched out along the bank of a swift-flowing stream . . . [with] its lush spring grass, brilliant wildflowers, and towering ponderosa." Now the town has "a thriving business district . . . with glass windows, and roofs of tin and tar, while brightly colored signs advertised everything from beer to boots, cigars and stoves." Pursued by a forest fire, Buck leads a mule train to miners stranded in the mountains, perhaps the last time mules will be needed for a rescue mission because in a year there'll be an easy wagon road.

Finally, Matthew P. Mayo's "Bloodline" takes us all the way west to the California mountains at the close of the 1800s. Although the U.S. government announced the end of the frontier, those mountains are still the frontier as far as its young narrator is concerned. His grandfather hates him for his half-Indian heritage. One beating too many forces the boy to flee in the perhaps futile hope of reaching his father's tribe, if it still exists. The harrowing hunter-hunted chase is grippingly intense, a microcosm of the violent conflicts that shaped the West.

★ ★ ★ ★ ★

David Morrell is the bestselling author of *First Blood,* the novel in which Rambo was created. David thinks of that book as a contemporary Western in which a wandering gunfighter isn't allowed to hang up his weapons. A former board member of Western Writers of America, he writes frequently for WWA's *Roundup Magazine.* His *Last Reveille* is a historical Western about "Black Jack" Pershing's 1916 military expedition into Mexico in pursuit of the bandit Pancho Villa after Villa's men had raided a New Mexican border town. David writes in other genres, as well. His espionage novel, *The Brotherhood of the Rose,* became the only television miniseries to be broadcast after a Super Bowl. He has Comic-Con, Inkpot, Macavity, Nero, and Stoker awards as well as ITW's Thriller Master award and a Bouchercon Lifetime Achievement award.

★ ★ ★ ★ ★

THE BUFFALO TRACE
BY LARRY D. SWEAZY

★ ★ ★ ★ ★

1.

April 1, 1807—Indiana Territory

I held the paper behind my back, trembling with excitement, like it was a secret I couldn't wait to share. Pa looked at me sideways, over wire-frame glasses with deep summer blue eyes, then smiled. "Well, there you are, young miss. What do I owe the pleasure of your company?"

He called me young miss—whether I liked it or not—instead of by my name, Hallie Mae Edson, when he was in a good mood. Whenever I heard my full name come out of Pa's mouth, I knew I'd done something that had riled him. A rare occurrence most days, but I was more than capable of turning his face beet red with restraint on my stormy days. Today, however, was not that day. I was young miss, the apple of his eye, his one and only favorite daughter. I dared to hope that I had half a chance of getting what I wanted.

I stepped inside his workshop and ignored the strong smell of sheep tallow simmering in the iron pot the best I could. Pa was a candlemaker, a trade most often pursued by womenfolk. He had taken up the task after the death of my mother and found more success at it than he'd planned. With new folks moving into the territory everyday, he was busier than a bee working a field of bloomin' spring flowers. He had six broaches going, long pieces of planed wood with multiple cotton wicks that were hand-dipped and trimmed over and over again until the candle was formed. I was glad that the tallow was sheep instead of pig. The stench of pig fat made my stomach roll and the smell would never leave my clothes. School days had been troublesome enough without me smellin' like a market-ready hog. Numbers and letters bored me. I longed to shoot and hunt with my brother, Tom, so it was those things that I took to. Learnin' inside a schoolhouse made me feel like a goat bein' pulled around on a leash.

"I got a question to ask you, Pa," I said, fightin' to hide the paper behind my back. I had never wanted something so bad in my life.

Pa stopped the dipping and studied me right close. "What you got there, young miss?"

"I know you need help here in the shop, Pa, and I can still dip for you. Me and Tom both. We won't be slackin' in our chores none. I promise."

"You're acting like you got ants in your pants on Christmas morning, Hallie Mae. Now why don't you calm down and tell me what has got you all possessed. You haven't been sneaking glances at Will McIntyre again, have you?"

My face flushed red. I could feel the color change rush to my cheeks, then dart to my toes. The mere mention of Tom's best friend gave me a head twirl and an instant sunburn. "This ain't got nothin' to do with no boy."

Pa's face tightened and he settled back in the chair with his spine so straight I feared it might snap. "We don't say 'ain't' in this house, Hallie Mae. You know that. We're not barefooted, uneducated Hoosiers. We're proud, hardworking folk who respect our language and ourselves. I've had this talk with you before and I don't expect to have it again. You're not an ignorant girl. A sloppy one sometimes, but not ignorant. But I figure you'll grow out of that with time and training. Now, tell me what this is all about. I've still got two hundred candles to dip before the moon rises."

14

I looked down to my toes to avoid his glare. Regardless of what Pa had said *I was* barefoot, since it was spring. Any thrill of the mention of Will McIntyre had left my entire body with the tone of admonishment given to me by my pa. I sure did hate to disappoint him. My mouth got ahead of my brain some days. Now it was so dry I couldn't utter a clear word. I had no choice but to hand him the paper.

Pa looked down and read it silent with his eyes, not giving me a clue to what he was thinkin'. I moved my lips when I read. His index finger shivered, giving the announcement an unintentional tap. It was the sign I was looking for. I lowered my head in defeat before he said a word.

"Tom wants to do this, too?" he said, still eyeing the paper like it was the devil come to take me away.

"Says so," I said to my feet.

"You're just a girl, young miss," Pa whispered.

I shook my head. "I'm nothin' like Abagail Peterson, all frilly with ribbons and bows, and acts like she's gonna grow up to be the Queen of England."

"She might be."

"Impossible. Just like it's impossible for me not to be nothin' but what I am. You say so all the time. 'Be yourself. That's the best you can be.' So, I am. I can skin and gut a squirrel faster than any boy around, including Will McIntyre, whose face goes pale at the first sight of blood. I can outshoot him and Tom, and the rest of the boys, too. You made sure that I could fend for myself. Didn't you?" I exhaled to calm myself down, to keep from getting ahead of myself and overstepping my bounds with Pa. I was shocked he hadn't said so yet.

"I know everyone's upset about that Larkin baby," Pa said with a long sigh. "I know the troubles that incident has sparked. I hear it everyday I step outside this shop. The mister is dead with the Indians taking the missus and their children captive.

All five of them, including the baby. Cries of fear have washed up and down the Trace louder than a mob of blue jays pursuing a marauding hawk." He stopped and looked at the paper again. "I fear this struggle with Tecumseh and his brother, the Prophet, will fall to no good for us all. So, this is the response from Governor Harrison? A call to arms putting our young men on the road to make the travelers feel more secure?"

"Young women, too. Calls for us all. Says so right there." I pointed to the paper knowing full well that Pa had read the words I was referencing. He'd chosen to ignore them for as long as he could.

"You're just a girl," he said again.

"And that's all I'll ever be if you keep on saying that." The words jumped out of my mouth unbidden. I wished I could take them back by the cause of pain that flashed across Pa's face, but I couldn't. What was done was done.

"A militia?" he said, relaxing his spine. My heart raced. I saw an opening.

"The Indiana Territorial Rangers," I said with so much excitement my fingers curled around an imaginary trigger.

"And they want you to patrol the Buffalo Trace from Vincennes to Louisville?"

The Buffalo Trace was a wide path pounded into the ground from migrating buffalo making their way to the salt licks in Kentucky. It was a timeworn trail that offered an easy ride from the Ohio River city, Louisville, all the way to the capital of the Indiana and Illinois Territory, Vincennes. Except when whites crossed paths with Indians, and they took it upon themselves to cause troubles and fear. We lived right square between Vincennes and the river, outside of a small dot in the Trace called Cuzco.

"There's to be three divisions," I said, giving Pa more information than was on the paper. Tom had filled me in because of what Will had told him. "Captain William Hargrove and the First Division is gonna patrol from the Wabash River to French Lick. Our own Samuel McIntyre is dustin' off his uniform, and will head up the Second Division, based here in Cuzco."

"So, that's how you know all of this, tagging after Tom?" Pa said.

I wasn't going to let my feelings show any more than I already had. I never tagged after Tom. I was with him is all. And joinin' up with the Rangers had nothing to do with Will McIntyre. At least that's what I was telling myself, and tried to convey to Pa. I could help. Make a difference. Have an adventure that wasn't full of side-mouth gossip and silly giggles.

"Couldn't say," I answered. I rushed past the thought of Will and continued on with what I knew. "Second Division will patrol from French Lick to the Falls of the Ohio, and the Third Division has the east route along the river from Lawrenceburg to the Ohio border."

"You'll be gone for days at a time," Pa said, setting down the paper next to him. He stirred the tallow without looking at me. I wasn't sure what was to come next from him. "Paper says the pay is a dollar a day. That's a fair wage even though you have to supply your own horse, ammunition, and a tomahawk."

"Gotta have a belt and two knives as well. A long and a short."

"You don't have a long knife."

"Tom's out fetchin' one for me. At least finding out if he can find one that's fittin' for me."

"And how do you expect to pay for such a thing?"

"I was hopin' you'd loan me the money against my wages. I'd pay you off first thing before anything else, once I got my first dollar."

"You really want to do this?"

"I do. More than anything. It's the first thing that's come

along that I can stand shoulder to shoulder with Tom and the rest of the boys, and do what I do best. They haven't found that Larkin baby yet. Rest of 'em escaped the Indians, but if somebody don't find that child, he'll grow up a savage, or worse, not grow up at all. I can track a coon on a moonless night better than anyone around. You know I can. Meat's on the table more from my efforts than Tom's."

"That's because he's pining after Nell Jenkins."

"And he's lazy."

"Be nice to your brother."

"I am most days."

"I've thought of that baby, too," Pa said, then stood up and walked toward me, "out there all on its own." He stopped and put his hands on my shoulders with his elbows extended all the way so we was face to face. "You know I couldn't bear losing you. Your pride, confidence, and beauty remind me of your mother everyday. I see so much of her in you that it makes my heart ache sometimes. Just the thought of something happening to you shatters my spirit. Tom, too. But especially you."

"I know I got chores to do, and I'll do my best to keep 'em up, but please don't say no," I whispered, trembling all over.

He shook his head. "I won't tell you no. Tom, neither. I'll get some help with your chores if need be. If your mother was still alive, she would do anything she could to help find that baby and help keep everyone safe. She would have been out the door so fast the wind couldn't have caught up with her skirt. If you want to do this, then go ahead, but you have to promise me that you won't do anything to put yourself in harm's way, and you'll come back to me as soon as you can."

2.

When breakfast came, I was giddy as a ten-year-old on the last day of school. I wasn't sure that Tom had slept any more than I had, which had been about two winks. I knew I wasn't doing myself any good, but I was so ready to start Ranger training that I went to bed in my clothes. All I had to do was wash my face, grab my bag, and walk to the breakfast table like it was any other day. Pa looked like he'd tossed and turned all night, too.

Tom glared at me when I sat down across from him at the eatin' table. "What's the matter with you, you old grouch?"

"I ain't speakin' to you," Tom said. He was a shorter version of Pa, except he was gangly, hadn't grown into himself yet, and clumsy as a mule drunk on soured corn. His curly brown hair was unwieldy and his eyes, the same color as Pa's—all full of summer and clear skies—were most often tinged with kindness. Except when he was mad. Then they was as dark as granite.

Pa looked over his shoulder from the fireplace, but said nothing. He didn't have to. Tom jumped in and corrected himself before anybody could utter another word. "I'm not speaking to you, sister."

Sister. That was my angry name from Tom. Between his pet names for me, and Pa's, sometimes I had to wonder who I was. "And what, pray tell, I have done now, brother?"

He started to say something, but clamped the corner of his lip to contain the words inside his mouth.

"Well, what is it?" I said. "A horse step on your toe? A fly slip down your throat?" Tom was easy to goad and I couldn't help myself. My excitement for the coming day was bubbling over.

"That's enough, Hallie Mae." Pa stopped the fun and sat down two bowls of boiled oats on the table. His eyes looked tired and his face held a grimness that was usually reserved for funerals. His tone snapped the joy out of me as quick as it had come on. "They found the Larkin baby," he said, turning his back to us, tendin' to the fire. We didn't have to ask what the outcome was. Pa's gray face was a shroud of grief.

I was sad before I knew it and I couldn't eat one spoonful of the oats. Tom, on the other hand, ignored the heavy pall in the room and dug into his breakfast and ate like another meal would never come. I let the silence settle between us the best I could. All sorts of songbirds were singing outside the door, welcoming the bright, sunny day that had been bestowed on us. Cardinals, blue jays, sparrows, and yellow canaries were celebrating their wings. They didn't know no better than to be happy at the sight of the sun.

"Why are you mad at me?" I whispered to Tom. Pa was six feet away from us. It wasn't like he couldn't hear me. I was trying to get Tom to answer me.

He took a big swig of milk to wash down the porridge, licked his lips, then returned the glare that had welcomed me when I'd entered the room. "Are you deaf?"

"I can hear you fine."

"I'm not talking to you."

"Yes, you are."

"No, I'm not."

"I guess, I'm hearing things."

Pa turned around from the fire and stalked out the front door. He'd had enough of us. I couldn't say that I blamed him.

Tom watched the door pull shut, then said, "You told him

about the Rangers. You was supposed to wait till I got home."

"Did you get it?" My excitement rekindled itself, sparked by my craving for a new knife.

"Get what? I don't know what you're talkin' about."

"Yes, you do. The long knife. It's all I need."

"So, if I say no, then you'll have to stay behind?"

I leaned forward with my chin over my untouched oats. "So, that's what this is all about. You're afraid you'll get shown up by a girl."

"Am not."

"Are, too."

Tom exhaled, sat back, and crossed his arms. "I got it."

"Good. 'Cause it sounds like we got some Indians to go after."

"They're long gone."

"You sure?"

"Or hidin' out with the British. Ain't no justice gonna get served to those heathens and everybody knows it."

"You shouldn't say . . ."

"And you shouldn't tell Pa things you promised not to." Tom bit his lip again. There he'd had his say. He was pleased with himself. But he was still mad at me.

"I'm sorry," I said. "I was wrong to do that. I couldn't help myself is all." I meant every word I said, too.

"Well, I guess it's my own fault. I know you can't keep a secret any better than an owl. You're always goin' about say who, who, who?" Tom cracked a wry smile then, and I knew we were all right, that he wasn't mad at me no more. "You better eat up. Captain McIntyre don't like recruits bein' late."

I took Tom's advice and started to eat. He did, too. I eyed Pa through the window, standing outside the door, staring off into the distance, toward the cemetery where mother laid in her eternal rest. I saw him there sometimes, talking to her, asking her opinion, nodding as the squirrels chattered above him, as if they were giving him the answers he longed for. I understood his melancholy, his newfound sadness even though he tried not to show it to me and Tom. The loss of the Larkin baby weighed on him, touched his skin like fire to an open wound. Death gave him the shivers. Me, too, but I tried hard not to think about it too much. Losing mother knocked me off my feet, and I've struggled to stand upright ever since she died.

For every bite Tom took, I took two. It was only a few seconds before he caught on to what I was up to, then the race was on. Even though he was a year older than me, he was always trying to catch up to me, beat me at every task. But like most challenges, I won this one easily. I jumped up and washed my plate before Tom could set his spoon on the table. I didn't want Pa to do any more of my chores than he had to if I was gonna be a Ranger.

3.

We assembled outside of Cuzco at the McIntyre place. The morning air was cool and fragrant with the ripe possibility of spring. What was once brown was now transformed into a vibrant, showy green. Grasses shot up in the paddocks, dotted with the spiny leaves of dandelions yet to sprout a bloom. I always thought the flowers looked like tiny suns. All sprinkled together they made a bright yellow blanket that glowed at night. Some folks, like the McIntyres, tended the dandelions to make wine. Pa never took to drinkin' any kind of liquor, but I worried he might get a taste for it after mother's untimely death. He held out, though, I think for Tom and me. Mushrooms were abundant in the woods that skirted the McIntyre's well-kept farm; spongy brown fungus that had to be soaked overnight in salt water to rid the holes and crevices of bugs and dirt. Fried in butter the mushrooms sure were tasty. Titus Findlay ate one of those brown ones with a thick stem and nearly died. You had to be careful which ones you put in the skillet. I heard tell he suffered mightily from stomach pains, producing gas so rank that a new litter of pigs fainted when he struggled to the outhouse. Will McIntyre told me that. I don't know if it was true or not, but I believed everything he told me.

The McIntyre family had come into the territory as soon as it was opened up from somewhere in Virginia. Where exactly never mattered much to me. I was only glad that Will and his family lived close enough for me to see him with some regularity. There wasn't a girl around who didn't stop talking and take notice of Will when he passed by. He was tall with well-formed muscles from hard work, skin bronzed by the sun, and blue eyes that could look right through you and see what you was thinking. To him, I was Tom Edson's little sister, a tagalong that never seemed to annoy him. He hardly acknowledged my presence except when it came to shootin' or knife throwing, then he tried to beat me like I was any other boy. I was glad of that, but sometimes, as long as those times was secret, I wished he would look at me like he did Abagail Peterson—who, to my surprise, had gathered up a horse, long knife, and all of the requirements to be a Ranger, and showed up in the paddock with the rest of us. Of course, she had pink bows in her hair and a tiny bit of rouge rubbed on her cheeks, like she was gonna get all gussied up and be whisked off to Paris, France, instead of protectin' travelers on the Trace. I had to say, I hadn't never seen her in pants before. I had to put my hand over my mouth to keep from laughin' out loud at the first sight of her. She looked like a ragamuffin in the school play from the neck down. I figured it was her brother, Miller's, pants she was a wearin'. They were twice the size of her waist and the cuffs were rolled up on the legs so she could walk without trippin' over her proud self. I wondered how long she was going to last in the hot sun. I figured she'd wilt like a dandelion set to boil.

"I bet you could wrestle her to the ground in two shakes," Tom whispered. He was as amused as I was by the sight of Abagail Peterson lookin' like a toad tryin' to be a frog.

"One shake," I said after seeing Will take notice of Abagail, too.

"You're probably right."

Captain Samuel McIntyre was father to a brood of six boys and two daughters, all younger than Will. They all stood watch from the porch, drawn out by the excitement and most likely the relief of not being under their father's command for the rest of the day. Samuel was an organized man who shared in Will's good looks and strong build, but unlike his son, he took himself serious. He was dressed in the remnants of a Virginia militia uniform and stood straight as a broomstick, watching the dial of his gold pocket watch tick away the seconds, tappin' his foot in wait to call his assembled troops to order.

There were ten of us who had answered the call to arms. Eight boys, me, and Abagail. The boys congregated in the middle, jabbing elbows, guffawing, actin' like the fools they were without taking direct notice of us girls. Abagail stood on one side of the mob and I stood on the other. She ignored me and I offered her the same slight in return. I figured she'd realize what she got herself into once the real training started. I had never seen her run, more less fire a long rifle. I wondered if she'd faint at the first sight of blood, like Will McIntyre.

The captain looked up from his watch, and yelled, "Assemble!" His jaw set hard and he stared in front of him without offering any more instructions.

A few boys kept on talking, Jacob Hopmeyer and Edward Vance in particular, troublemakers since the day they'd arrived in the territory. My guess was their fathers had sent them to join the Rangers to gain some discipline. Lord knew they needed it. The rest of us jumped at the command, forming a wiggly line five feet in front of the captain.

"Straighten up!" Captain McIntyre said. I had never heard him yell before. His voice sounded like a booming drum, and gave me a quick learnin' not to cross him. I didn't want to catch the full force of his attention. No, sirree, I was gonna do everything he said.

Everyone but Jacob and Edward obeyed. They were still engaged in some kind of finger-wrestling contest. Captain McIntyre didn't take kindly to being disobeyed. I heard Will let out a slight whistle, which, in my experience, meant those boys were about to get a thrashin'.

The captain lurched forward and grabbed Jacob by the ear faster than a frog's tongue snatchin' a dragonfly out of the air. "You listen to me, young man," he said. "When I say move, you move and keep your mouth shut. If I have to tell you again, I'll send you straight home to your pa and he can deal with you because I won't. There's too much at stake here. Do you understand?" To emphasize his seriousness, the captain gave Jacob's captive ear a good twist. He offered the boy a look that dared him to yell out in pain.

To my surprise and relief, Jacob mumbled a, "Yes, sir," and stood there and took the ear twist like a man even though he was a few years from that in my mind. We all were under the age of twenty.

Captain McIntyre let go of Jacob, then returned to his place, heading up the middle of the line. "That goes for the rest of you, too. Do I make myself clear?"

It was as if we all had been joined at the hip and sung in the church choir since we was nothing more than babies. "Yes, sir!" we all said in unison. Even Abagail showed enthusiasm.

"That's more like it," the captain said. "Bein' a member of the Indiana Territorial Rangers is serious business. There's Indians out there heartless enough to leave an infant to fend for itself against the bears, and we're gonna put a stop to that. Understand?"

"Yes, sir!" Our voices reached heaven on wings forged of disgust and anger. Pa hadn't told us what had happened to the Larkin baby, but the captain saw fit to make it our business now that we had an official reason to know.

"Good," he said. "We're gonna train hard and fast for two weeks, then you'll be set to the road. One on horseback, one on foot, carrying the long rifle. Don't matter if you're a boy or a

26

girl, everybody that signed up has to qualify in both tasks. Looks like we'll have five sets, that is if the lot of you don't go runnin' home like whimperin' pups shoved off a teat. This is tough work and you'll earn your dollar a day twice over. Understood?"

"Yes, sir!" Even Jacob and Edward wore serious faces now. There was a reason the captain took himself serious and the McIntyres were some of the best-behaved children in the territory. The captain said what he meant and meant what he said. I liked him.

It wasn't long before we were lined up single file, waitin' to show off our horse-ridin' skills. Me and Tom had been riding since we was old enough to stand. I wasn't sure about anyone else other than Will. He was as good as they come on a horse. He rode a roan mare who listened to him like the rest of the girls. She was as captivated by him as any human, and sometimes, I thought that horse could read his thoughts, for there wasn't a move he needed to command her to make. She knew ahead of time which way he wanted to go and how fast he wanted to get there.

Will was up last, so I would have to wait to watch his grace on that mare. Jacob Hopmeyer was first up, directed by the captain to run a route around four rain barrels front to back, then opposite. Fast, then slow, counted off by Tom who had been appointed as the timekeeper. Captain said it wasn't no race but, if there was time involved, it sure seemed like a race to me. I couldn't wait to get into the saddle of my ride, a trusted brown I called Ol' Hank. He was a hefty boy, up to pulling a plow as much as he was made for ridin'. Considering Pa was a candlemaker, there wasn't much need to farm other than the fresh garden we needed to get through the seasons. Ol' Hank had a mind of his own but he liked me well enough, as long as I didn't yank too hard on his bit. He had soft teeth.

Jacob rode a draft horse that was as slow as spring comin'

on. Good Lord, you have to wait forever for the cold and snow to go away. That horse didn't know the word *hurry*. Captain McIntyre frowned as he watched Jacob traverse the barrels.

One after one we went. Edward, Abagail, then me. Abagail was a better rider than I thought her to be. Her horse, a skinny little black mare, cut low and fast on the turns, and for a second, I feared she was gonna get a better time than me. That mare kicked up some dust, and gained a nod of approval from the captain, until she took a straight run and failed to give the horse its head. It fought her then, and went into a braying fit. I was relieved even though I knew better than to celebrate someone else's failure. I had something to prove.

I whispered in Ol' Hank's ear askin' him not to be his stubborn self. I needed a win. Can't say for sure if he understood or not, but he didn't moan when I took to the saddle. I ran him hard, cut deep myself, then freed him to run on the long stretch. Wind in my face, eyes focused on the barrel, I didn't think a whit about that Larkin baby, or why those Indians left him to die. I rode to win, to be free, to become something I wasn't. When I crossed the finish line, Tom quit his countin' and a bead of sweat slid down the side of my ear. I swear it hit the ground and cried out in pain. Captain wasn't givin' out times 'til the end, but when I ran past, I could tell he was impressed with my turn at the barrels. That was all I wanted, other than beatin' Abagail Peterson.

Tom went then with Will takin' over with the timin'. He ran a good lap, but didn't elicit any kind of response from the captain. Neither did Will when he ran, even though it was obvious to everyone—grace married to the speed of thunder—that he was the best of us before he came to a sidestepping stop. If it had been anyone else, I would have thought they'd cheated, run the course before anyone else had had a chance. But it was Will McIntyre, and he weren't no cheater.

The captain didn't announce the winner, to which we were all relieved and disappointed. He said there'd be another chance tomorrow. Then the day after that. We was gonna run to the end, then we'd have one race to set the winner in stone. I liked that idea. Gave me time to improve, to watch Will's line as he curved around the barrels.

All the trainin' was gonna be like that. Short knives. Long knives. Rifle shootin'. We'd all compete with ourselves day after day, until the end, then we'd find out who was who, and what we was gonna be on the Trace. Captain said a flower didn't bloom in a day and he was right about that.

4.

Every night before I fell asleep, I wished to dream of my mother. Her voice was like the distant wind. I had to strain to hear it in my memory. Some days I dropped my own voice a might deeper, hopin' to hear something of her words come from my own mouth, but nothin' ever did. I missed her something fierce. I knew Pa and Tom did, too. They didn't say so, but I could see it in their faces and on their shoulders. Other days, I tried to catch a glimpse of Mother in my own reflection. I suppose it was there as much as it was in Tom's eyes, too, but it was like I was blind to her. It was, however, my good fortune to have her blanket in my possession. I didn't sleep with it or use it for warmth. I kept the soft blue wool cover in a wood box under my bed. Along with my wish, I'd sneak a deep sniff of the material and try and breathe in her scent as much as possible, then I'd lay flat on my back and try to conjure an image of her. Sad to say, she never came to me in the middle of night to offer me comfort or love. After a dreary long winter and a few short months of spring I had started to understand that dead was dead. She was gone forever and there was nothin' I could do to bring her back. My heart broke for those Larkins and I couldn't help but cry myself to sleep one more time.

Trainin' days wore me out, but I had promised Pa that I would still dip for him in the evening. The flood of folks comin' west needed candles to light their way. After twelve-hour days in the sun, if it was nice out, or in the rain if spring was bein' spring, I'd head straight out to the shop after eatin' a bit of supper. The McIntyres put on a big dinner spread in the midafternoon after a mornin' of marchin', shootin', knife fightin', and the like. Will was a lucky boy to have a momma who could cook for her own brood and ten more mouths, and not notice or complain about the extra effort. She said she was accustomed to cookin' in oversized batches, and I suppose that was the truth. She made fatback and beans, cornbread, young nettle salad picked straight from the woods behind the house, and baked a rhubarb pie that was near the best I ever remember. There wasn't a thing about Missus McIntyre that reminded me of my own mother, other than the joy she took in the care of her children and all of us Rangers that were donned on her to look after now that we had come under the captain's charge. Missus McIntyre was thick and wide as a milking cow, and wore the same kind of soft, understandin' brown eyes. She smelled of flour, salt, and freshly turned garden soil, and like the captain, I was enamored with her, too. It was easy to see in her perpetual cheerfulness that at some point she had been a pretty girl. Time and birthin' children had dimmed her looks, but not her spirit. She was the sun in the house and her light touched everyone around her. Even the captain, who I wouldn't have thought liked playing second fiddle to anyone. But he did to her, to My Lady as he called her, with grace and kindness. Will was a fine combination of them both, and it wasn't no surprise that he had a glow of his own.

With all that went on in my days, it was surprisin' that I didn't fall asleep standing up with a broach in my hand and thirty more candles to dip. But somehow, I managed to meet the demand of my days as a Ranger and my nights as a candlemaker's daughter. Tom, too. We both worked harder than we thought we were capable.

The days passed through rain, sunshine, and a baby's funeral.

His fragile body given back to the soil and his soul offered up to heaven. It was a sad, gray day, and all of us Rangers stood together in a tight formation, shoulder to shoulder, our faces washed of youth and replaced with the hunger for justice, and revenge—until Elvira Larkin stood and begged us to give up our arms and any thought of continuing violence. She was a Quaker and did not believe in an eye for an eye. For a moment I considered heeding her words, but I couldn't help the feelin' I had, that Baby Matthew had been robbed of seeing a full life only because his family had set foot on the wrong side of the Trace. Even in the deep hours of the night when I laid awake in my comfortable bed, all I could hear was dirt cascading down on that small wood coffin. I knew I couldn't do anything to bring that baby back any more than I could my own mother, but maybe I could stop a tragedy from happenin' to someone else. I would wake more convinced that my longin' to be a Ranger was the right thing, a good thing, and that would spark my feet to the ground into a run straight to the McIntyre's place.

It was hard to believe that time had passed so quickly. Our two weeks of trainin' was almost up. Three more days, then we'd be out on patrol, ridin' up and down the Trace doin' our best to bring peace of mind to the near constant band of travelers who were on their way to one place or the other. Edward and Jacob had fallen in line, goofin' around only when time called for it. Jacob turned out to be a fine horseman and it was pretty easy to see what job he was gonna get. The rest of the boys learned pretty quick to take me as a serious threat to makin' them look bad when it came to shootin' and handlin' a short knife. The long knife was my bane. I'd never toyed with one much. Well, not at all, until Tom brung me home one. I wasn't the worst skilled one among us, but pretty close. I was near top of the pack with the rifles, tight behind Will, which was no surprise. The greater surprise was that Abagail was still holding her own. She was a fair shot, a decent rider, and capable of fending off attacks with both knives. Her momma had taken her clothes more serious since Abagail had put herself forward into the heap of Rangers. She spoke to me when she had to but most of the time she shadowed Will, hopin' to catch his eye. I tried to hide my jealous tendencies, but I was a duck out of water when it came to that. There wasn't no foolin' anybody about how I felt about Will McIntyre, and that uncontrollable emotion caused me a great deal of grief and embarrassment. Tom teased me unmercifully. Even the captain took time to note my infatuation with his son, warnin' me to focus on duties at hand and quit searchin' for rainbows over Will's pretty head. I didn't shoot worth a darn that day.

5.

"Where's Tom?" I said to Pa. Tom was nowhere to be seen, his spot at the table empty and untouched.

Pa was stirring the oats, had his back to me, his shoulders sagging with permanent exhaustion, dressed for his day in the shop. "He went on without you."

The quick response struck me as odd. Me and Tom always walked to trainin' together. We talked about the day before, what we had to do, how things were goin', that kind of thing. Bein' a Ranger had brought us closer together, put a lid on our sorrow, gave us somethin' in common we'd never had before. From what I could tell, we was matched as even as the tassels on summer corn; only the wind made one higher than the other. I hadn't said anything wrong or done nothin' to shame Tom that I knew of, so I was bewildered by his absence.

"He say why?" I said.

"No." Pa was stiff, didn't move a muscle other than what was required to attend to his duty in the fireplace. The cabin was stuffy, humid, like all the air had been sucked out of it when Tom had left. My gut said something was amiss, but Pa's tone and attitude warned me off of pursuing the question any further. I was sad for a second longer, then I realized I was more hungry than anything.

"That's all right," I said and sat down in my spot at the table.

Pa served me my breakfast and left me to eat it all on my own. I wanted to rush out after him as he hurried to the shop, but I knew he was focused on his work, had to ready the dipping pots for the day. He's weary from all the work. That's all it is. Nothing is wrong. I told myself all of this even though I didn't believe it. After mother passed, I saw a crack of gloom in every ray of sunshine. So did Pa and Tom.

It wasn't long before the air hung low with the faint smell of sheep tallow, a new fire, and the curiosity of a sour mood held familiar court over the world. Even the clouds drooped with grayness and promised turmoil in the hours to come. A spring storm was brewin' over the trees; thunderheads reached and roiled in the tumultuous sky, growing by the second. But that didn't mean that trainin' would stop. Just the opposite. Captain said we had to be versed in all kinds of weather. Danger and travelers didn't stop 'cause of the threat of rain or discomfort. If that was the case, none of us would be here.

I finished up my breakfast and gathered myself together quicker than I usually had to. Tom's absence had caused me to linger longer than normal. I rushed to the barn, saddled Ol' Hank, and made sure I had my short knife secured in my belt. It was the only weapon I carried at the moment. Captain's tack stall served as an armory for our rifles and long knives. Once I was settled in the saddle, I hurried away from the cabin, leaving the smell of candles and Pa's sullenness to hisself.

Ol' Hank took pleasure in the early mornin' run. Our cabin was a good ways away from Cuzco and even farther from the Trace. To get to the main road, I had to go north about half a mile, down a ravine and up another, then rush a stretch to the McIntyre place.

The path to the trainin' field was nothing more than that, a deer path worn wide over the years as folks came and went to buy candles, peddle wares to us, or visit during happier times. I knew the dirt and turns like the pores in my skin. A hard right here. A run through a good fishin' creek there—fingerin' off the

Wabash—dotted with monstrous sycamores spotted white and brown by thin, peeling bark that seemed to glow in the summer sun. The leaves on those ol' trees were as big as plates and with the wind riled up, they flapped like fans, pushing the air against my face like they were born of a distant tornado. To make things even worse, the light had dimmed deeper, grayed by the storm clouds and the new batch of leaves that had already began to deprive the ground of a constant source of light. Thunder clapped in the distance and I urged Ol' Hank on. I sure did wish Tom was with me.

I wasn't afraid. At least I thought I wasn't until I took a turn on the edge of the Russells' cow pasture—our nearest neighbors. Once I cleared the curve, I came full on into a roadblock. I had to pull Ol' Hank to a sudden stop, which he complained about with might and disdain; whinnying and snorting like he'd been gouged with a red-hot poker. Poor horse gave me a spiteful look, but obeyed the evil bit in his mouth.

Two men dressed in travelin' garb, one tall and the other short and round, stood with horses nose to nose, blocking my way past. More thunder roared in the distance—but it was growing closer. Wind slapped my face and I could hear my heart beating in my chest. They didn't look friendly, not friendly at all.

"Well, well, looka here, Miles, we found us a girl in a hurry that ain't goin' nowheres," the tall man said.

"Looks like," the short one said. They both wore dark hooded cloaks, had scraggly beards, onyx eyes, and faces I'd never seen before. Neither of them had a welcoming tone. They looked at me the way a cat looks at a mouse before it claws in for the kill.

The hair on the back of my neck stood on end and I didn't like the way I felt. Ol' Hank felt the tension through the reins and danced to the right a bit.

"Best get that horse under control, girl," the man called Miles said.

Ol' Hank snorted and lifted his tail to drop a load. I liked his response. My instinct said I should make a run for it. These men were up to no good. Pa had found opportunity in the flood of travelers makin' their way into the territory and so had men like these. Bandits. Robbers. Thieves. Call 'em what you want, but they was the reason there was a need for Rangers. Them and Indians. As if we didn't have enough to worry about . . . Illness took mother, not men with evil intent.

I looked over my shoulder to check for a way free and my heart dropped. Two more men had appeared, dressed similar in clothes and demeanor as the two in front of me. Something told me they were all together, working as a team to trap me.

With the way behind me taken away as my way of escape, my eyes darted to the right, then to the left. One side of the road offered a deep wooded ravine peppered with blackberry thickets, and the other side dropped straight down to a shallow creek, the sides sandy and unstable. The four men had picked their spot well. I wasn't going anywhere.

Miles handed the round man the reins of his horse, a young gelding that had midnight eyes like its rider. I had to make a decision quick. He was coming for me, I could tell.

With that thought in mind, I spun Ol' Hank around and jumped off him. We were heading back the way we came. I slapped the horse's solid behind and yelled at him to run. He did exactly what I told him to. I knew with a distant whistle, the horse would come back to me like a loyal dog. Ol' Hank ran straight through the two horses, pushing the men to the side of the road, saving themselves from being trampled. I darted to the sandy side, jumped over the edge, and slid down to the creek before any of the men could gather themselves to come after me. I disappeared into a thick stand of grass that was unaware that the new leaves and shade overhead would drown out the sun soon—but at the moment, I was glad for the presence of it. I could hide, wait for the men to make their next move. Which didn't take long. Two of them came after me, Miles and the round man.

I scurried across the creek and pulled out my knife. I ran faster than I ever had in my life, heading north, toward the safety of the McIntyres' land. I was close, but I didn't know these woods like I knew my own. I did know my way in the woods, though, since I'd spent a good part of my life under the canopy of elms, oak, and sycamores. Spotting a game path was second nature and I found one quick. But the bad thing was the weather. Morning had turned into night; the sky was black as the rot on a pig's foot and thunder brought forth more lightning than I wanted to see. I feared a tree strike or worse. A bolt needlin' to the ground and catchin' me on fire. Death would be quick, unlike what faced me if I let myself be caught by the men giving me chase.

I ran fast, but Miles ran faster. I was on a climb upward, close to a paddock or field, one that I hoped would lead me to help. I started screaming my fool head off. But it didn't do me any good. Most likely, it slowed me down. I felt a hand on my shoulder, then pressure that forced me to stop. I was spun around against my will. Caught. In danger. I didn't have time to recall everything I'd been taught in the last two weeks. I couldn't think. It was all I could do to push away my fear so it wouldn't paralyze me.

I was panting, he was panting, but I had my knife out, ready to fight, and the man wasn't about to let me go after workin' so hard to catch me. Before I knew it, he had both his hands on my wrists, binding the movement of my hands with his power and strength. I could have given up, since the threat of the knife—which I still held—had been rendered useless. But I knew better. I stepped back and with all of my might, I jumped up, raising my wrists to my chest with all of the strength I had. The move, showed to me by the captain, proved effective and gave me my freedom as I broke out of the man's grasp, though not without a cost. My knife fell to the ground.

I had another quick choice to make. Stand and fight, or run.

I chose to run. There was no way I could survive four against one. That's what the captain said. "First order of business is to keep yourself alive. Do whatever it takes. Stand and fight if you only got a chance of winnin'." Seemed simple at the time he said it. Not so much now.

I tore away from Miles as quick as I could and headed toward the field.

Once I was at the top of the ridge, facing blowing wind and rain, I came face to face with another man. Only this time I recognized him. It was Captain McIntyre, still as a statue, eyeing me like he was judgin' a cake in a church bakin' contest. I was pale with terror, shaking with fear, but relieved to feel rescued. I stopped before him, trying my best to catch my breath and tell him that danger was on my heels, heading our way. I had never been so happy to see a man I knowed in my life.

He nodded, and said with a calm voice, "You did good, Hallie Mae, except one thing. You left 'em your knife."

"What do you mean I did good?" I said between heartbeats.

"This was a test to see how you'd fare on your own," he said, "how you'd react to an attack or bein' held up. Only thing you did wrong was let go of your weapon and give it to the enemy. I bet you'll be more careful next time, won't you?"

"Yes, sir," I answered as I came to grasp that what had happened had not been real, but an exercise, a test, to see what I had learned and nothing more. I thought I was going to die—or worse, be taken in by men who would do unmentionable harm to me.

Miles and the other men showed themselves, came up into the field as the storm came to a crescendo over our heads. They were friends of the captain's, no more a threat to me than a lamb was.

"Come on," Captain McIntyre said, "let's get inside before this wind blows us all away. Don't worry about your horse. The fellas will bring it back."

We all headed toward the house, equal in step and stature, relaxing from the fear of attack by the men, but still concerned about the weather.

6.

Pa took time out of his day to come see Tom and me graduate into bein' full Rangers. It was a proud day, clear of storms, bright and sunny, perfect for a ceremony and a grand feast put on by Missus McIntyre. Roast chicken, new potatoes, fresh cream gravy, asparagus, bread, and rhubarb pie. All the other women brought a dish to share. All Pa had to offer was his presence and a free candle for all the graduates and the captain. It was enough, I think, since I'd been busy with trainin' and couldn't make somethin' myself. The table sat out in the air in front of the house was so pretty I almost hesitated to take anything and put it on my plate. I'd never seen so much food in my entire life.

All of us, in one way or another, had been tested by the captain. Our worthiness to take to the Trace judged as capable, or not. Eight of us had made the grade. To no one's surprise, Edward and Jacob had failed to stand up to the demands set forth to take on the Ranger way of life. But to my surprise and everyone else's, Abagail Peterson had passed with near honors. In my defense, she dropped her knife and was captured by Miles and his gang, but she had escaped after the round one took a swift kick in the you-know-wheres—somethin' I noted to remember. Her desire to stay in Will's company and impress him with her skills—still a shock to me—was higher than I had anticipated. So, six boys and two girls formed Captain McIntyre's Indiana Territorial Rangers division. Only two other girls had attained status in the other companies, with ours being the only one with a multiple of females. Even though my companion was Abagail, I was proud of that fact.

After our meal and a few kind words from Captain McIntyre, we was paired up in four teams. Tom was put with Abagail straight away, to which I was relieved. I stood in wait to see who my partner would be, hoping on one hand it would be Will, and on the other that it wouldn't. I feared his presence would distract me from the seriousness of the business of bein' a Ranger, now that I was official. When it came down to it, I got exactly what I wanted. Me and Will McIntyre was gonna ride and walk the Trace together. I could tell by the look on Abagail's face that she had no plans to speak to me ever again. And that was fine with me. I didn't care if she whispered a song in my ear at that moment. She could fly away with Tom and be as silent as a polecat—and as stinky—for all I cared. It took all I had to contain my excitement and glee. Especially as the menfolk walked off, taking to their smokes and small talk, and I was left to help Missus McIntyre, her two daughters, and mothers of the other Rangers to clean up. Oh, Abagail lingered back, too, but she was too sullen to speak with anyone. Her job was cleanin' plates in piles, savin' the leftovers, and sortin' the chicken bones for garden fertilizer.

"You done yourself right proud," the captain's wife said. "Are you up to it?" She looked at me with concerned blue eyes, soft and penetrable, just like Will's.

"Yes, ma'am, I am. Wouldn't have come along to train if I didn't think I could hold my own."

She nodded. "I've watched you from afar. You have fair skills for the weaker sex." She held my gaze and something in her face changed. I wasn't sure what it was. A hardness of some kind. Jealousy, maybe. Or fear. I wasn't sure which or what. I didn't have much experience with readin' faces or words that weren't spoke.

"Pa made sure I had the skills I needed in case he wasn't around to look out for me. This ain't Philadelphia."

"Isn't."

"Yes, ma'am."

"Your pa has done a good job with you and Tom. Your mother was a dear woman. Bless her soul in heaven. I wonder if she would have been so enthusiastic in your endeavors?"

We walked along the table slow as snails, collecting plates as we talked. Our voices were low. No one was paying us any mind. I wasn't sure why the missus was concerned, especially now, after I'd won my place among the Rangers. If she had reservations about my welfare, I would have thought she would have expressed herself before now.

"Did I do something wrong?" I said.

Missus McIntyre stopped. There wasn't a spot of anything splattered on her bright white apron. She was put together in a perfect way from head to toe, but her face looked so hard that it was about to shatter. "No, dear, I'm concerned about you is all." She put her hand on my shoulder. "Out there in the hinterlands, on the Trace to protect folks with knives and guns. I worry that any of you are up to the task."

"You're worried about Will, aren't you?" I almost regretted sayin' such a thing to an elder, especially in the tone that flittered out of my mouth.

"Of course, I am. But I'm more worried about all of the dangers you two will face alone."

I examined my toes hidden inside my walkin' boots and hoped my face didn't flush red at her suggestion. It wasn't somethin' I hadn't thought about myself, but I didn't want to admit such a thing aloud.

"We got us a job to do, ma'am, and I 'spect Will and me can do that, like we was two boys, if that's what worries you. It was

43

the captain's wisdom to set us together, and beyond that, it was Governor Harrison who had to give way to boys and girls bein' able to serve in a protection corp."

"You're a smart girl, Hallie Mae. I'll expect you to mind your manners is all. Am I clear?"

"Yes, ma'am." I stopped and looked past her, into Abagail's green eyes—who was standing close enough to listen—and said, "Am I dismissed now?"

Missus McIntyre didn't answer, she kept on walking.

I turned and ran to join up with the men and Tom. I needed to be where I belonged more at that moment than any other.

7.

Me and Will had never spent much time alone. A moment here, when Tom had to go after something, or a moment there, when we was waitin' on one thing or the other—usually Tom. But never hours at a time. Much less the thought of a whole day, or days, as far as that went. The thought of such a thing made me giddy, but deep in my heart I knew I had a job to do and this adventure had nothing at all to do with spending time with Will McIntyre. Even though it did.

Me an Ol' Hank were teamed up and Will was on foot. Captain's orders. We started out at Cuzco, early on a fine April mornin' with the air fragrant with honey locust, solomon's seal, and the promise of a new day ahead of us. The sky was streaked with clouds that looked like wiggly first graders' lines, puffed on the sides by unseen and unfelt wind. Birds were busy building nests, or tending to their new broods of hungry mouths. Bluebirds sat atop trees, singin' their hoarse robin's song to the world, letting everyone in earshot know that everything was well and good even if they were a bit weary. Which was fine with me. I would have hated to have started out on a stormy day.

My saddlebags were loaded down with enough food from Missus McIntyre's kitchen to last three days even though we were only going to be gone for two. That was the plan. A short trip to start. Once we returned, Tom and Abagail would take our place. We would rest two days, or in my case help Pa catch up on the candle dippin' I missed out on. After a few trips,

45

we'd extend our tours to three and four days, but never more than that. Three teams would be out at once with one in for a rest. It was a smart system, all managed by the captain, who took his own turn patrollin' the Trace with one or another of us. Along with the Rangers, there were four couriers, one assigned to each of the three divisions and one to the headquarters in Vincennes, to send instructions and communicate between all of the captains and the governor. I had feared being placed as a courier until I realized that none of them were girls. Couriers rode alone. That would never do for a girl. There was no escapin' special considerations for boys. I didn't say nothin' to no one about that. It was the way of the world. At least I was on the trail, on the adventure, keepin' the fine folks of the territory as safe as I could.

Will was outfitted head to toe with weapons and ammunition. Like all of the Rangers on foot, he carried a Harper's Ferry Model 1803 rifle. The same muzzleloader that Lewis and Clark had carried with them on their expedition west. Will was a fair shot, but I was better, and that was no empty boast. My targets shattered twice the number of times as his. He was a little clumsy with the load, which even to me was a complex series of maneuvers, but so was everyone else. Loading and firing took time, and one of our chores was to practice at least once a day while we was out on the Trace—even the riders. Along with the rifle, Will carried a measure, a powder horn, a pouch for the wads and gunpowder, his long and short knives, and his tomahawk. He had the heavy burden of carrying the rifle. Ol' Hank bore the brunt of my assortment of weapons and necessaries, exceptin' the short knife sheathed on my right hip. Put simply, we was cocked and loaded for bear, bad trouble, or a long boring ride, which was what we both hoped it to be. I wasn't quite up to a run in with Indians or men like I had thought Miles and his gang to be.

Since it was still spring and the air prone to be cool, we both wore buckskin jackets and pants. I had on my floppy brown felt hat with my hair braided and stuffed down my back. Since I was a skinny girl, I could pass for a boy until you got close up on me, or I had to speak, which I left to Will if the need came. Wasn't nobody's business that I was a girl. I wasn't gonna show 'em what I was in case they thought me less, weak, or unfit to be a Ranger.

We was a load of miles down the Trace, headin' for the Falls of the Ohio, before we encountered our first travelers. It was nigh on toward the falling tilt of the sun. It wouldn't be long before we set out to find a spot to strike camp. They was a man and a woman, goin' the same ways as us, ridin' in a cart stacked with all of their earthly belongings, pulled by a muddied old gray ox that didn't look none too pleased at the chore he'd been yoked for.

We caught up with the pair easily, and they seemed inclined for a bit of company, so they pulled over to the side, and welcomed us to talk a bit.

"Where you boys headin'?" the man said with a wave. His arms were skinny as a broomstick and his head was as bald as a hairless and pink baby mouse. His wife was twice his size with a sad look painted across her blubbery face. She worried a wad of chew of some kind in her left cheek, and spit every once in a while.

I smiled inward, of course, at the deception of boys, other than it wasn't no deception. Not really. My disguise, if it could be called that, was more for my own safety than anything else.

"To the river," Will answered. "We're Rangers. Indiana Territorial Rangers, put here by Governor Harrison to keep you safe."

"You? And that gnat of a boy there?" the man said.

That didn't make me smile.

"Yes, sir," Will said. "Only she ain't no boy. That there's a girl. Governor Harrison seems to think the Trace is a fit place for us all. I'd be inclined to disagree, but I've knowed this here girl since I was a tot, and I'll tell you, she can outshoot any fella in the territory."

"Is that so," the man said.

"Yes, sir."

"Then how come you're carryin' the rifle?"

"Because she's better throwin' a knife."

It was a fine comeback and I was proud of Will for bein' so quick to my defense. I held the man's gaze, then dropped my fingers to the hilt of the short knife on my hip. He looked away real quick.

"Well, then, I'm glad to know there's a patrol on this road. Makes me feel better," the man said.

"Do you have news?" Will said.

"You heard of Tecumseh and that brother of his gatherin' in Greenville?"

"No, sir, I didn't."

I sat atop Ol' Hank and watched and listened. The woman in the cart looked bored, like she'd heard everything the man said a hundred times over.

"Well," the man continued. "I heard tell there was a mass of Injuns there. A thousand from one man, while another said the number was closer to four hundred. Now, you know there's no good that can come from that many Injuns bein' in one place, no matter how benevolent Harrison is to 'em. That Prophet is fillin' their heads with all kinds of nonsense about magical powers and witchcraft of the like. I don't know nothin' about that, but there's concern all the way to Washington. I heard tell there's a half-blood Shawnee that took a letter from the president to Tecumseh to try and smooth things over. Tecumseh sent the man away and told him to tell the president to come there and meet him face to face. Can you imagine such a thing, a heathen tellin' the president what to do and where to go?"

"No, sir," Will said, "I cannot."

"That's all I know for now. There's a storm brewin' among the tribes. Miami. Delaware. Shawnee. All being pulled and played by the French and British. Like I said, I sure am glad that you two are out here, but I sure hope you're outfitted enough to take on what's comin' for you, 'cause I don't think ya are. Don't matter if that girl's a good shot or not. You gotta get the ball down the barrel and powder in the pan before one of them savages comes for your scalp."

Will nodded and took into consideration what the man said. "We're ready. And if you're not in need of our services any further, we'll be on our way."

"Are there more behind you?" the man said.

"There will be. Now, don't you worry. Something unseen happens, you send up some smoke and we'll come a runnin'."

"I'll do that. I hope you get there in time. I don't want to end up captured like those Larkins."

"That's why we're here," Will said.

8.

We stood high on a ridge looking west over an abundance of treetops bathed in the fadin' light of the day. Fresh tender leaves, tinted gold as if they had been touched by an unseen god, stretched out for as far as I could see. Striped clouds lined the pale sky overhead, drained of blue, almost white, touched by fire hot enough to melt gold. The sun was gone, tucked in under the horizon. There was a little breeze; a caress wrapped around us causing only the slightest flitter of anything tethered. A fire crackled behind us with a comfortable flame. Awaiting next to the spit made of fresh green sticks was a skinned and gutted rabbit. Will took it with one shot to the head. I was impressed. Of course, he could have blown the thing to bits and I still would have been impressed.

Will was transfixed by the view. One of the finest I had ever seen. I'd never been this far down on the Trace so it was a new world to me.

"They say a squirrel can go from treetop to treetop all the way from the Mississippi to the ocean out east without ever touchin' the ground," Will said. "It won't be like that forever."

"Why do you say that?"

"Look at the land around Cuzco. Every time someone moves in, they fell trees and plant a plot of corn. More people come, the less trees there will be. Less trees, less squirrels."

I looked at Will's face all awash in the golden light, his hard chin jutted forward, his summer blue eyes glistening with an extra dab of moisture from peekin' into the future too hard. His brow was furrowed with worry instead of the possibility of youth. I had never seen him so serious. Ruminatin' on the state of the world was a side of him I had never seen before. It was almost like I was lookin' at a different person. For all the years he'd exchanged shadows with Tom, at that moment I discovered that I didn't know Will McIntyre at all.

"You sound like a sympathizer to Tecumseh and his like," I said.

"I'm defending the way of life I love. Aren't we the same, me and him?"

"You ain't spreadin' lies about magic powers like him and his brother are doin'."

"He don't know no better," Will said. "He's protectin' what's his and what's always been his. Now, here we come changing things that have been the same for hundreds of years. Look at this road we're a standin' on. Where's the buffalo that made it? You ever seen one?"

"No." I looked to the ground, to the Trace, and tried to imagine what a herd of buffalo on a trek to a salt lick looked like. I couldn't see such a thing in my mind because I'd never seen such a thing before me. I'd never seen a buffalo in my life.

"They're all gone is why. Or near gone. How does that happen?"

I shrugged and looked away. I didn't want to think about such things. As much as I hated to give up the view, I turned and made my way back to the fire. It was past time to eat.

Will stood still as a statue for a long time, looking out across the expanse, thinking thoughts I never knew he was capable of, seeing things I had no idea of, and dreaming of a life that included me and everyone one of us back home. If I had liked him before from a distance, I liked him even more up close.

After we ate, our night passed with one of us standing sentinel over the other. An owl hooted in the distance, and another hooted back. A coyote yipped. Something growled down the hill, its discomfort floating upward in the air, too far away to reach us with its claws. I watched over Will as he slept, and I eyed the Trace for any comers. Through it all, I wasn't afraid nary a bit. I was exactly where I was supposed to be. It felt right. And I knew bein' a Ranger suited me. I liked seein' folks take comfort in my presence.

The next day, another blessed relief of calm weather with a sky as cheerful as a China doll's face, greeted us as we turned around and made our way back to Cuzco. We passed travelers, assured them that they were safe, gathered what news there was, and arrived home without any scars of confrontation or encounters with bad luck. Captain McIntyre was happy to see us and sent Tom and Abagail straight out onto the Trace in our place.

I headed home to our cabin, knowing full well that I had work to do there, candles to dip, time to spend with Pa and assure him that this new way of life would work out for us. He looked even wearier than he had when I'd left. I wondered if it was possible for exhaustion to spread in two days, as quick as a fever?

"Are you all right?" I said, studying Pa's face in the dim light of the shop. His shirt was wilted and his face looked like it was gonna melt right off. I had also got the first whiff of pig tallow, and I wasn't real happy to be reacquainted with the smell. He must of used up all the sheep tallow and had to resort to the pig. He'd been a busy man.

"More orders keep coming in," he said, dipping and talking at the same time, solidifyin' my assumption.

"Maybe you could hire a boy. Jacob Hopmeyer's brother. He's a good worker. You said so yourself."

"I have two children of my own."

"We're not children anymore, Pa. Some girls my age have done got married and brought a baby or two into this world."

"You're not gonna, are you?"

"Well, I hope to get married some day, but not anytime soon, if that's what you mean."

Pa froze in his movement and stared at me, examined me from head to toe, still dressed in my Ranger garb; buckskins soiled from the road, my hair still in a braid, Trace dirt under my fingernails. No boy would look twice at me if he was in his right mind. After a long take he looked away, put the broach down, and sat down in the chair next to the dipping pot. "You're right, Hallie Mae, you're not a child anymore, and neither is Tom. Both of you have grown into fine adults while I've been standing over this vat of pig fat dipping away the future and the past. I'm sorry. I suppose it's natural for a pa to want his children to stay young for as long as they can."

I knew better than anyone that Pa had lost part of himself the day he buried Mother, that his work had occupied him through his grief. But I could see that it was getting to be too much for him, that what weighed on him was more than the unfilled orders stacking up on his desk. He was lonely and sad, bound to an occupation and a way of life that had grown into a heavy chain, while his children longed to see the world and have an adventure or two for themselves. Spring had passed Pa by and landed square on my shoulders.

"I'm thinkin' I might give up the Ranger days," I said. I didn't know where those words came from. It wasn't a thought I had considered until I saw Pa's face after bein' gone. I felt more selfish at that moment than I'd ever felt in my life.

"You don't mean that."

"Maybe I do."

He judged me one more time and shook his head. "Maybe I will go talk to that Hopmeyer boy. I think you might be right. I can afford to hire a hand. You're not giving up this Ranger business. I won't hear of it. Not on my account. Now, you go on in and wash up for dinner. I put a stew on the stove for you. It should be ready."

I started to protest, but Pa read my face like it was a well-worn psalm.

"Go on," he said. "Do as I say, and don't argue with me. You've helped me settle something in my mind. Go on."

I couldn't argue no more. I was tired and wore out myself. I did as I was told, and gladly found my way to familiar food and a soft featherbed. I know I was only gone for two days, but it felt like it had been a week.

9.

My two days of rest passed like one deep sleep. I hugged Pa goodbye as I left for my next tour, but he was well into a lecture with the Hopmeyer boy on the right and proper way to stir tallow. I was relieved that Pa'd brought himself some help into the shop. It would be one less thing for me to worry about while I was away.

When I rode up to the McIntyre house, I was happy to see Tom and Abagail's horses hitched up in front of the porch. It seemed odd, though, that there were more horses than usual tied about this early in the mornin'. There were six, all told, beyond Tom and Abagail's mounts, peppered in front of the well-kept house. I wondered if the captain had called a meeting of some kind that I wasn't aware of. There wasn't any friction in the air that I could taste. It was as nice a day as you could ask for; pale blue sky lackin' any clouds or wind, and the birds were happy to go about their business tendin' to their early broods. I didn't think anything was wrong until I walked into the house and saw Tom sittin' in the parlor surrounded by a bunch of grim-faced men.

I stopped sudden, like I'd ran face-first into a wall. The men looked up, saw me, and stopped talking, allowing silence to cut my way and stab me with a dreadful feelin' I'd had before. Something was wrong. Death was afoot. I knew the look like it was a long-lost uncle come home to borrow money.

It took me a second to work up the courage to walk into the

room, headed up by the captain, who had no interest in looking me in the eye. Tom, neither. One step in, someone took my shoulder from behind. Not in an angry way, but a gentle way, saving me from stepping over a ledge of some kind.

I spun around and came face to face with Will McIntyre.

"They took her," he said, real soft. A forbidden whisper on the tip of butterfly wings. Not the sweet nothing that I had dreamed of, but the announcement of something I could not imagine. I had to strain to hear him, but I did. I knew what he'd said and didn't need the details, even though I wanted them in a desperate way.

Will's face was pale and his eyes were streaked red; a taint of no sleep in the corner of each eye. He was dressed and ready to ride, save his boots. He was in his socked feet. I had to comprehend for a moment that this was his house and the headquarters for our division of Rangers, too.

He led me away from the parlor, willing me to keep my mouth shut with a stern side-glance that meant nothin' but keep your trap shut. He'd inherited the talent for command from both parents, though he favored his mother. I didn't need a book on how to read his face. No, sir, I didn't. The last thing I was gonna do was bring any undue attention to myself.

"You're the last person they want to see," Will whispered, leading me outside. We stopped on the porch with our backs to the house.

I clinched my teeth with foreboding. "We have to go find her."

"You're not going anywhere."

"What do you mean?" I knew the answer to the question before it had left my mouth.

"They can't afford to lose another girl."

"You're sayin' that to get me good and riled up, aren't you?"

"It's the truth of the matter, Hallie Mae. Momma was gonna

be the one to break it to you, but she lit out to comfort Abagail's mother and tend to her needs. She's in a dither and worried sick."

"While the men sit and talk about what to do instead of going after her? Who wouldn't be in a dither, Will? That's foolishness is what it is." I looked out to Ol' Hank and caught Will's eye in the process. He seemed to know what I was thinkin'.

"You can't go after her," he said, reaching out like he was gonna grab me and drag me back inside. That was the last place I wanted to be.

"Says who?"

"The captain. Me and you is to stay here while they go on the hunt for those savages."

"So, it was the Indians?"

"That's what Tom said. They stole her away while he was sleepin' and she was standin' sentry. He feels real bad, and all, like it's his fault that she got took. Her screams woke him up, but the fire had dimmed and it was too dark for him to get a look at anythin' other than buckskin and feathers. And then they were gone. Off on horses, with the night as black as that ewe over there."

I let my vision follow his nod to a pen of sheep the captain kept for wool and nothing more. Something didn't seem right, but I couldn't figure it out. I needed to talk to Tom myself and get his side of the story, but that was impossible. He was trapped in an inquisition with far more threat than I could offer. I felt sorry for my brother. I knew how he must of felt. But I was more worried about Abagail, and the rest of the girl Rangers, for that matter. This might be the end—just as it was gettin' started.

"Where'd they take her at?" I studied Will's face for the slightest hint of blame on my brother. I didn't see any judgment at all. Only concern.

"At the first switch that heads to the river," he said.

The river always meant the Ohio River. I knew of the switch, but I'd never traveled it. Tom had, so I wasn't surprised that he'd stopped there to set camp for the night. "He looked for her?" I said, noticing a rising chorus of voices from inside the house. Men argued a lot before they ever got around to doin' anything of value if you ask me.

"Says so," Will answered. I believed him.

"Okay. He's gotta fend for himself, then." I headed off the porch.

"Where you goin'?"

"Home," I lied.

Will knew a falsehood when he heard and saw it. He looked down to his socked feet, then to me as I hurried to Ol' Hank. I had to get out of there before he stopped me. There was no way that I was gonna sit back and let anyone else go after Abagail, especially with Tom's reputation on the line. If that girl turned up dead it would follow him all his life. Captive as he was to the head men, I had no choice but to save his honor . . . and Abagail's life, if I could.

With that in mind, I jumped into the saddle like I had a hard wind helpin' me upward. Ol' Hank shuddered at the suddenness of my arrival, but he knew the press of my legs and the hard grasp of the reins meant business. It was time to run, time to fly, time to do what I set out to do. Be brave, be on an adventure, be a Ranger.

10.

It didn't take Will two shakes to grab his pair of boots, put them on, and rush after me. But if there was one thing Ol' Hank loved to do, it was run with his head all to hisself. I had a good lead on Will, kickin' up dust like I was, and I couldn't see him clear enough when I looked over my shoulder. I didn't know whether he'd betrayed me and set off an alarm to the other men, or not. I knew he was on my tail and that was it. I urged Ol' Hank to run faster than he'd ever run before. I was damned if I was gonna let Will drag me back to the captain and pin me down in the kitchen, or worse, the cellar. Pa wouldn't like my use of strong language, not even in my head, but I feared for Abagail's life, and I knew I could help. Nothin', nor nobody, was gonna stop me. Not even Will McIntyre.

I rounded a lazy curve in the road and lost sight of my pursuer. I chuckled at the thought. Of all times to get what you want, Will chasin' after me, I could have cared less. Now all I wanted to do was get away from him. Life sure does have a sense of humor that I don't think is funny at all.

Ol' Hank was havin' the time of his life gettin' lathered up, so I leaned forward in the saddle and joined him in the race. I gave up my worry about Will, the other Rangers, and the whatevers that was goin' on in that meetin' room. I was ridin' the high wind of desire. I had a taste of freedom and I wanted more. I didn't lose sight or thought of Abagail, neither. My run was about her more than it was about me.

Settled in on a good run, I turned over the hard part to my horse. He'd stay straight in the middle of the road as long as I held fast, and let me wander in my mind for a bit.

If you would have told me a month ago that I was going after the Indians to try and rescue Abagail Peterson because she was ridin' the Trace as a Ranger, I would've laughed till I fell over. But Abagail had proven herself worthy, more skilled with knives and rifles than I ever thought possible. Until then she had been the spoiled daughter and lone child of a traveling minister who came and went, leaving his daughter home with her mother. Abagail was an only child, a rare situation on the frontier. Most folks had a load of children. But whatever the reason, Abagail's parents had only brought her into the world. They doted on her somethin' terrible. I don't know if that's a sin or not, but Abagail seemed to have an endless supply of frilly dresses, gewgaws, and the like. I haven't got a clue how she talked her mother into lettin' her try out for the Rangers, but my guess was what Abagail wanted, Abagail got. And it wasn't so much an adventure the girl was after, but Will McIntyre hisself. I swear she hated me for gettin' to ride with him on the Trace, but she restrained herself and her cat claws—which was a good thing 'cause if she'd a come after me, I'd a given her a lickin' like she'd never had before. Fightin' wasn't her way. Instead, Abagail worked harder at bein' better than me at everything. I liked her for that, but on my part, I wasn't about to cede my affections for Will McIntyre without showin' effort of my own. I'll have to give it to Abagail, gettin' herself captured by Indians sure put her at the center of the attention. Seems to me I only had one choice in the matter, and that was goin' after them savages and bringin' Abagail home.

I should have been payin' more attention to the road behind me, for it wasn't long that Will caught up to me. Like everything else he took his hand at, Will McIntyre was an excellent horseman. If there was ever a war to come, I was sure he would go off and make his pa proud. He rode like a soldier, and obeyed orders like one, too, which I assumed were to bring me back to headquarters as soon as possible. I gouged Ol' Hank with my knees at the thought, but Will outrode me. He eased up aside me on his roan mare like she had wings instead of hooves. Without askin', Will reached over, grabbed Ol' Hank's reins, and yanked my horse under control. We both stopped at the same time. I didn't try and get away. It was no use.

"What in tarnation are you doin', Hallie Mae?" Will said.

I glared at him with as much anger as I could muster. My lips were sealed so tight I feared I'd never say another word in my life.

"You have to go back," Will continued. "We both do."

I shook my head no.

He squared his strong shoulders and jutted his chin like he was about to bark an order, but he didn't say anything. He seemed to think better of what he was about to do, and relented. "You can't go out there all on your own. I ain't gonna let that happen, more less be responsible for such a thing. The captain'll skin my hide if I let anything happen to you."

"Nothin' is gonna happen to me." I relented. Will's tone had changed. It was more a plea than a command. Add that to the concern on his face, and the direct look into my eyes, and he could melt any iron courage I could have forged inside myself. "I have to save Abagail. Every second those men take making plans is one more second she's closer to trouble, if that hasn't already come to her."

"Don't say such a thing."

"Any creature that'll leave a baby to fend for itself in the wilderness isn't gonna show no care to a pretty girl like Abagail. They took her for a reason, and I shudder at the thought of what that reason was."

"Don't say such a thing," Will repeated, looking over his shoulder, back toward home, back toward the rest of the men who made the decisions. "Okay," he said with reserve, "we'll go after her. Me and you. That's the way it's gonna be."

I didn't argue. How could I? "Let's go," I said, taking the reins from Will. I urged Ol' Hank on, who was ready to have another go at the run, especially now that he had a mare to show off for. Will was at my side in a wink, joining me in my quest to save Abagail. I hoped we weren't too late.

11.

Night fell as we reached the switch. The first clouds of bitin' bugs hovered over tender bottlebrush grass waiting for a disturbance, waiting to attack or for a shift in the wind. There'd been no sign of Abagail on the Trace, but Will and I hadn't expected any. We did encounter a few travelers heading in both directions, but none of them had seen or heard anything of a girl taken by Indians. One man, a pot and pan salesman with a wide belly and suspicious eyes, warned us of the French, though. That brought a rise of alarm in Will, and after the salesman went on his way, Will argued that we should turn around and go home, that we were in enough trouble the way it was. I know he feared his father, I woulda, too, if I was him, but I argued back that all would be forgiven if we brought Abagail home. I rode on and Will followed. I was starting to like that, but I felt bad deep inside for the plan I had formed in my mind to keep Will from gettin' in any trouble at all.

"We should strike camp," Will called out from behind me.

I slowed Ol' Hank so Will could catch up, so we could talk while looking at each other. "Let's find Tom and Abagail's exact spot. See if we can figure out what happened."

Will looked at me like I was half-crazy, then turned his attention to the dropping sun. "We don't have much time."

"No, we don't."

We stopped in the middle of the road. No one was about. The only other living creature witness to our presence was a lone squirrel, plump and sleepy, stretched out on the branch of an oak tree like it had nothin' better to do. Songbirds chatted in the distance and the clouds of bugs hadn't found their way to us. The sky was an array of pinks and yellows, dotted with thin clouds that looked comfortable enough to sleep on. All in all, it had been an easy day of travel, considering we'd leapt off on the road on our own. I knew Will was only here because of me and I felt bad about that. I didn't twist his arm, but he was my partner, so from his point of view, I supposed, he didn't have much of a choice but to come along with me on this journey. Authorized or not. I wasn't sittin' this out because the captain was afraid of losin' me, too.

"You know they're not too far behind us, Hallie Mae." Will looked over his shoulder toward home, then back to me, his face flushed with fear and concern.

"I 'spect they'll be here anytime. Till then, I think we ought to do our best to find Abagail."

"You'd make a good captain if you weren't a girl."

I didn't even acknowledge the comment. I let it fly right by me as I nickered Ol' Hank to a trot. If Will wasn't gonna help me find the camp, I'd find it on my own.

Will caught up with me real quick, passed by me without sayin' a word, rode about ten yards, and turned into the brush, following a wide deer path down a mild hill. I hoped the path was used by deer and not bear. Neither one of us had a rifle. We weren't set for bear. I had my knives and tomahawk, and so did Will. Neither of us had mentioned our lack of gunpowder or lead balls on our ride here. I suppose we didn't think we'd need it, or if we had, then that would have stopped our plan dead cold. There was no way to get a rifle from the Ranger armory without the captain's approval.

I followed Will, who'd come to a stop in a wide spot in the path. It was an often-used camp, the ground marred black by more fires than I could count. The grass was tamped down, stunted in its growth, and there was even some firewood left behind for our use. A narrower path led farther down the hill where a healthy creek ran, populated by the snowmelt and spring rains. Everything was luscious, green, and lonesome for as far as I could see.

Will jumped off his horse and started to strike camp right away by stringing a stay-line for the horses. I followed suit, setting to work on building a fire. I'd eyed that plump squirrel with moist and hungry lips and I would have had him for dinner had there been a rifle on the ride. But there wasn't, which meant we'd have to scrounge for food another way. It wasn't long before the pinks and yellows turned black and the only light around us glowed orange from the fire. Will had been able to fetch some crawdads from the creek and I'd boiled some tender young nettles and mushrooms for a soup in our tins that'd been packed on the horses, ready for duty. At least we had that. We supped in silence, keen to every sound we heard coming from the Trace. We were off it a bit, but easy to find for any riders searching us out. So far, there hadn't been any visitors and I was glad of that. I wasn't ready to be dragged home for a tongue-lashin' and possible dismissal from the Rangers.

"I didn't see no sign of Abagail's presence," Will said, breaking the long silence between us. "No shred of clothes, nothin'."

"I saw broken branches but that could have come from anybody. The light was dim. We'll have a better look in the mornin'." Somewhere deep in my mind I heard an admonishment from Pa about fibbin', but I ushered it away by focusing on Will's sweet face.

"I'll take watch after we finish eating. You can sleep all night and get some rest."

"Not all night. You won't be worth a hoot tomorrow if you don't get no shut-eye," I said, bein' as stern as I could. Call me

Captain Hallie Mae Edson. "I'll take the first watch, then I'll wake you up halfway through the night. Fair is fair. That's what we done on our first ride out, this here isn't no different the way I see it. This is a mission. Maybe more important than any we may ride." I made sure my voice was hard and unwavering as I held my right hand behind my back with my fingers crossed.

"Have you ever lost an argument in your life?" Will stood up with a humph, the sweet look all gone from his face, walked over to his horse, and unstrapped his bedroll. He was mad as a bee-stung mule from the sound of his stomps, but his question was a question I didn't have to answer and I wasn't going to. I could see I'd advanced my plan and I didn't want to ruin it.

Will made his way around me opposite the fire, unrolled his bedding, and got himself comfortable with some snorts and pulls. I almost giggled at him, but I wasn't a giggling kind of girl, or I tried not to be, so I held my breath.

"You promise to wake me up?" he said.

"Yes." I crossed my fingers tighter.

"All right then." He rolled over with his backside to the fire.

"Don't let the bedbugs bite," I said, then watched and waited until I knew he was deep asleep. When he gave a solid row of snores, I armed myself with my knives, secured my tomahawk, then made way down the path to the creek as silent as a weasel stealing into a henhouse.

I pulled out a piece of material I'd found trapped low in a thicket of blackberries and studied it by the light of the moon. I couldn't say for sure that the shred belonged to Abagail, but I was taking a bet that it did. When Will woke up to find me gone, facing a crowd of Rangers and his father, all he would have to say is that he came after me, didn't want to leave me out in the wilderness alone, and he'd be free of trouble. Me, on the other hand, I had to find Abagail, if she were still alive, and whisk her away from the savages that took her with my scalp still intact.

12.

It helped that the moon was almost full. I could see a good ways in front of my feet to follow all the game that had gone before me. I feared steppin' into a groundhog hole, trippin' over a branch or some other obstruction I couldn't see, or stumblin' across one of them night cats that I'd heard howl on occasion, out on the hunt for fresh meat. Every creature around had young mouths to feed and I knew I was as much prey as I was a predator travelin' at night like I was. I lacked any good advantage to survive.

I wasn't huntin' for no food this time out. I was huntin' for a girl that I hoped still breathed. Each step took me farther away from Will, from the safety of my scream callin' him to rescue me. I was alone, on my own, and that was the way I wanted it. I had been out of earshot before, but never this far from home, never this deep into the night, and never when there was the threat of Indians at hand. Pa kept us close when word of a raiding party spread through Cuzco. Now I wanted more than a sign of their presence. I hoped I wasn't being too reckless.

The air was cool and free of biters and bloodsuckers at the moment. Young nettle scratched against my ankles, but it wasn't near as itchy as it would be when the plant was waist-high and full of needles that stuck under your skin. I tried to be as quiet as I could, but I didn't have the stalking skills of no redskin. I've always envied them Indians from afar, and hoped I had the fortitude and courage I would need if I found them. I would need some luck, too. A lot of luck if I was to be honest with myself.

I walked a good five miles without coming across anything that lived. Darkness ticked darker and the moon headed for the horizon like a sleepy yellow face achin' to lay its head to the pillow. I hoped Will was still comfortable in his dreamland, but I pushed away any worry beyond that. I traversed creeks, then edged a swamp thick with cedar trees that looked like giant skeletons with their thick shaggy arms draped with moss; remnants of clothes from a former life flittering in the breeze. The shadows looked like they was made of nightmares. No game without fins or flippers could skim across the swamp's black water. I didn't know how deep it was and I sure as heck wasn't gonna find out. The last thing I wanted to do was wake a sleepin' snake. I trusted the trail and followed it deep into the ways of tall trees and more scratchy weeds, away from the swamp, farther south, if I judged correctly by the twinklin' stars over my head. It was there that I caught the first whiff of woodsmoke.

I stopped to gather myself and to make sure I was really smelling what I thought I was. There was a bundle of smells in the woods and swamps in the springtime. Rot and moisture, mixed with standing water, could confuse a nose sometimes. I had broken into a small sweat, not only from the effort of walking, but from the recognition that I didn't know where I was. Biters appeared out of nowhere, drawn to the nectar that only they could smell and fed on my fear.

I was lost as a blind newborn pup inches off the teat. At the moment, my plan to rescue Abagail was startin' to seem like a fool's errand. Me and my big pants, tryin' to be somethin' I wasn't: As brave and strong as any danged boy, is what I was tryin' to be. Maybe Pa was right, maybe I was just a girl. I almost worked myself up to a cry, but I warded that off with the stomp of my foot. Then I heard Pa say something else, call me young miss in my memory. He always said girls didn't have to be no rugs in this world. He sure didn't treat mother like she was property like most men did their wives. Pa and mother were partners. He was heartbroken is all, but in the end, he had believed in me, set me on the path to become a Ranger because I had wanted it so bad. Cryin' like a baby lost in the woods wasn't goin' to get me nothin' or nowhere. I guess doubt and fear was expected, normal, but I knew I had to get ahold of my courage. There wasn't no time to feel sorry for myself. I'd come this far. I had to find out if the smell of smoke would lead me to Abagail.

I stood tall and drew in a few deep breaths to calm myself. I couldn't see the glow of any fire, which was no surprise. Indians were masters at hiding their presence. I was sure the smell was woodsmoke, though, and I had no choice but to follow it if I could. It was the first sign of human life I'd come across since leavin' Will to his dreams.

A slight breeze pushed out of the southwest and the smoke was riding on that. I turned and pushed back to the edge of the swamp with my short knife in my hand, ready for anything to jump out and try to take me down. Each step was as quiet as I could make it, and I tried extra hard not to snap any twigs or weeds that blocked my way. It would have been easier if Will was with me, but then he wouldn't have had no excuse to offer the captain if we came up empty-handed.

The farther I went, the more I was sure that the smoke was from a burning fire, albeit a small one. I moved like a wary snail, but before I knew it, I had gone a long way. When I looked over my shoulder, to the east, a thin line of light had nibbled out some of the darkness. Morning was coming. Daylight would give me away soon. I had to hurry.

A hint of voices drew my attention and darn near stopped me

from breathin'. I had to strain to make sure I was hearin' what I thought I did. I had expected Indian gibberish, but what I heard was a language I'd heard before. It was French.

Before the Indiana Territory was carved out of the Northwest Territory, the land I walked on was controlled by France. But that had changed, especially since a man called Napoleon took over that country in somethin' Pa had called a coup. The French still had a relationship with the Algonquin and other Indian tribes in the area. I heard tell them Indians was cozying up to the British and French as a way to annoy Governor Harrison, who it seemed to me had his hands full enough with all the travelers comin' into the territory, along with Tecumseh and his brother stirrin' up all the other Indian tribes into what looked like a war on the horizon. The troubles were more than a nibble. The French, as Pa said, were troublemakers and not to be trusted. I hoped they was nothin' more than wayward travelers and didn't have anything to do with Abagail's disappearance. Regardless, I had no choice but to sneak up and take a look. One good thing, I was sure bein' sneaky would be easier against the French than it would be a camp of Indians.

I followed the smoke smell and the voices, which were low as whispers but carried on the breeze like the first morning call of the robins. Every creature stirrin' could hear life and movement if they was awake. Even though I hadn't had any sleep, the presence of people in the darkness jolted my eyes wide open. It was like a shot of lightning had gone through my entire body. I had one other desire propelling me forward, and it was the hope that the French would be more considerate with a young girl like Abagail than the Indians would be.

I skittered from one tree to the next, stepping easy so I wouldn't leave no sign of movement in the flowers and weeds. I hid behind an old oak tree, then moved on to a stand of hickories as the voices grew louder, closer. I didn't understand a word of what was bein' said, but I could tell it was easy talk between men, most likely the change of watch, drinkin' a chicory coffee, exhangin' boredom from one to another. There was an odd smell to the smoke and I figured that was it, mornin' doin's, breakfast and such bein' readied for the day.

I got close enough to see the glow of the fire, a flicker climbing up the side of a tree. I was glad I was thin, hiding like I was behind one oak and then the next. I stopped when I could see the shadows moving. I counted three men and could make out two lean-tos made when camp had been struck. The lean-tos were covered with branches full of tender leaves to keep out the night air and the possibility of any rain away from those that slept.

More birds started to sing as the dawn light grew brighter. I wasn't going to be able to count on darkness to hide me much longer.

I wanted to get closer so I could see if there was anyone else in the camp, to see if Abagail was somewhere I couldn't get a look at. But I knew every movement I made could be my undoing, could alert the French that I was close by. Even if the Indians hadn't taken Abagail, I could end up in as much trouble if I was taken by the French. Then Will and the rest of the Rangers would have two girls to rescue, not one. That would be the end to my adventures once and for all. I would be stuck dippin' candles with Pa for the rest of my life—if I was lucky enough to survive at all. For all I knew these men wouldn't think twice about killin' a Cuzco girl.

I couldn't help myself. I bounced from one tree to the next until I ended up ten feet from the camp. I was so close that I could see all of it. And to my relief and fear, I saw what I had hoped not to: Abagail Peterson sitting cross-legged inside the lean-to, her mouth gagged with a tight linen and her arms tied behind her back.

13.

The three men who hovered around the fire were all that I could see beyond that. It was possible that there was another man or two on watch somewhere, or a scout out that could come back at anytime. I'd have to factor the unknown into my plan to rescue Abagail if I was as smart as I hoped I was. I knew the odds were against me, that the best thing I could do was run back to Will and get help, not try and do this myself. But the problem was I didn't know what the men intended to do to Abagail, and finding my way back to camp would take some doing. I wasn't exactly sure where I was. What I did know was that I was running out of time. If I was going to act, it had to be soon, before the sun took away all of my shadows to hide in.

I took another look at the men to size up the situation again. There was one man sitting with his back to me, while the other two sat on each side; all of them faced the low fire, watching the pot come to a boil. The lean-to Abagail was stowed in was opposite the man with his back to me. Somehow, I needed to let her know that I was here to rescue her, see if she could help me in some way or another. But doing that risked showin' myself to the French. And then what? Well, I figured I had no choice but to come up behind the man with his back to me and prepare myself to slit his throat if I had to. First, I would press the sharp knife against his skin, draw blood if I had to. I took a deep breath and asked myself a question I'd never considered until that moment: *Do you have it in you to kill a man, Hallie Mae? Do you?*

I didn't know the answer, wouldn't know until I had to face such a thing, but I couldn't let my fear of the unknown stop me. I didn't come this far to bear witness to somethin' bad happenin' to Abagail Peterson.

My first piece of luck came straightaway. One of the men got up and wandered off into the woods without sayin' a word. I figured he was gonna relieve himself, but I wasn't too worried about the cause, all I knew was that now I only had two men to worry about.

Abagail's eyes followed the man, tall and limber, with a flow of dirty black sweat dipping over his collar, until he was out of sight. When she turned back to face the remaining two, I peered around the trunk of the oak I was hidin' behind enough for her to get a good look at my face. Good thing she had a gag on her mouth because she let out a gasp, and her eyes brightened. As it was the noise from her drew both men's attention for a splatter of a second. Abagail was smart enough to look to the ground as quick as she'd reacted to seein' me.

The two men, one plump, the other skinny, both dirty as pigs from trekkin' in the woods for an unknown amount of time, looked around to make sure they was still alone, then went back to starin' at the pot on the fire once they was satisfied there was no threat about. I melted into the tree the best I could, glad that I'd worn the darkest clothes I had. The sun was startin' to light the tops of the trees, sending a glittering glow of soft gold through the new leaves. It was going to be a fine day, but I needed the mornin' to take its time. It wasn't the first time in my life that I wished that I could stop the world from spinning.

Not only did I plan on holding one of the men hostage, I planned on throwing my long knife behind Abagail with the hopes that she would be able to reach it and cut through the rope that bound her hands. That was all I knew to do, other than fight to the death if it came to that.

I gripped my short knife and started my sneak out of the woods, moving as quiet and undetected as I could. I was a foot from the man with his back to me before the other man noticed my presence. But it was too late. Before he could sound the alarm, I was behind my target with my blade pressed hard against his throat. "You move an inch and you're a dead man. You," I said to his partner, "say a word, and he's dead before you can say boo." I tried to sound as mean as I could. The man with the knife at his throat swallowed hard and shivered. At least he was scared. That was a good sign.

The other man, the plump one, said, "She ain't nothin' but a girl."

"A girl that means to set her friend free no matter what it takes," I said, as I tossed the long knife behind Abagail. It landed six inches farther away than I wanted it to, but she understood my intent and scooted back to get it, grabbed it up, and started to saw away the rope. "Trouble's comin' your way fast, fellas," I continued. "A whole troop of Rangers is on my tail." I hoped that wasn't a lie. I couldn't imagine Captain McIntyre sitting around waitin' on us to return once he figured out me and Will went to look for Abagail on our own.

The plump man spat and stood up. "You lie, *petite fille*. There is no one but you."

I didn't panic. I pressed hard enough against my prisoner's throat to make him squeak out a plea for me to stop. The plump man stopped where he stood, eyeing me with anger and tension growing in his face. He looked over his shoulder, toward the direction where the other man went to relieve himself, but he restrained from calling out for help. All I could think of was not to lose my weapon. No matter what, I couldn't give up my knife.

Then the plump man looked to Abagail, who was making quick business of freeing herself. He started to move for her. I told him to stop, and to my surprise, he did what I said. I guess it doesn't matter if you're just a girl as long as you got a knife to someone's throat.

I had everyone where I wanted them but time was moving slow. I needed Abagail's help. I needed her to be free. Before I could do or say anything else, things got worse. The other man walked back into camp, focused on buttoning his trousers, not paying any attention to where he was going or what was going on. He looked up and said, *"Qu'est-ce que c'est que ça?"*

I could only imagine what he said. I didn't understand French. He looked to the other lean-to and it was then that I saw their rifles lined up inside. I yelled, "Stop!" and cut into my prisoner's throat hard enough to draw blood. The new man's attention was all on me. So was the plump man's. They looked like they were about to rush me, until I heard something whiz through the air. It was my long knife, spinning fast like a falcon chasing after a sparrow. The knife hit its target with a square-on thud: the new man's chest. He didn't even have time to scream out in fear. The blow knocked him backward into the brush.

Abagail was free and rushed straight into the lean-to after one of the rifles. I pushed away the skinny man and lunged at the plump one as he came for me. I caught him in the shoulder with my knife. I buried the blade with all of my force and we toppled to the ground in a bundle, each of us fighting for our lives. That gave Abagail time to grab up the rifle, but there was no time to load it. Instead, she used it like she was trained by the captain when it came to a situation like this. She swung the butt toward the charging plump man. She caught him upside the jaw and sent him tumbling. I was still on the ground, trying to keep hold of my knife, but that was getting harder as the skinny man was trying to wrestle with me. I punched him in the face with my free hand but that seemed to give him a taste of encouragement. He had my hand with the knife in it, prying at it with his strength, which was pretty darn considerable. He was gonna win—until I took one last run at savin' myself and kneed him as hard as I could in his boy parts, like Abagail had during her test with Miles and the round man. That won the battle, but I knew he'd come for me once he caught his breath, so I took advantage and jumped up off him. There was still a war to win.

I heard a row behind me like thunder had unleashed itself, except that it didn't make any sense 'cause it was as nice a day as you could ask for. A quick glance over my shoulder answered any question I could have and gave me the relief I'd been looking for. It was the captain, Will, Tom, and the rest of the Rangers come to save us. But they didn't need to. Me and Abagail could have takin' care of the French men all on our own.

14.

A month had passed before me and Abagail was allowed to return to duty. There was a lot of meetin's in Vincennes with a lot of arguing for and against the idea of girls ridin' with the Rangers. In the end, Governor Harrison prevailed, had his way, and set everything in place like it was from the start. I couldn't have been more relieved. I'd been helpin' Pa dip candles with that Hopmeyer boy, while Tom got to continue his duty. They all determined that he didn't do nothin' wrong, that it wasn't his fault that Abagail had been captured. The French had waited until Tom was asleep before they swooped in and took her. It seemed their intention was to blame the whole thing on the Indians to get everyone all riled up. Instead, one of them ended up dead, and another injured. Me and Abagail came out of the thing all right, except Abagail was a little disturbed by the killin' she'd done. Turned out she'd never even killed a squirrel, so takin' a life was new to her, no matter the reason. Still, she shook it off pretty quick, took to the attention that came her way like a pig to mud, and decided right quick that she was gonna ride with the Rangers again, too, if the captain would have her. He did, and he would for as long as she wanted to ride.

I walked into the shop to the comfortable smell of sheep tallow simmerin' in the pots. More and more folks kept floodin' into the territory and it was gonna be a long time before Pa got caught up, if ever. I was glad he had help, but I was also glad to get away on my own. Candle makin' wasn't for me.

"There you are, young miss," Pa said, stopping a stir. "I see you're dressed and ready to ride."

"I am," I said.

"You're sure about this?"

"As sure as I'm standin' here breathin' before you. There's folks out there that might see trouble if I sit back and do nothin'."

"I suppose you're right, but I wish you weren't. That's not the world we live in, is it?"

"No, sir, it's not." I turned to leave, stopped with my hand on the door, then spun around and hurried to Pa and gave him a tight hug. I'd seen death close up and it had woke me a bit about how fragile everything around me was. I wanted Pa to know I love him.

I took off before we both melted into a pool of tears. Ol' Hank was outside waitin' for me. So was Tom. It was me and him on this tour. Will was ridin' with Abagail on the next ride out. That didn't bother me much. I had other things on my mind. Boys and who liked who didn't seem so important when there was Indians and the French out in the world stirrin' up any kind of trouble they could.

"You ready to go?" Tom said.

I didn't answer. I climbed onto my horse, settled myself, kneed him enough to let him know that it was a run I wanted, then pointed his head toward the Buffalo Trace. I had the wind at my back and the future waitin' ahead of me. I couldn't have been more excited and happier to get back to doin' what it was I was put on this earth for. I was a Ranger and, at that moment, that's all I ever wanted to be.

AUTHOR'S NOTE

The Indiana Rangers, also known as the Indiana Territorial Rangers, were a militia formed by Governor William Henry Harrison in 1807 after the Larkin family was attacked by Indians as they traveled the Buffalo Trace. Well-trained men and women made up the three divisions depicted in this story. The Rangers protected the Buffalo Trace for eight years. They were disbanded in 1815, a year before Indiana became a state, at the end of the War of 1812.

ABOUT THE AUTHOR

Larry D. Sweazy is a multiple-award author of fifteen western and mystery novels and over eighty nonfiction articles and short stories. He lives in Indiana with his wife, Rose, where he is hard at work on his next novel. More information can be found at www.larrydsweazy.com.

★ ★ ★ ★ ★

TWO OLD COMANCHES
BY JOHNNY D. BOGGS

★ ★ ★ ★ ★

I

Tatsipï stunk. But then, that was how he got his name. In the language of The People, *tatsipï* meant skunk bush, although Ecapusia knew that Tatsipï, a worn-out holy man more bones now than spirit, smelled worse than any reeking shrub, or even a dozen riled skunks. Not that Ecapusia's name sounded any better. Skunk Bush and Flea? Yes, with names like that, they must be dangerous warriors, so the bluecoats had no choice but to send those two old Comanches to be imprisoned inside this strange Fort Marion.

Ah-kes, the girl who had seen nine winters, had been imprisoned, too. And also her mother, though Little Prairie Hill had not been born to The People. She was a Mexican, or had been, until The People adopted her as one of their own.

But it was not Flea's fate to be imprisoned next to Little Prairie Hill and Ah-kes. Or Always-Sitting-Down-In-A-Bad-Place. Or Black Horse. Or any of the other brave People, those who sang fine songs, who counted many coups, who had fought with Quanah until The People had no choice but to surrender or starve to death. No, Flea had no such luck.

Which is why he wished he were dead, although it was Skunk Bush who kept moaning so pitifully: "I am going to die today." The holy man began rattling the chains and shackles that had been on him practically every day since *Totsiyaa Mua*, the Flower Moon. "I am going to die today."

The chains on Flea's own arms clattered as he raised his hands to squeeze his ears. "Then die already," he snapped. "Sing your death song. Your passing will at least put me out of my own misery."

A thick wall separated the dungeon of Flea from Skunk Bush's cell, but this prison had been built of what *taibos* called *coquina,* bits of shells from the strange, giant pond with waves that constantly crashed onto the sand beyond this Fort Marion. Such soft rock did nothing to dull Skunk Bush's moaning. *Coquina* could not even lessen the stink of the holy man, which overpowered the foulness of dampness, of salt, of rot, even the odor from Flea's miserable body.

If Flea guessed right, this must be *Yuba Mua,* the Fall Moon, but he could not be certain because the seasons in this world *taibos* called Flo-ri-da rarely changed. And Flea and Skunk Bush had been chained and shoved into darkness long before they had arrived here. As soon as Quanah had brought the last Kwahadis to the bluecoat fort called Sill—in the heart of the land of The People—Flea, Skunk Bush, Tail Feathers, Black Horse, Always-Sitting-Down-In-A-Bad-Place, and many others had been put in irons and shoved into an icehouse. Once brought out of their cold, dark prison, they had been loaded into wagons—with Cheyennes, Kiowas, two Arapahos, even one Caddo—and taken east to the Fire Wagon Road. There, after being herded, like cattle or sheep, into rectangular houses on iron wheels, they endured long days and nights in stinking, smelly, smoking *taibo* machines known among The People as Fire Wagons. Flea preferred to call those *Pisups*—for all Fire Wagons stank, like one of Skunk Bush's farts.

Skunk Bush began singing.

"That is a Kiowa death song, old man," Flea told him. "You are of The People."

"I have no death song," Skunk Bush fired back. "For I am no

coward, like you are. I sing no death song. I will die, yes, for I am of the true people, and no one lives forever. But I will not die here." So he sang:

> *Let us travel on the warpath.*
> *Everyone now sing.*
> *We are going to see a land*
> *One we have never seen before.*
> *We shall soon enjoy*
> *Feasting on a colt.*

Skunk Bush's singing stunk, too, so Flea began his own song.

> *Where you go*
> *I do not care*
> *What you do*
> *I do not care.*

For a long while, they battled this way, raising their voices, trying to drown out the other's. Eyes closed, singing, though, old as they were, neither had the voice of, say, Telling Something. Or Pile of Rocks.

They refused to surrender, lighthearted now, words making no sense, no melody, songs without reason. Until someone down in the bowels of Fort Marion screamed at them: *"Cierra la puta boca. El ruido que haces hace que mi cabeza explote."*

Both fell quiet, but from the other cells, Comanches, Kiowas, and Cheyennes cheered. Not for Skunk Bush and Flea, but for the little voice that had chided the old men into silence.

"Who said that?" Skunk Bush said, much softer, so only Flea could hear. The words that stopped their song had been spoken in Spanish, but The People understood much of that language, having raided Mexicans for so many years.

"Little Prairie Hill?" Flea guessed.

"No," Skunk Bush said. "The voice was much younger."

"Ah-kes?"

Skunk Bush sighed. "Yes. But that is ugly talk from a child so young."

A moment later, the holy man began chuckling, which echoed across the dungeon, and soon grew into a chorus of Kiowa, Comanche, Mexican, Cheyenne, and Arapaho laughter. Eventually, even Flea joined in.

The jangling of an iron key in the heavy lock awakened Flea, who rolled off the blanket onto the dirt floor. Dim light sneaked through the window's iron bars in what was no lodge of The People, but what the bluecoats called a "casement"—and Flea's home. Rising, rattling like some *taibo* machine from his long chains and shackles, Flea waited for the door to swing open. The bluecoat with the long gun stepped into view and yelled, "Chow time."

These bluecoats were becoming careless, for this one no longer aimed his long gun at Flea, but kept the weapon slung over his shoulder. *I could kill him easily,* Flea thought, although he had doubts. Besides, even if he killed this man, what else could he do? Climb the walls of this Fort Marion? Then what?

Before he had a chance to decide anything, that red-bearded bluecoat with the two stripes on his blouse stepped inside. This one never showed carelessness. He kept a revolver in his right hand.

Two Stripes said something to the other soldier, who stepped aside and began unlimbering his long gun. Yes, Two Stripes was not a fool like most bluecoats. Flea almost smiled at the sour-faced soldier who could read the mind of one of The People.

The leader of these bluecoats studied Flea, aiming the pistol's barrel at the two buckets, one of water, the other of . . . Flea's foulness. Knowing what was expected of him, Flea picked up

90

the handles of the two buckets, his right holding the water container, his left the one of his own urine and excrement.

"Keep him outside for a minute, Mattox," Two Stripes said. "I want to look around here for a minute."

Although he did not understand what Two Stripes had told the younger bluecoat, Two Stripes's tone worried Flea. The long gun now waved, from Flea's stomach to the door, and he had no choice but to step out of this casement, his chains clattering again, to join the assembly of other prisoners.

Standing outside the open door, Flea kept his head straight— for bluecoats insisted on this—yet his eyes watched Two Stripes, who stood by the blanket on the floor, studying it closely.

"Criminy, Corporal Zachary," the bluecoat with the long gun said. "Let's get this over with, for Christ's sake."

With a grunt, Two Stripes kicked the blanket and moved out of Flea's sight. A long while passed before the wise bluecoat stepped out of the casement, sliding the revolver into the holster on his hip.

"Move," he said.

Into the courtyard of the lower level, Flea walked straight toward another bluecoat's gun.

"Stop," Two Stripes said, and Flea obeyed. After months of imprisonment, Flea had learned a little of the white man's tongue: *Move. Stop. March. Up. Down. Right. Left. Thirty minutes. Stand up. Stretch your legs. For Christ's sake. Piss pot. Shithole. Son of a bitch. Chow time.*

He knew to wait, to keep his eyes now trained on the floor, at his filthy moccasins. Behind him, Two Stripes moved to Skunk Bush's cell. The heavy key ground against metal and, after a struggle and two of Two Stripes's "son of a bitch" commands, the door opened. "Move," Two Stripes told Skunk Bush. At length, Flea heard and smelled the holy man standing behind him.

Surrounded by bluecoats, the prisoners marched into sunlight, leaving their water buckets by the cistern, and carrying the foul-smelling containers to the little cart with the big barrel in the back that was pulled by two mules and guided by a bony, old Mexican.

They say he is blind, a Cheyenne signed with his hands.

But his mules see for him, Tail Feathers signed back.

One would have to be blind to take this job, Flea thought, *hauling the wastes of men to some faraway spot day after day after day. He would be blessed if he had no sense of smell, too.*

Flea emptied his waste bucket into the large barrel, stepped off the two-wheeled cart, set his empty bucket where he always did, and waited for the other prisoners to finish this degrading chore. All the while he thought: *I see bluecoats go to those small houses to empty their bladders and bowels. Yet they do not wish our urine and excrement to mingle with their own.*

He smiled. *The white men even fear our piss and shit.*

The rest of the morning became rote. Stand in line, grab a tin plate, walk down another line, single file, no talking . . . while bluecoats, looking silly with hats on backward and white dresses hanging down the front of their shirts and pants, slopped what the white men considered food worth eating. Bacon. Molasses. Potatoes. This was their Morning Eat, day after day, day after day. Sun Eat? Tripe, rice, soup. No buffalo. No pemmican. Some of the prisoners had even decided to eat fish—which The People would never touch. The bluecoats even wanted their prisoners to eat some bugs from the water called oysters, which tasted like snot no matter how they served it: raw, boiled, or fried. Evening Eat never strayed from beef and beans. Always bread for all meals, along with the one thing Flea felt that the bluecoats cooked well—*tuhpaé*—coffee to drink. Even with sugar.

After eating, the prisoners moved into the sunshine, to walk—

"ex-er-cise," the bluecoats called it—although Flea did not understand how they were supposed to "ex-er-cise" with their wrists and ankles still shackled.

Flea moved off the hard stone floors to the center of Fort Marion, liking the feel of grass underneath his moccasins, although after a summer of imprisonment, the grass no longer looked so green. In fact, in several spots, the grass had died. The sun, however, warmed his face, made the dampness and pains in his bones evaporate. Wherever this Flo-ri-da was, this, at least, felt good. Above the high, gray, lifeless walls, he saw the funny tops of the strange trees, bending with the strong wind, with the unusual bark and queerest of leaves. Odd white birds flew over this Fort Marion, squawking like rabid coyotes. Flea liked the big birds the best, the ones with the giant, crazy-looking beaks, but spotted none this morning.

On these days, Flea did what he always did. He followed the rectangle's edge, on what was left of the grass, but just inches from the slabs of stone. He stopped at the stairs, counting the steps that turned past the large barricade the bluecoats had constructed. Two other bluecoats stood behind the wooden structure. More steps beyond that . . . to what the bluecoats called the "gun deck." Before the bluecoats became suspicious, Flea moved to the corner, and looked at Two Stripes, who leaned against the wall, rolling tobacco in his little yellow paper. Two Stripes stood four hands taller than Flea, and even taller than Skunk Bush.

Then again, most *taibos* were. Even Cheyennes, Arapahos, and Kiowas grew taller than any of The People. The People were short, round, but no Cheyenne, Kiowa, or Arapaho acted braver, and no one—anywhere—rode a horse better.

Flea frowned. How long had it been since he had felt the wind in his face while a fine, stolen horse carried him toward a herd of buffalo?

The memory faded, and the frown darkened, for at that moment, Flea saw Skunk Bush.

II

Cutting diagonally across the grass, Flea walked with purpose, as fast as tired, manacled legs could carry him. He paid no attention to the young Cheyenne who wanted to talk to him—Flea knew what the Cheyenne would say and he had no time for this today—and did not stop until he stood in front of Skunk Bush.

He had not seen him while in line—just smelled him—and had ignored him during their morning meal, because, well, Skunk Bush's odor alone soured one's appetite. But to see him while you ate . . . ? Now Flea felt shame for ignoring his longtime friend.

The weathered holy man coughed, shivered, and adjusted the blanket wrapped over his shoulders. The cough came from deep in the lungs, bringing with it phlegm and ugliness. Skunk Bush's eyes appeared rheumy. The braids had turned grayer since the last time they had been brought to ex-er-cise on the grassy yard.

Those thin lips hardened like Skunk Bush's eyes. "I am not dead," he whispered to Flea, before coughing again.

Flea raised his left hand, running fingers over those lips before turning his hand over to inspect his fingertips.

"There is no blood," Skunk Bush said. His Adam's apple bounced, but swallowing came hard for the holy man. "Yet," Skunk Bush added.

Rubbing the fingers against his thumb, Flea said softly, "We will speak of this later," turned, and walked away from the old man. He saw a puddle in the far corner from one of the recent rains. That was another thing different about this Flo-ri-da than in The People's home, where rain came rarely, though often in violent outbursts. Here, rain fell steadily, almost daily, but never hard or for long periods. He knelt, and lowered his face toward the small puddle. The reflection revealed the blueness of the sky, white birds, gray walls, and his own ancient face. His own braids showed more white than black.

Flea sighed. "You are old, too," he told himself.

The whistle blew. Flea stood, heard Two Stripes yelling what he always shouted, so he marched, not speaking, not even looking across the spots of grass and onto the stone floor, and found his place behind Always-Sitting-Down-In-A-Bad-Place. He heard and smelled Skunk Bush as the holy man stepped behind Flea. This time there were two lines, with Flea in the longer one. He kept his head straight, the way the bluecoats liked, but turned his eyes at the other line.

Today, those prisoners would cross that strange bridge. They would see something strange, yet wonderful. And they would come back cleaner. But Flea would not see this giant pond with the splashing waves on this morning. He would not feel salt water on his face, or try to catch one of those funny bugs that had a giant pincer for one hand and a much smaller claw for its other hand. No, bluecoats knew better than to let all of their prisoners outside the tall walls of Fort Marion at one time. Instead, they sent smaller parties outside to bathe. Flea and Skunk Bush would have to wait for their turn to wash. If Skunk Bush still lived.

On this day, Arapahos and Kiowas got to leave the walls of the dreary soldier fort, to see the giant water, the funny trees, other oddities. They would even have their chains removed, if only long enough to bathe with the harsh *taibo* soap.

Afterward, they would join their wretched fellow prisoners and fall into line to be served more bad food.

Shortly after the lucky prisoners walked across the little bridge and through what the bluecoats called a sally port, the mules pulled the Mexican, his two-wheeled cart, and the barrel of foulness out of Fort Marion, too, hauling the reeking cargo to wherever a *taibo* disposed of such wretchedness.

After eating what the bluecoats called "supper," Flea knew what to do. He picked up his water bucket in his left hand, the slop bucket in his right, and followed the Cheyennes and Skunk Bush to the well.

Two bluecoats lifted the heavy covering, and minutes later, with all water buckets filled and slop buckets emptied, they moved back to the casements, water sloshing over the sides, and stood in front of the doors, waiting. Flea knew to keep his head down, his lips tight, as Two Stripes opened the first door. His eyes moved to find Skunk Bush, head also down, coughing, trying desperately not to drop the heavy bucket of water. When Buffalo Meat, a Cheyenne perhaps older than Flea or Skunk Bush, had dropped his bucket early during their imprisonment, the bluecoats had just laughed. They had no intention of letting him return to the well, even though it would have taken only a few minutes, but White Bear, the Arapaho, poured half his water into the Cheyenne's bucket. Which had silenced the bluecoats' amusement.

Yet Two Stripes showed that he had a heart, for, seeing Skunk Bush's troubles, he stopped at the holy man's door first, watched him enter, pushed the door closed, turned the key in the lock, and stepped toward Flea's cell.

"You're next," Two Stripes said. Flea stepped inside, still holding the buckets till the door scraped on the hard rock and closed tightly, the key grated, Two Stripes barked, and bluecoats and prisoners moved to the next "casement."

He waited until the last of the doors opened and closed, until the bluecoats moved away. Then he set the buckets on the cold floor, found his blanket, and slowly worked on moving part of the piece of *coquina* that hid his means of escaping this place of death.

The rope he had woven rolled in his hard hands. Two Stripes had noticed something different about the woolen blanket. About the width of one's hand shorter than it had been the last time Flea had been taken to bathe in the never-ending pond. Over the months, Flea had managed to splice together wool, his own hair, strips from his shirt, from other blankets, bits and pieces of material he had traded beads and feathers with to the Cheyennes, and Kiowas. He had even used the purple sash he had taken from the body of one of the *taibo* killers of buffalo in the land of The People—a time that seemed so far ago, Flea sometimes wondered if that life had been a dream. He remembered his wife, their lodge in the Wichita Mountains. He remembered his ponies. And his sons, long dead from the spotted death the *taibos* unleashed upon The People.

"They would never have defeated us," Flea whispered, "without their *tásia.*" What *taibos* called smallpox.

He had four feet of rope. Not even that, really. Which might support the weight of Flea, even Skunk Bush, or not. It might break with someone who weighed even less than tiny Ah-kes.

Four feet. Maybe three and a half. Maybe even not quite that. He looked through the window, between the iron bars, and saw the birds flying over the gray, forbidding walls. He thought of Two Stripes leaning against that wall. Pictured another bluecoat standing on Two Stripes's head. And another. And another. By Flea's reckoning, the wall rose thirty-five feet high.

Four feet of rope, a pathetic string of life, in five moons. Skunk Bush would be dead before Flea had enough to fashion an escape.

Escape. Survive. Flea whipped the woven softness against his dirty, mangled, worn blanket. He used the language of The People with some of Two Stripes's favorite words: "For Christ's sake."

Even if he had a real rope of hemp, something made by the women of the summer village in the shade of the high hills of the land where he had been born, escape was hopeless. Was he just to walk through this door? Slip between the iron bars of the window. Pray for Skunk Bush to use his powers to walk through the walls made from broken shells. Could they walk right past the guards, throw the rope like *taibos* did on their cattle with the long horns? Climb up the rope—without breaking their necks—to this forbidden gun deck? Lower the rope to the other side, and climb down, into the water below—the moat of Fort Marion? Climb the other wall and stare briefly at the most water Flea had ever seen, with waves crashing all the time—not just during a thunderstorm, or when the wind blew hard across the plains?

Then find their way home?

He had earned his name. Flea. Yes. How fitting. For his brain could have fit in a flea's tiny body. Over the nights, he had envisioned many ways of escaping. Now, he saw the futility of all of his ideas. So much time had he wasted trying to braid a useless, worthless rope.

Flea screamed at his own incompetence, and brought the back of his head against the wall.

"Son of a bitch," he said, using Two Stripes's words, and lowered his head, while bringing the fingers on his right hand through his damp hair. For such soft rock, the shells hurt, and he felt the blood, along with the knot that already had started to rise.

Nearby, the Kiowas laughed.

Beyond the thick *coquina*, Skunk Bush chuckled.

"Be quiet, Old One," he snapped.

"You are older than I am," Skunk Bush reminded him.

"Yes. By two summers. But . . ." He held his tongue, realizing he was about to remind Skunk Bush of how sick he looked, how puny and pathetic. His heart felt heavy, and the sadness started to overtake him, replacing the anger. Yet he could not let the haggard holy man think he had gotten the better of Flea.

"I am older than you, it is true," Flea began. "But I do not stink like . . ."

He stopped suddenly, and forgot all about the rope, the *co-quina*, the tall walls that reached to the blue sky. His mind began to race . . . again.

III

The next morning, after the *taibo* "breakfast," Flea spoke to the young Cheyenne while they ex-er-cised. Walking back and forth, about as far away from the bluecoats as they could get, they stopped when they were maybe ten feet from one another, speaking quickly with hands and fingers. They talked this way for Flea knew only a few phrases in Cheyenne, and this young Cheyenne understood no Comanche.

The Cheyenne: *How do you catch those funny bugs? One bit my toe and it hurt.*

Flea: *You turn yourself into obsidian and forget the pain. The bugs let go after a while.*

Before the bluecoats grew suspicious, they walked past each other, looked at the gray wall, turned around, and moved again in opposite directions. Again, they stopped, and spoke without uttering a word.

What is it the bluecoats call the bugs? the Cheyenne signed.

"Fiddler crabs," Flea answered, whispering the *taibo* words, then using his hands and fingers quickly to explain: *They are different than the mudbugs we find in the land of The People.*

I have never eaten a mudbug.

I would not eat a . . . Flea had to whisper the bluecoat words again: "Fiddler crab."

On the next pass, Flea spoke first.

Would you like me to catch one for you?

The young face brightened. *What do you want in trade? I found a giant fang on the beach.*

Again, they strode away in silence. Flea had seen the fang. The Mexican interpreter for the bluecoats called it the tooth of an alligator, and that if any Indian misbehaved, he would be fed to the reptile. Turning at the edge of the grass, Flea saw Skunk Bush staring at a gray bird that flew overhead, and one of the bluecoats who seemed to be focusing on the young Cheyenne. Even *taibos* were not foolish. Flea and the Cheyenne must be careful.

With his back to the suspicious bluecoat, Flea signed to the approaching Cheyenne: *No more talk. Bluecoats watch us.*

The soup the bluecoats served had the white flesh of the other sea bugs. Shrimp, he heard one of the servers call it. Flea ate only the tripe and rice, but Skunk Bush seemed to enjoy the soup, even with the bugs from the horizon-stretching pond. When the holy man looked up and wiped his mouth with his dingy shirtsleeve, Flea whispered, "I have a plan."

The old man wet his lips with his tongue, then pointed at the untouched bowl in front of Flea. Understanding, Flea nodded. Skunk Bush's shaking hands reached across the hard wooden table and found the bowl. As he dragged it back toward him, he said hoarsely, "You will get us killed."

"Perhaps." Flea picked up the cup of good coffee. "But would you rather rot to death here?"

From somewhere in this area, Two Stripes hollered: "Whoever's talking better shut the hell up or we'll feed him to the gators." The words made no sense, but the tone could not be misinterpreted.

He stood in the center of the grass, looking up, watching the birds fly over . . . so many of them . . . so white, circling as though mocking Flea and the other Indians below, showing off their freedom. Eventually, the Cheyenne stood across from him. He too raised his head, but his hands and fingers moved in sign.

I offered you a giant fang for a bug.

Flea turned his head away from the Cheyenne, as though following the flight of another bird, but his hands and fingers flashed.

I need no tooth. I want freedom.

A bluecoat approached, the Cheyenne walked away while Flea stayed, staring at the birds until the bluecoat stood in front of him and grunted. When Flea looked at the scar-faced man, the bluecoat said many unintelligible words, pointed and barked, and spat out the brown juice. So Flea headed to the large stack of round balls, heavy, leaden items, no good—too heavy—for games, and began to move them to another place.

They did this, some *taibo* joke, every few days. After Flea and the other prisoners had first arrived at the strange bluecoat fort, a Mexican with many tattoos on his arms had explained that this was one of the bluecoat ex-er-cises. To keep The People, all the Indians, healthy. *If they wanted to keep us healthy,* Flea thought, *they would have left us in our land.* "If they wanted to keep us healthy," Skunk Bush often said, "they would never have brought the spotted death to our country."

But the ex-er-cise on this day would work to Flea's advantage. Because when those selected Indians moved the heavy balls from one end of the grounds to the other, the women sang, in Comanche, Kiowa, and Cheyenne—there were no Arapaho women, and the poor Caddo was alone with no woman of his own blood at all. They sang, and a few even danced. Therefore, no bluecoat listened to the singing or even watched what Flea and the young Cheyenne signed before they hefted the heavy balls and moved gingerly across the stone slabs and remnants of grass:

Cheyenne: *What is the cost of this freedom?*

Flea: *Wait. It occurred to me that I have been impolite. I am called . . . Flea.*

Cheyenne: *Flea? You are much larger than such a puny parasite.*

Flea: *I was small when I came out of my mother's womb. But even then, my heart was big.*

Each grabbed a ball and trudged to the other side of Fort Marion.

There, the young Cheyenne sighed as he set a big ball atop another, then turned and signed as Flea stretched his aching back. *Your dreams are big, too. To be free. I am called He Walks By The Light Of The Moon.*

No longer encumbered by the weight of those *taibo* toys, they crossed the open spaces of the soldier fort slowly, moving hands and fingers at their sides. This was a difficult way to talk, considered rude, because they could not look at each other, and sometimes it took two or three passes across the grass before they understood.

Eventually, the bluecoats ordered the ball movers to the shade, where they could rest while other prisoners moved balls, chains jangling. Flea, He Walks By The Light Of The Moon, and the other sweating, aching laborers drank water from gourds and ate the white man's hard, dried, tasteless beef. Oh, what Flea would have given for a handful of pemmican.

But now the bluecoats watched the others who moved the balls for no reason. Flea could tell the young Cheyenne what he wanted done, when, and how.

What is your price? Flea signed. He expected the Cheyenne to laugh at the absurdity of the request, to call Flea a fool, or ask to be taken out of this Fort Marion, too. Instead, the young Cheyenne answered after no more time than it took a white bird to fly over the soldier fort: *Your freedom will cost you two of the strange bugs.* He Walks By The Light Of The Moon smiled.

The following morning, after taking their morning meal of the same old *taibo* slop, Flea and Skunk Bush fell in line behind He Walks By The Light Of The Moon and three other Cheyennes. Led by Two Stripes and followed by six other bluecoats, they passed the blind Mexican as he waited for the rest of the wretched-smelling buckets to be emptied into his cart. They crossed the bridge, went through the tunnel in the *coquina* walls, and moved to the sandy shore of the giant pond.

The skies turned cloudy this morning, with a brisk wind, and misting rain. Huddled together, the bluecoats in rubber ponchos tugged their hats low, and one whined to Two Stripes: "Why don't we just let them stand in the rain, Corporal, and wash that way?"

" 'Cause this mist won't knock the stink off 'em," Two Stripes grumbled as he fished out the ring that held the key to their manacles.

What worried Flea as Two Stripes removed the iron bracelets from Skunk Bush's ankles, then his wrists, was that the rain might make it harder for him to find the two fiddler crabs Flea owed He Walks By The Light Of The Moon. But as they marched, unencumbered by the irons, toward the crashing waves, he saw them—hundreds and hundreds of the small, strange bugs running through small puddles the waves had left on the wet sand.

At the edge of the sand, the bluecoats motioned with their long guns, and the four Cheyennes, Flea, and Skunk Bush began disrobing. Flea disliked being naked in front of Two Stripes and the white men, but there were many things Flea did not like in this bad place. The hard bar of the soap the bluecoats made them use was one such thing he despised, but holding what *tai-bos* called lye, he walked toward the never-ending pond, feeling the mist from the clouds and waves dampen his face, body, and his long braids.

First he stopped by one of the puddles, where those bugs, those fiddler crabs, the largest of them no more than two inches wide, scurried about like ants. Other Indians gathered around, and one of the Cheyennes jumped back when a tiny bug waved its big claw at him. Everyone, even the bluecoats, laughed. But Flea handed his lye soap to Skunk Bush, saying, "Hold this."

He knelt, the sand coating his bare knees, and lowered his right hand to the horde of bugs.

"Ai-yeeee," another Cheyenne cried, although it was Flea's finger—not the Cheyenne's—that the first of these fiddler crabs latched its big claw on. Flea raised his hand, admiring the bravery of the tiny thing that would attack such a giant monster. A fiddler crab, he thought, has the courage of a Comanche. As he turned to the four Cheyennes, two of them leaped back. The bluecoats laughed even harder, but He Walks By The Light Of The Moon cupped his hands together and extended them toward Flea.

Shaking his hand, Flea watched the fiddler crab drop into the young Cheyenne's hands, and his comrades gathered closer as Flea went back to catch another bug. *Or am I letting this bug catch me?* he thought, and laughed.

After he shook the second bug into the young Cheyenne's hands, Flea watched as the other Cheyennes gathered around. Even two bluecoats stepped closer, and He Walks By The Light Of The Moon began singing, dancing in the rain and on the sand, and held out both hands, with a fiddler crab holding on to each of the Cheyenne's pointer fingers.

"He has the power of the mudbugs now," Skunk Bush whispered. "Thus this Cheyenne will be a fine leader among his people. For such a tiny animal to have courage to attack a human being . . . these things have much *puha*." Skunk Bush looked down at the hundreds of crabs. "And when the Cheyenne lets those bugs return to their village, they will have much power, too."

"Get in the water, you sons of bitches," Two Stripes cried. "We don't have all morn."

Two bluecoats stepped toward the six Indians, holding out their long guns, and Flea and Skunk Bush walked into the waves. After He Walks By The Light Of The Moon let the fiddler crabs down into a small pool of water, he and the other Cheyennes followed.

IV

He loved the power of the waves, the taste, feel, and smell of salt. The chill of the water lasted only a short while, and Flea rubbed the white-man soap over his arms and chest. Turning around, he let a wave slam against his back, almost knocking him to his knees.

All of the Cheyennes sat in the big water much closer to the shore, and Skunk Bush stood only a few feet in front of them, up to his thighs where the foamy water moved toward the fiddler crabs, the Cheyennes, and the bluecoats standing in the sand.

"You go too far," Skunk Bush said over the roar of the waves.

"I know what I am doing," Flea called back. He motioned. "Come with me."

When he saw the blind Mexican's cart turning onto the beach, he waved desperately, "Hurry."

His heart pounded so fast, Flea thought it might explode out of his chest, and his hands balled into fists so tightly that his arms began to shake. Hesitantly, Skunk Bush stepped toward the breaking waves, closer to Flea. Now Flea's concern turned to the Cheyennes. Had He Walks By The Light Of The Moon played a cruel joke on him? Had he garnered power from the fiddler crabs at Flea's expense? Those suspicions shamed Flea when one of the Cheyennes rose from the shallows and walked with the waves back to the beach.

He Walks By The Light Of The Moon stood, shouting something that Flea could not hear for a larger wave crashed behind him, almost knocking him off his feet. When he shook the water from his eyes, he spotted the other Cheyenne kneeling beside the camp of those wonderful mudbugs.

He Walks By The Light Of The Moon came straight for the Cheyenne.

The bluecoats tossed away their smoking papers.

The blind Mexican with the cart hauling excrement and urine leisurely moved down the beach.

Suddenly, Two Stripes snapped up, pointed directly at Flea, and screamed: "Shark. It's a damned shark."

Soldiers and Cheyennes scurried about in confusion, moving like fiddler crabs, while Flea reached out and grabbed Skunk Bush's hand, pulled him forward, then stepped back as another monstrous wave swallowed them.

When they came up, coughing, spitting out salt water, moving away from the beach, Flea turned around. He held Skunk Bush tightly, for the old medicine man had grown too weak, too sick to swim in such an angry current. That's when Flea saw the point of a lance gliding across the blue-gray water. No, that dark, brownish gray triangle, maybe three feet high, was too big for a lance point.

What had Two Stripes called it? A shark? It certainly was no alligator, but definitely moved as though it were alive.

"Get out of the water." Two Stripes's unfamiliar words barely reached Flea's ears after the pounding wave crashed.

The triangle disappeared as the next wave emerged, lifting Flea and Skunk Bush high, so high both Comanches could see He Walks By The Light Of The Moon and the other Cheyenne fighting, rolling across the mudbugs, while the bluecoats gathered around them. Two Stripes no longer looked at this shark or Flea or Skunk Bush. He ran to stop the Cheyennes from killing one another—or so it seemed.

The Mexican's cart rolled along without concern toward the south, the wave dipped, and the world turned blue, white, and dangerous as furious water drove the two old Comanches into the pounding surf again.

They came up briefly, coughing, gasping for air, only to be slammed hard by yet another massive wave. This time, when Flea stood, he realized Skunk Bush was no longer with him. He glanced toward the shore, where all four Cheyennes now fought, saw the soldiers trying to stop them, and the cart moving farther down the beach. He whirled to find Skunk Bush struggling as this strange current in this never-ending pond seemed to keep sucking the holy man farther and deeper—away from their once chance of freedom. And closer to that triangle that again cut through the water's surface beyond the pounding waves.

Somehow, Flea managed to grab a tight hold on Skunk Bush's left arm, and pulled him closer. They went under, came up, and Flea spotted a large white bird—one with the huge pinkish beak—floating on the surface, its big dark eye surrounded by yellow, focusing on the crazy fight on the beach. He also saw the tip of the lance, but it changed directions, disappeared beneath the surface, and Flea reached out with his right hand—the one not clinging to the coughing, struggling Skunk Bush, and grabbed water, pulled it behind him, and let the next wave lift him up and carry Skunk Bush and him closer to the shore.

The big-beaked bird spread its wings and rose into the rainy skies. Flea's mouth dropped open when the largest fish Flea had ever seen—a monster with a lance point on its back—leaped out of the water. Its huge teeth clamped down on the strange bird's large feet. The bird screamed, then disappeared in a foamy eruption of water that swallowed bird and beast. Flea glimpsed the giant tail of this—shark—before the wave broke, driving those two old Comanches into the sand beneath roiling water.

Coming up, hearing the screech of whistles, Flea staggered, collapsed to his knees, and felt himself driven forward by another vengeful wave. Quickly, he rose again, blinking out the burning salt water, gagging. He shook his long braids, tried to call out Skunk Bush's name, but only coughed. He moved blindly back toward the deeper water, and heard Skunk Bush moaning to Flea's left.

Turning, Flea glanced over the rising waves but saw neither the strange bird with the large beak nor the monster fish. He took hold of Skunk Bush's arm, and held on to him as the next wave pushed them forward.

He felt his feet on sand now, and heard Skunk Bush wheezing. Moving on his knees, soaked with water, he asked, "Can you run, old man?"

"I can barely move," Skunk Bush replied. "Leave me."

Instead, Flea folded the shivering holy man over his right shoulder, rose with a grunt, and moved at an angle. He looked to his right, seeing the bluecoats surrounding the Cheyennes, and focused on that slowly moving cart. Waves assaulted them, but the two old Comanches had moved beyond the murderous assault. Chest heaving, Flea made himself keep going. Closer to the sandy shore, the waves turned into mere trickles, but the rain became steadier, icier, and the wind blew hard against their sides. Yet that worked to Flea's favor, because the blind Mexican tugged on the lines to the mules, slowing the cart to a crawl.

When they reached the rear of the cart, Flea stopped long enough to set Skunk Bush down on his own bare feet. The sick man still clutched the bluecoat soap.

"You fool." Flea pried the slippery bar from his friend's hand. "Do you think this would help you swim?"

Skunk Bush only coughed, and Flea turned to pitch the lye away, but thought better, and tossed it onto the cart's floor. "Move," he said. Once they caught up to the cart, Flea climbed into the low back first, holding onto the top of the rim of the stinking barrel, and pulled Skunk Bush into the cart. The holy man stumbled, driving Flea back into the hard barrel.

"Quiet," Flea whispered. He looked north to see more blue-coats running from Fort Marion through slanting rain, hurrying to assist Two Stripes and the guards with the still-fighting Cheyennes.

"You are my brother," Flea whispered to He Walks By The Light Of The Moon, "and I will sing songs of your honor when I am back with The People."

Hurriedly, he spun back, grabbed the bony waist of Skunk Bush, and hoisted him up. "Hold your breath, old man," he said above the wind and pounding bullets of icy rain. "Here is another bath for us."

Then, Flea climbed up the barrel, and lowered himself into putrid filth. He vomited onto the gagging Skunk Bush's gray hair before he sank into the barrel's foulness.

V

For most of eternity, Skunk Bush and Flea alternated, lifting themselves up on tiptoes as close as they could get to the lip of the barrel without risking being seen by some passersby, letting the rainwater bathe them while they sucked fresher air into their lungs, and then sinking back down into chest-high filth. They retched. When there was nothing left in their stomachs to purge, they merely gagged.

He expected Two Stripes to stop the cart, and prayed that if the bluecoats did, none would think to look inside a barrel of human waste. Yet the Cheyennes must have fought hard, taking all the attention of the bluecoats. And maybe since Two Stripes had seen the great beast, they might assume that the shark had eaten Flea and Skunk Bush, instead of a weird, large-beaked bird.

But the filth of the barrel might yet kill them both.

Even Flea had his doubts that they would survive such misery much longer, yet just when he thought he might pass out and sink beneath the brown waste, the cart stopped. The rain came down, pounding now, driven by a strong wind. Flea tried to breathe, waited. He looked up, feeling hard drops pound his cheeks and forehead, but seeing gray clouds, and knowing that nightfall remained a long ways off.

The voice startled him: *"Está bien que ustedes dos salgan del barril ahora."*

Mexican words, spoken by that blind hauler of shit. When Flea gasped, the taste of manure and urine almost made him dry heave again.

Skunk Bush whispered, "He knows we are here."

"I heard him," Flea said, too loud.

"He wants us to climb out," Skunk Bush said.

"I know—" Flea turned, lowered his head, coughing out saliva and the sordid taste that might never leave his tongue.

Louder, the old Mexican said: *"No voy a lastimarte. Tienes mi palabra de honor."*

"He gives his word that he will not harm us," Skunk Bush said.

"I . . ." Again, Flea turned to gag, spit. His own bowels quaked.

When he could see and hear, he turned in the filth and saw his old friend struggling to climb out of the barrel. Flea started to wipe his mouth, quickly stopped, and waded through the grotesque mixture; then reached up, placed his hands on Skunk Bush's buttocks, and began pushing. Eventually, he had to climb out first before he could help his struggling friend down. The Mexican stood at the side of the cart, too blind to offer to help Flea. Or maybe just too wise.

Skunk Bush stumbled onto the cart, knocking Flea into the wet sand. Flea rolled over, barking in anger and confusion, and came up to his knees to see the old Mexican before him, water rolling off his battered old straw hat and dark poncho.

"*Buenas tardes,*" the hauler of human waste said.

Flea did not answer. He stood, letting rainwater wash away the filth, and helped Skunk Bush off the cart.

The holy man sat on the edge of the cart, with rain bathing him for a wonderful few minutes, before looking at the Mexican.

"I thought you were blind," Skunk Bush said in Spanish.

"My eyes do not see," the old man said. "But my brain does. It tells me what is near, so that I do not step into the manure I haul. Besides, I may be blind. But . . ." He grinned. "I hear very well."

"You see not with your eyes?" Skunk Bush asked.

"My brain senses my surroundings," the hauler of human waste said. "When I was younger, I saw all, colors, people, faces. Then I hit my head on a rock wall. After that . . . just darkness . . . but my eyes are good. The doctors tell me there is just something wrong . . . here." He touched his head.

"Why would you help us?" Flea spoke sharply, always suspicious. "I have taken the scalps of four Mexicans myself."

"But you have never harmed me," answered the blind man who saw things without seeing. "And I would not wish upon the cruelest of my enemies what you endure in *Castillo de San*

111

Marcos." Which was what the Mexicans called Fort Marion.

Flea looked around, seeing sharp-bladed grass that grew on the slope that led away from the never-ending pond, at the sand, and the trees with the odd leaves. Mostly he saw the clouds, felt the rain and sharp wind. The waves rose higher, and pounded the shore with a fury.

"Where are we?" Flea asked.

"Two kilometers from St. Augustine." The Mexican pointed. "This is where I dump the contents." He pointed to a channel that ran from the inland into the big water. The blind man pointed farther. "I live another kilometer in that direction." He nodded at the cart. "You will help me empty my barrel. Then I will be on my way."

"Where are we to go?" Skunk Bush asked.

"That does not concern me. I got you here. But I will not be locked in chains in *Castillo de San Marcos,* which is where I will wind up if the soldiers catch me with you." Grunting, he pointed at the barrel.

As the channel's current carried the waste from Fort Marion to the giant, maddening waters, and the empty barrel rested again on the back of the two-wheeled cart, the blind Mexican stepped to the seat, picked up a bottle, and walked back to the two Comanches. He held the bottle out to Flea.

"This," the blind man said, "is the medicine I use to endure the filthiness of my cargo." He nodded at Skunk Bush, who sat in the sand while unbraiding his coarse hair. "It might help your friend."

Ashamed of his own nakedness, the stink that covered his body, but mostly feeling completely destitute, Flea said in Spanish, "I have nothing to give you in return."

The blind man grinned. "You have given me stories to tell my grandchildren. That is payment enough."

Moments later, the mules carried the blind Mexican who sensed but did not see across the putrid channel. The rain and wind turned even harder, so Flea moved to Skunk Bush and handed him the bar of soap.

"You were wise to bring this with you. Clean yourself. As best you can. But save some of the white-man soap for me." He began removing the braids from his hair, and lifted his face to let the rain begin to cleanse him.

Naked, they moved through grass and weeds, trying to follow an animal path as far away from the channel as possible. Rain and wind pounded their backs, but neither man complained, knowing it would take rivers full of water to wash away the foulness they had stood in for what felt like ten lifetimes. When they cleared the brush, Flea let Skunk Bush sip from the bottle the blind Mexican had given them.

"The fire burns my mouth and warms my belly," Skunk Bush said, and handed the bottle to Flea. "Now that you have freed us from the dismal place, how do we not drown from the water that drenches us or be blown to the ground by the wind?"

Flea nodded north, back to the *taibo* city called St. Augustine. "We walk," he said. "With the rain and wind on our backs."

"We return to the bluecoat fort?"

"No, but that is the way to the land of The People."

Skunk Bush shivered and reached for the bottle. Flea let him drink again, after which the holy man held the bottle to the west. "That," he said, "is our way home."

"But it is not the way we got here." Flea took the bottle, and this time, returned the cork.

"We are naked," Skunk Bush reminded him.

"You are not speaking to the Mexican who cannot see with his eyes," Flea chided, but breathed out his anger, and spoke in a calmer voice. "Rain and wind will cleanse us. And we are also of The People. We will not be naked for long."

Which made Skunk Bush's eyes beam with delight.

They stole a blanket off the bench in front of a small, wooden home on the outskirts of this St. Augustine. Flea draped it over Skunk Bush's shoulders. The holy man, now shivering, thanked Flea, and they pushed on.

Realizing they were walking toward the terrible Fort Marion, or, as the blind Mexican called it, *Castillo de San Marcos*, Flea turned Skunk Bush west, and they followed a dirt path until the brutality of wind and rain forced them north again.

Now the wind roared, and the drops slammed harder. Flea had trouble remembering how the bluecoats had gotten them to the dreary place of the *coquina* walls. This storm would be the death of them, he feared, but it also protected them.

The streets of St. Augustine had been abandoned, with practically every building shuttered, doors locked. No one roamed the streets but two old Comanches. Raindrops felt like rocks thrown by small boys. The cobblestones bit into their bare feet. Briefly, they ducked into an opening in one of the ugly buildings, where Flea handed his friend the medicine bottle. He turned, and stared at the window, barely making out what some *taibo* had put out for others to see.

He let out a war cry, and turned to Skunk Bush. "Let me borrow your blanket," he said, which he removed while the holy man struggled with slippery, wet fingers to remove the cork from his medicine bottle. Wrapping the wet blanket tight around his right arm, Flea smashed the window.

"What do you do?" Skunk Bush shouted over the roar of the storm.

Flea let the blanket fall onto the ground. Grinning, he turned around and shoved a large sombrero at Skunk Bush.

"I would rather have a breechcloth," the man said bitterly.

"And a blanket that would not cut my wet back with shards of glass."

Flea slammed the other sombrero onto his head, too big—Skunk Bush's was too small, so they swapped, though neither hat fit well. And they had to hold the sombreros on to prevent the storm from stealing them. Then Flea stepped into the wind and rain and shook the now-heavy blanket as best he could before giving it to Skunk Bush and taking back the bottle of medicine.

They walked through the village where people hid from the storm. Pants they found at another place where again Flea busted the window, and Flea reached inside, cutting the top of his forearm slightly by the sharp edges of the glass, but retrieving two colorful sashes they needed to keep the *taibo* britches from falling to their ankles.

"Do you know where you are?" Skunk Bush asked as they waded through the flooding streets.

Flea did not answer, would not answer, because he did not know where he was until he stumped his toe on the iron rail that was covered with water. When he looked up, he saw the markings on a stone building, and smiled.

"Yes," Flea said, as he helped Skunk Bush cross the rails. "We are on our way home."

They moved up, to higher ground, where running water no longer covered the rails, and came to the building of tan stone, empty, dark, unattended. It was what *taibos* called "the depot."

"I see no Fire Wagon," Skunk Bush reminded him.

"But look at that." Flea pointed.

VI

He remembered everything so clearly.

Sitting next to the Kiowa named Straightening An Arrow and another Cheyenne—not *He Walks By The Light Of The Moon*, but an older man, face hard, scarred, the Cheyenne who calls himself *Three Wolves*. They have been taken off the stinking, straw-filled Pisup at the taibo village with the funny sounding name of Chattanooga.

They wait on this "siding" for the next Pisup to take them farther from their own country. Bluecoats stand and smoke, joke, laugh. One plays music on the small silver thing that he moves between his lips. Music? It sounds like a wailing coyote that is so sick it is about to die.

Then Three Wolves points at a strange, small-wheeled vehicle that rests on the iron road near Pisup-Wagons that have neither ceilings nor walls, and the strange red house on iron wheels that taibos call a "caboose."

"We ambushed one of those," Three Wolves says with a grin, speaking in the tongue of The People, "when the pale eyes built the iron road that the first Iron Horse followed through our country." He tilts his head back, remembering. Finally he says, "Eight summers ago."

Laughing, he continues. "We struck down the talking wire, knowing the pale eyes would send men to fix it. Then we used hackamores and muscle, and, of course, our horses, to pull up the bars that made the iron road. After that, we sat and waited. In the darkness, the pale eyes came in one of those wagons, pumping the handle. We saw the light from their wagon, and heard them. Heard the squeaking of that strange thing, the clicking of the wheels on the iron road. Then we heard the men screaming when they saw what we had done. I took a scalp that night, only to lose it while mounting my horse. My first scalp."

"What color was the scalp?" Flea asks.

"A golden red." Three Wolves nods. "I remember it well."

In the rain in the *taibo* city of St. Augustine, Flea stared at the strange wagon, remembering the one Three Wolves and his Cheyenne brothers wrecked so many years ago.

"*Later, an Iron Horse raced through the darkness,*" Flea remembers Three Wolves saying, "*and it wrecked even better than the tiny wagon. We killed more white eyes, burned the cars the Iron Horse carried, and tied pretty white-man cloth that we found in the wreckage to the tails of our ponies as we rode away. It was a fine, fine night for the Cheyennes.*"

Yet Flea cannot take his eyes off the strange wagon. "*How does that go?*" Flea asks, pointing at the wagon with the long iron lever rising off its wooden bed. "*It has no chimney for the black smoke, no place for fire.*"

"*You pump that handle,*" Three Wolves answers. "*Up and down, up and down. Sometimes it must take two pale eyes to make it go, but that is because they are weak, pathetic creatures. A Comanche.*" He nods at Flea. "*A Kiowa.*" He nods at Straightens An Arrow. "*Or even a Cheyenne boy could do this by himself.*"

After helping Skunk Bush onto the That Which Does The Pumping Motion, Flea looked through the darkness and the raindrops at the sign that swings back and forth on the wooden beam that struts out from the doorway of the "depot."

ST JOHNS RAILWAY
St. Augustine, Florida

Yes, he made himself believe, *yes, this is the place where we were removed from the* Pisup. *That* . . . he nodded and looked west . . . *is from where we came.*

Flea pulled himself onto the cold, soaking floor of the car, and knelt beside Skunk Bush, who sat on the side, away from the heavy levers that Three Wolves told him were how *taibos* made this thing move.

"How do you feel?" Flea asked the shivering man.

"Like I have drowned." Skunk Bush sniffed, spat, and coughed.

"Hang on tightly, my friend." Flea squeezed Skunk Bush's shoulder, and pushed himself up. He grabbed the handles to the lever that pointed skyward, and pushed.

Nothing.

He tried again, and again, then felt the anger surge through his body. He would not go back to living in squalor in a dark cell with *coquina* for walls. He would not listen to Two Stripes's condescending mockery. He would not disappoint Skunk Bush. And if a *taibo* could work one of these wagons, then so could Flea, no matter how tired he was, how cold, how wet, or how old.

This time, the lever lowered, and slowly, eventually, the strange little *Pisup* wagon moved west, with the wind and rain at Flea's back.

The muscles in both arms and shoulders screamed in agony, but Flea kept pumping the lever, up and down. Rain had turned into a drizzle, and the wind shifted directions more north and east. The That Which Does The Pumping Motion followed the Fire Wagon Road west in the darkness, for clouds hid the moon and stars. Exhausted, Flea kept moving the lever down, letting it raise his arms, and pushing down again. Every movement, he decided, got him farther from bluecoats and Fort Marion.

A moment later, he felt the sudden change in direction, no longer following the straight line west, but turning sharply to the north. Ahead he saw nothing, but sensed the danger. Letting go of the lever, he stepped back, then to his right toward the side where Skunk Bush had curled into a ball, wrapped in the stolen blanket, and snoring peacefully.

"Skunk—"

But that was all Flea said.

Drizzling rain woke him. That and the bits of daylight that

escaped through the gray clouds hovering close to the towering trees surrounding him. Hard rocks bit into Flea's bare back and through the stolen pants. His head pounded, and he fingered stickiness on the back of his head, knowing that dried blood caked parts of his long, unbraided hair.

Slowly, he filled his lungs with air—breathing in just enough that nothing caused any sharp pains. He turned his head to see the Fire Wagon Road, looked the other way, and found the thick trunks of tall trees. The fingers of his right hand curled gently, relaxed. His left hand and arm hurt like a horse had stomped both, but still he could feel the fingers bend, and straighten. Both ankles worked, twisting his aching feet north, south.

At length he realized that, yes, he lived.

Fear punched him.

"Skunk Bush?"

That hurt, too.

"Skunk Bush?" The intensity of his statement made him wince, but he rolled over onto his side, off the gray rocks and into tall grass, and pushed himself up, like some snake lifting its head out of the weeds.

Fearfully, he found himself standing, but the world spun for several breaths, and he thought he might collapse, or fall into the blackness that would consume him forever. When that passed, he remained standing.

"Skunk Bush," he said again, but no answer reached his ears. Turning he saw the massive pile of wooden beams *taibos* used to keep the heavy rails of the Fire Wagon Road from sinking beneath the earth when the *Pisup* rode through this country. The sharp breath he took pained him after he spotted the strange vehicle he had used to speed toward his homeland. It lay on its side, off the iron rails that seemed to go nowhere past the mountain of wood. The main tracks continued west, so what cruel trick had the *taibos* played on him? Making him go this way instead of straight. He saw a few small ugly buildings, a wagon but no horses, mules, or oxen, and the broken bottles and trash *taibos* left everywhere. He looked back at the stacks of wood, and stumbled toward it and the wrecked That Which Does The Pumping Motion.

On the other side of the wooden mountain, he found Skunk Bush.

"My friend." His ribs protested his decision to speak, but Flea continued. "Are you alive?"

"No," came the answer. "I am waiting to kill you before I walk with my ancestors."

Leaning Skunk Bush against the still-wet blanket he had placed against the stacks of wood, Flea found the bottle. It had landed in thick grass, away from rocks, and iron, and other bits of broken tools and garbage from the men who made the *Pisup* go. He pulled out the cork with his teeth, and handed the bottle to the holy man.

Skunk Bush needed both hands to get the medicine to his lips, but that told Flea that the old man had not busted any bones in his arms, his back, or his ribs, for the man drank two swallows without pain. He would have consumed more, but Flea pulled the bottle away.

"Save some," he ordered. "We are not home yet."

The old man's laugh carried no humor.

"We will never see our home or buffalo again," Skunk Bush said.

The words troubled Flea, but not as much as that deep weariness that the holy man showed every time he exhaled, and the wheezing when he tried to fill his lungs with air.

It was not how a healthy man breathed. It sounded like the

rasps of one about to travel to The Land Beyond The Sun. Then, Flea heard something else.

They walked, Skunk Bush leaning on him, following the path of iron bars, wooden beams, and painful rocks, heading west, toward those mechanical moans. But their feet had grown accustomed to the pain, and if they stepped from plank to plank, and not on the rocks, traveling on the Fire Wagon Road felt not so harsh. Besides, whenever Skunk Bush started to complain, Flea reminded him: "Are you not one of The People?"

Eventually, they came to a *taibo* settlement both Comanches remembered, and they saw the big river, the floating raft, and the rope that stretched across the deep water to the far bank. There, across the wide river, floated the source of the loud groans that they had heard. Smoke belched out of the black pipes above the *taibo* canoe with a wheel of paddles on the back that pushed that Water Board House that smoked and smelled just like a *Pisup*—only without the terrible noises of iron and rails—upstream and downstream. Just the occasional belches to let others know that this Water Board House was nearby. They had traveled on a similar giant canoe on their way to Fort Marion.

"They will not let us cross without paying them," Skunk Bush reminded Flea as they watched what *taibos* called a ferry bring more white men, and white women, from the place on the far side of the river to here, on the eastern banks, where a *Pisup* would carry them to the place of the never-ending pond, and the fiddler crabs, the bluecoats, and The People and Kiowas, Arapahos, Cheyennes, and the one Caddo still inside the dark place called Fort Marion.

"We will not have to pay them." Flea pointed at a smaller canoe, with no wheels or paddles, and no tubes from which it breathed dark smoke. It floated in the shallow waters next to a wooden bridge that went no more than ten feet into the river, and a pitched-roof building painted green and white, but mostly covered with rot.

At night, they crawled out of their hiding places in the trees and weeds, and used the stars that eluded the clouds to find their way to the ugly *taibo* house and the bridge that had not been finished. Skunk Bush hesitated before getting into the rocking *taibo* canoe.

"A Cherokee once invited me to ride in his canoe," Skunk Bush said.

"How did it ride?" Flea asked.

"I refused to ride with him," Skunk Bush said. "I told him that when a Comanche wants to cross a river, he rides his pony."

"We have no ponies for you to ride," Flea told him.

Eventually, before the current took them farther downstream, Flea figured out how the sticks with the flat ends made the *taibo* canoe move.

"Flea," Skunk Bush said. "The water is up to my ankles."

Flea paddled harder.

He almost let out a tremolo when the front of the canoe hit the banks on the other side of the deep water. He stepped out, surprised when the water reached his nipples. He had never seen a river so deep in the land of The People—except the big mud-filled river that stopped the land of *Tejanos* from stretching farther north into The People's country. After helping Skunk Bush out, and listening to the old man accuse him of trying to drown him once again, they crawled out of the river, up the bank, and moved north toward the lights of the Water Board House that would leave with the dawning of another day in Flori-da.

"They will not let us on their Water Board House unless we pay them," Skunk Bush reminded Flea when they could see the big, smoking canoe.

"They will not see us this night," Flea said.

He had to steady the wobbling medicine man as they eased across this "gangplank"—Flea remembered the *taibo* word the bluecoats had used—and onto the Water Board House. All round him came ugly snores. He spotted crates, barrels, and boxes, some covered with canvas, at the curved edge of the ship that pointed north.

"Here," Flea whispered to Skunk Bush. "We will hide here."

The canvas would protect them until the Water Board House stopped at that *taibo* city where they had left the Fire Wagon for this *Pisup*-Canoe. Leaning against sacks that smelled so wonderful but foreign, Flea pulled the heavy canvas over Skunk Bush and himself. He felt like singing a song of going home.

VII

"I am hungry," Skunk Bush said.

"Be quiet," Flea whispered. "It is after dawn. And *taibos* walk all around us."

"I said nothing," Skunk Bush said, but this time kept his voice low. "It was my stomach that spoke."

Grumbling, grinding his teeth, Flea used his left hand to feel around the coarse sacks that had been his backrest, his pillow, and his salvation. Eventually, he found the opening to one of the sacks, and snaked underneath the canvas, feeling, finding something soft and slick. His fingers slid up a few inches until it hit the end. Or, perhaps, the bottom. But he twisted, turned, heard the tearing of something like a vine, turned his wrist and his arm, and pulled out a curved something of green. This he held to Skunk Bush.

"Here. Eat this."

"What is it?"

"I do not know." He looked and studied what he held in his

hand. "I have never seen anything like this. But it smells like something a *taibo* would eat."

"*Taibos* eat snot they call oysters," Skunk Bush reminded him.

"And you ate bugs called shrimp," Flea said.

Skunk Bush took the slightly curved thing, sniffed it, licked it, and frowned. "Bad taste," he said, and handed it back to Flea.

Looking at it, Flee turned it around, felt it closely, and brought his hand to the top of the stem, where he had pried it loose from the others that the sack held. Suddenly, he grinned. "It must be skinned first," he said, and began twisting the top. Once that broke open, the rest proved simple. Pull one edge down, then another, and another. The insides kept a green tint, but the flesh looked more yellow—though how green or how yellow Flea could not guess since the canvas that covered them and this cargo kept out most of the light.

Skunk Bush leaned closer, and Flea held it out to the holy man. Eventually, the old Comanche bit into it, and began to chew. He swallowed.

"Hard," he told Flea, "but soft. Like a potato after being cooked underneath hot coals, only softer. Sweet like an apple." He tasted it again, and smiled. "Better than snot or shrimp."

He took another bite. Flea let him have that one, but reached back into the sack to try one.

"My belly hurts," Skunk Bush said.

So did Flea's own, but he gave his friend the sternest of looks. "Be quiet. Control the noise your stomach makes. *Taibos* scurry about like fiddler crabs in the rain."

The canvas covering popped up, and brilliant sunshine blinded Flea. He covered his eyes with one arm, heard Skunk Bush cry out in shock and anger, followed by strange words coming spoken by a *taibo* with a rough accent.

"Bloody stowaways."

The toe of a boot bit into Flea's calf. Flea brought his leg up, the stiffness of his joints paining him worse than the bruise forming on his lower leg. "Up, damn your bloody hides. Worse than English bastards. Stowaways. Miserable stowaways. Eating green bananas bound for Savannah and Charleston. Well, the marshal will soon have you two sneak thieves in chains."

The boot struck again. And again. Flea rose, still fighting the bright light, and when he heard the boot striking Skunk Bush and the holy man's cries, he spoke sharply to the bearded man with the funny hat.

"Shithole. Son of a bitch. Piss pot. For Christ's sake." And in the language of The People, he barked, "Touch Skunk Bush again and I will cut out your heart and eat it before life fades from your green eyes."

The tall man with green eyes backed away, and Flea bit back the pain in his leg. Helping Skunk Bush to his feet, Flea whispered: "I have failed us both. We will not get back to the land of The People." He wanted to break into his death song, for he knew that once they returned to Fort Marion, Skunk Bush would lose the will to live. And it was all his, Flea's, fault.

"Jiminy, Moynilam," said another *taibo*, shirtless in the heat, revealing the blackness of his skin except for the undersides of his hands and whites of his eyes. "Look at those wretches."

"Aye," said the one with the iron toe and green eyes.

"Capt'n Fitsmorris will give them forty stripes less one," the black white man said. "And that's before the white law take these old . . ." He shook his bald, black head.

The other said, "No." He turned and spit over the side of the Water Board House, which Flea now realized had pulled next to the shoreline of the bustling, noisy, angry place where they had left the Fire Wagon Road to float down the river on the Water Board House on that long journey to Fort Marion. "No," the lighter one repeated. "No, he sha'n't." He sighed, stepped back, and told the black white man, "Busy yourself with the tarp, mate. And be fast about it." Once he turned back to Flea and Skunk Bush, he said, "Off me deck and be damned quick. For if the capt'n sees you, he'll lay your backs raw for all the mates and every bastard and strumpet in Jacksonsville to see. And the same to me if he spies you before you get off the *Gary Hardee.*"

While the words made no sense to Flea, he understood what this thin but wiry strange-looking white man—with an earring hanging from one lobe and a cross, more green than copper, dangling from a thong around his neck that shined like a beacon against his hairy chest. Flea saw the gangplank, and the crowds of *taibo* men and women, and men and women of other colors who lined the docks of this Jacksonville.

"Go." Flea gently nudged Skunk Bush.

The old man started, but stopped, and handed the bottle the blind Mexican had given them an eternity ago. Skunk Bush had been wise enough to nurse the medicine gently, so perhaps a quarter of fiery liquid remained inside. In the language of The People he said, "This is for you." Skunk Bush repeated it in Spanish, but Flea could tell the hairy white man understood neither language. Yet his eyes widened at the words on the bottle, and he took it gingerly, withdrew the cork, and smelled the opening.

Laughing, he turned back toward the house that rose from the center of the Water Board House, as though looking for someone. Quickly whirling back toward the two Comanches. "This is where you get off. Now move. You're home." He raised the bottle, grinned wider, and said, *"Céad míle fáilte."*

He drained the bottle before Flea and Skunk Bush had walked past him and onto the gangplank.

Shirtless, barefoot, their stolen britches ripped and torn, and the big sombreros gone with the wind after the wreck of the That Which Does The Pumping Motion on the Fire Wagon Road, Flea knew they had to make their way through the bustling riverfront before bluecoats or other *taibos* stopped them. Or shot them on sight.

His heart pounded, and with all these men, women, and children, the cacophony of screams, all the thunder and groans from the big Water Board Houses, he felt lost. Confused. The Fire Wagon Road that had brought them here from . . . he could not remember the names of the *taibo* villages, or, perhaps more importantly, the markings that told him which *Pisup* he would need to take west to return to his homeland.

The stone-lined street pained his already swollen feet. Skunk Bush began coughing, wheezing, and then some *taibo* boy ran without looking and stepped on Flea's toes. Crying out in pain, Flea whirled, wanting to find a rock and hurl it hard at the rude boy. But the kid rounded a corner before Flea could find a weapon, and like that—the anger vanished. For he knew that the boy had been sent to show Flea the way.

"Skunk Bush," Flea whispered when the old man stopped coughing. "What do you see?" He pointed his jaw north, across the street.

Some stringy, irritating music came from inside the building, and two men with tall hats came out, singing, turning, laughing, finally stumbling their way down the path made of boards. Flea paid them no mind. Skunk Bush whispered something, but the din of this Jacksonville drowned out the old man's words. Yet it was Skunk Bush who stepped off the boardwalk and began moving to the building of red brick and loud noises. Flea followed.

They were done riding Fire Wagons, Water Board Houses, and the smaller *taibo* canoes, or traveling in a barrel of piss and manure on the back of a small cart driven by a blind Mexican. And they would walk no more. At least not for a while. They would move west now the way The People preferred.

After loosening the leather reins from the hitching rail, Flea helped Skunk Bush into the saddle on the claybank. The holy man straightened as though he had been made forty winters younger as he backed the horse onto the busy street. Flea looked through the open doorway—for no one could see through the dirty glass that lined the front of the brick building. No one appeared to be paying attention, so Flea ducked underneath the rail, and moved east, past that rail, and to the next one. The sorrel with the white blaze and two white feet looked like it would carry him a long way.

Yes, Flea thought with a smile, and he dropped to his knees to remove the braided hobbles around the gelding's front feet. *Yes, the owner of this horse knows he has a good horse that many men would want to steal.*

Leaving the hobble of braided horsehair, Flea loosened the reins, and swung into the saddle with ease. Now, he understood why Skunk Bush had turned younger.

They were on the backs of horses. Horses stolen from their enemies. They again were living like The People. Skunk Bush kicked the sides of his claybank, and heard the iron hooves pounding against the stones on the *taibo* road. Flea quickly caught up with him.

With the sun over their heads, they rode west.

VIII

Finding a Fire Wagon Road that moved east to west, they rode toward home. At a farm, they stole *taibo* clothes hanging from a wire that stretched from post to post, and this was good, for they left with thick pants of the blue denim from Mexico, and pullover shirts of brightly colored cotton. Flea even found a scarf that he tied over his forehead.

"You look like you are Apache," Skunk Bush chided.

"But I do not wear the yellow blouse of a woman," Flea responded. "With lace around its collar and cuffs."

In the next town, they walked their stolen horses through that night, until stopping in front of a building. The markings painted in a semicircle on the glass window—*Little and Kimmel, Cobblers. Baldwin, Florida*—meant nothing to either man, but the *taibo* shoes they pulled through the busted glass felt better in the stirrups of the horses they had also stolen.

Those were fine horses, too good to be owned by *taibos,* but the claybank went lame, so the sorrel had to carry both men for a while. Although Skunk Bush began coughing from the hard nights and oppressive stickiness in the air, despite this being closer to Heading to Winter Moon, Flea felt confident. Because at another *taibo* house tucked in the thick woods, they replaced the lame and worn-out horses with a big black stud and a fine pinto mustang.

"Do you remember this place?" Skunk Bush asked as they rode through the forbidding forest of palmetto and pine.

Even in the darkness, Flea could not forget. He would not say the name of the Cheyenne who had died here, nor would he ever forget the old man. Gray Beard was how he was called among his own people, and on smelly *Pisup,* the bluecoats had put the prisoners, chained of course, in the covered wagons pulled by *Pisups* meant to carry men, women, and children, not cattle. In the darkness one night during the Flower Moon, Gray Beard had slowly opened a window, and as the *Pisup* slowed, he pulled himself out. The clattering of chains roused the bluecoat with the long gun who had fallen asleep. Now he screamed, waking the other sleeping bluecoat, but Gray Beard dropped outside to be swallowed by darkness.

So one bluecoat pulled the cord that moved along the walls of the rectangular house on wheels, and iron squealed, sparks danced in the night, and Flea and Skunk Bush felt themselves rammed into the seats where two other Cheyennes sat. The *Pisup* slid to a lurching, squeaking stop.

As bluecoats searched by their lanterns outside, Flea, Skunk Bush, and others whispered with excitement that Gray Beard might escape. The loud gunshot outside silenced those murmurs. He Walks By The Light Of The Moon broke out into a song, and the bluecoats brought the bleeding, dying Cheyenne into the car, laid him on the floor, and let Eagle Head cradle the old warrior's head in his lap for the next two hours, until Gray Beard left the Fire Wagon and the earth to join his mother and father, his grandfathers and grandmothers, and all the others in The Land Beyond The Sun.

As they rode on, all this time later, Skunk Bush tried to sing a song of honor for the dead Cheyenne, but only coughed.

The cough had grown worse, and Flea had to stop and let the shivering old man rest. When he placed the back of his hand against the holy man's forehead, Flea winced.

"You are burning up, my friend," Flea told him.

Skunk Bush tried to answer but his front teeth—those he still had—merely danced on the bottom ones.

The pot they had stolen from the back of the eating house in some other tree-shrouded *taibo* village came in handy.

"What are you cooking?" Skunk Bush asked when he finally awakened. He tried to sit up, but sank, and began shivering.

"I boil fever bark," Flea replied.

"How does . . . a Comanche know . . . of fever bark?" the holy man whispered, his teeth chattering as he formed the question.

"A Chickasaw told me about it," Flea said.

"You believe what a Chickasaw tells you?"

Flea stirred the pot. "I care not if the Chickasaw told me the truth or told me a lie," he said, although he wondered if he remembered the description of the tree from which the bark could reduce fever correctly. "For I am not the one who is sick."

"Do we still ride in this tunnel?" Skunk Bush called out.

The holy man lay in the back of the travois Flea had fashioned in the thick woods, pulled by the mule they had stolen in the big village with the name that must have been stolen from Indian peoples. Not Cherokee, but . . . Tal-, Talasee, no—Tallahassee. Horses were not as good here as the ones they had stolen back east. Flea rode an old dun that was blind in its right eye. But the mule remained strong, and pulled the sick holy man without complaint, obediently following the lumbering, half-blind mare.

Flea looked up at the canopy of pine branches and needles that blocked out most of the sun's rays. Oh, how Flea longed to be back in the land of The People, where a man could see exactly what he rode toward, where the only things to block the sun were clouds, where bugs were few, and the snakes at least warned you before they struck.

He remembered with sadness the copper-headed serpent that had sunk its fangs into the left leg of the valiant pinto, and how that horse had bucked Flea into brambles that ripped the cotton of his shirt and the flesh of his arms and back.

"There is no sunlight in this part of Flo-ri-da," Flea told Skunk Bush. He let out a heavy sigh. As dark as this place felt, he might as well have been back in the *coquina* walls of Fort Marion.

"It is not . . . a place I . . . wish to die," Skunk Bush whispered.

"Then do not die," Flea prayed.

He boiled the last of the fever bark that morning, his exhaustion bordering on death, and stuck the boiled hide of a tree into Skunk Bush's mouth, making his jaws work to chew until the holy man's muscles and joints responded and he chewed on his own.

"Flea?" Skunk Bush whispered.

"Yes."

"I saw the buffalo again."

Smiling, Flea lifted his friend's head and let him drink broth from the boiled fever bark. "I would like to dream such a sight," Flea said longingly.

"It was no dream. It was a vision."

"Vision?" Setting the empty bowl on the ground, Flea shook his head sadly.

"We will see a buffalo. It will bring us home."

"Home." Flea looked up, but saw only the path carpeted by pine needles, and that endless fissure leading to nowhere.

"José, ol' hoss. Today's your lucky day, *amigo*. Haab-low Inn-Glaish?"

Flea's eyes shot open, but the brightness of day pained him, and he saw just a shadow walking toward him, music coming from the thick, black, shining boots this *taibo* wore.

"You're exactly what I'm lookin' for, Mex. I'll make you rich, keep you in tee-kill-ah, and all the ladies ah-lay-no-chee you can afford."

Flea's head pounded. Waves of pain shot from his chest to his arms, his back to his neck, his knees to his feet. He blamed himself, his old age, his misery. He had fallen asleep in the saddle, only to wake up by this long-haired, wild-eyed *taibo* with a towering sombrero, and a large mouth surrounded by thick blond hair on top and bottom.

"By the gods of Neptune and Methuselah, this son of a bitch looks deader than John C. Breckinridge."

Straightening, shaking the cobwebs in his head, Flea turned as the singing boots carried the long-haired man past him. But the movement only startled the horse, which lurched to its left while Flea turned toward the man passing on the right. Flea felt himself in midair, feet out of the stirrups, and saw the hard-packed earth of the street rushing up to greet him.

"Well, how the hell are you feelin', ol' hoss?" the phantasm before him said. The bronzed face underneath the towering hat grinned, before a gloved hand brought a brown glass to his mouth. The head tilted back, the throat bobbed, and the man's wild head reappeared. "That was quite a fall you taken, boy, yes, sir, I do mean to tell you."

Flea wished this bellicose-mouthed *taibo* would lower his voice. His head shot left and right, then toward his feet, past the crazy man. He saw only walls, painted yellow, strange things *taibos* put in their lodges and such. Skunk Bush was nowhere in this room, and the room was small. If his friend were here, Flea would have seen him.

His heart shattered into millions of pieces. For he knew: Skunk Bush had crossed into The Land Beyond The Sun.

The crazy face appeared again, only inches in front of Flea's. The man's lips parted beneath the thick, shining hair, and Flea smelled the breath of hot spirits.

"Listen, to me, ol' hoss." The man burped, and the hideousness of the gasses made Flea's stomach roll over. He repeated words Flea thought he might have heard once before, though the language made no sense to one of The People. And likely, not to anyone who spoke all the tongues across the earth. "Haab-low Inn-Glaish?"

Getting no response, the face left Flea's view. "Emiliano, poor fay-vore, talk to this long-haired, poor, ol' greaser, will you, ol' hoss?"

The next face that came before Flea was older, wiser, and the breath did not reek like those of the Comancheros who traded with The People for supplies, whiskey, and, often, guns, in the Valley of Tears at Los Lingos Creek in the Llano Estacado.

"Buenas tardes. Me llamo Emiliano Ruíz. Estoy aquí para traducir las palabras del valiente coronel, David Thomas Robert Kirk, *héroe a millones."*

These words made sense to Flea, no matter how addled his own brain felt at this moment.

"The colonel would like to offer you a position of gainful employment," the Mexican said in Spanish.

Slowly, Flea raised his hand. *"Espere. Por favor,"* he said in Spanish. Then began speaking hurriedly, excitedly, before realizing he spoke not Spanish, but used the tongue of The People, bringing suspicion—no, understanding—to the bronze-faced man's eyes. Swallowing down fear and bile, Flea managed to smile at the Mexican interpreter. The Mexican was not the fool that this Colonel David Thomas Robert Kirk might be. The colonel thought Flea was Mexican. The translator knew Flea was of The People, but he also knew better than to betray Flea. "My brain," Flea said, and tried to tap his temple. "Forgive me." He breathed out, in, exhaled again, and said, "Where is my old friend?"

The Mexican's head bobbed, and tilted to a closed door.

"Doctor Bethell is tending to him now. Your friend is sick, really sick, pneumonia, other ailments that I cannot remember, but the doctor says *you* . . ." The Mexican nodded and emphasized the last word. "Yes, you. He says whatever you did, you kept that old man alive."

Much later, the brave colonel with the deep lungs, loud voice, and breath that smelled of the potent brew of Comancheros, Colonel David Thomas Robert Kirk, pushed Flea, sitting in the Chair On Wheels through the door to the adjoining room, and left him alone with Skunk Bush.

"They have stolen your mind and turned you into a fool," Skunk Bush whispered after Flea did his best to explain.

"These *taibos* are the fools," Flea said with a sigh.

Skunk Bush turned and studied Flea's face.

"You do not joke with me?" the holy man said.

"I am too tired to joke."

"They believe us to be Mexicans?" Skunk Bush spat with contempt.

"The Mexican is from Veracruz," Flea said softly. "I am sure he knows we are of The People, not of his own, but he fears we will kill him, scalp him, kill his family."

"Which we would do," Skunk Bush. "Where is this Veracruz?"

"It does not matter," Flea said.

"What exactly is it they wish us to do?"

Flea sighed. "To dress like we are wild warriors."

"The People?" The old man's face brightened.

"It does not matter to this colonel. The People. Cheyennes. Chickasaws. Cherokees. Apaches. Lakotas. They are all the same to him."

"I will not pretend to be a Cherokee. I will certainly not ride in a canoe when a horse can take me across a river."

Flea sighed. "You can be whatever you want to be. They ask us to beat a drum when we are told to. They ask us to chant and sing. They ask us to look menacing."

"Menacing? What does that mean?"

Flea smiled. "Like you are a warrior of The People."

"For how long?"

Flea did not answer. He said: "They will take us on the *Pisup*. From *taibo* village to *taibo* village. They will feed us. And they will get us closer to our home."

With a spit of disgust onto the floor, Skunk Bush turned away from Flea. "We do not need any help from some fool of a white man to get us home. We will get home in our own time, in our own way, by our own power. Or have you forgotten that in you and I the blood of The People flows freely?" The words came out angrily, and with finality.

Yet Flea shot back with his own wrath, and his own final words. "You are a fool, Skunk Bush. I do not know how you are even still alive. I have almost drowned you. I have almost let you be swallowed by a monster fish, and we likely both would be in that beast's belly had he not decided he wanted to eat a bird with a big beak instead of two old Comanches. Have you forgotten the man with the cross on the Water Board House? He would have sent us back to the place with *coquina* for walls. We have not reached this place but for luck. And, after all the days and nights we have traveled, do you, Skunk Bush, know where we are?"

"No," the worn-out old man said abruptly.

"We are in the white-man city of Pensacola. We are still in Flo-ri-da."

Skunk Bush pouted. He did not look at Flea. He stared at the silver ceiling over his head, and studied the designs the punched holes made.

But Flea leaned forward. "Skunk Bush," he whispered. "They

will pay us in *oaui,* too."

The holy man's eyes opened with curiosity. "White-man gold?" he asked.

"Yes, my friend, but there is more." Now, Flea grinned. "This Colonel David Thomas Robert Kirk and his party of fools . . . they travel with a buffalo."

Skunk Bush raised his head off the pillow. "I told you it was not a dream. I told you it was a vision."

"Yes." Flea laughed. He tried to remember the last time he had laughed. It felt wonderful. "Yes," he said. "That is what you told me. But you are the holy man. I am just an old warrior."

"Who is two summers older than I am," Skunk Bush reminded him.

IX

And so it was, that early one afternoon during *Toh Mua,* The Year Moon, on the date the white men called the Fourth of January in The Year of Our Lord 1876, two old Comanches named Ecapusia and Tatsipï—but called José and Tomás by Colonel David Thomas Robert Kirk and other members of his troupe, and, during performances in opera houses or underneath canvas canopies in fairgrounds, pastures, or baseball fields, also known as Sitting Bull, Captain Jack, Crazy Horse, Cochise, Satanta, Dull Knife, Savage Heart, Many Killer, once in a while Quanah, or whatever struck the colonel's fancy on that particular night—left aboard a *Pisup* from the station at Pensacola, Florida.

They ate well, and since there was little for them to do except smoke cigars, or what the colonel said was an authentic Indian pipe, and make their marks on programs for white women, men, and children, the two old Comanches grew fatter and healthier. On some of the trips, they left their Pullmans and settled in the cattle wagon with the old buffalo, blind in its left eye.

Tallahassee. Tampa. Jacksonville. Savannah. Charleston. Atlanta. Mobile. New Orleans. Baton Rouge. Houston. Jackson. Birmingham. Chattanooga. Nashville. And with temperatures warming, to Lexington, Cincinnati, Fort Wayne, Chicago for two weeks, Madison, Toledo, Cleveland, Pittsburgh, Columbus, Indianapolis, Peoria, Springfield, St. Louis, Memphis, Bowling Green, Louisville, St. Louis again.

In *taibo* lodges in the big cities, the colonel would ride his horse on the stage and tell stories that neither of "the two authentic savages from the frontier" could understand. Ecapusia and Tatsipï pounded drums. Or sang. Sometimes, they danced.

In such places, the buffalo waited outside in the streets, while one of the colonel's assistants charged men, women, and children copper or silver coins to touch the shaggy animal. In other cities, men, women, and children crowded underneath a giant canvas tent assembled in a dormant field, where the colonel would ride his horse in circles and tell "big windies"—according to the Mexican interpreter—about the buffalo, the West, and "the two authentic savages from the frontier" while Flea and Skunk Bush danced, whooped, beat drums, or just stood or sat and frowned. The men, women, and children who came always stared in awe, and fear, at the two old Comanches.

No matter what Flea and Skunk Bush did, or where they did it, they were given a gold coin when they returned to the *taibo* "hotel" or left on the *Pisup* for another big *taibo* village. They slept in *taibo* "beds," took *taibo* baths, ate *taibo* meals.

The Mexican interpreter, after consuming too much from a stoneware jug during one of the colonel's "lectures," said he was "damned tired of working in some dog-and-pony show." Skunk Bush said, "I wish there were a dog in this show."

Then they moved west. Jefferson City. Kansas City. Topeka. And took the "spur" to Wichita in southern Kansas.

It was there, during the night, that Flea and Skunk Bush walked out of the hotel, stole the colonel's two best horses, led the old buffalo out of the corral, and rode south, crossing out of Kansas and knowing that a cowardly fool like Colonel David Thomas Robert Kirk would never pursue them into *Indian Territory.* Besides, the colonel had to be in Hays City in three days.

Seventeen days later—for they traveled slowly, comfortably, not to rest their tired bones and backsides, they explained, but because the buffalo they herded was old and half-blind—they crossed Cache Creek and found the shade of the Wichita Mountains. They led the buffalo into the camp of The People.

Who, at first, feared that they were ghosts, because word had come from bluecoats that Ecapusia and Tatsipï had been eaten by a giant fish outside the prison of Fort Marion far away in Flo-ri-da, and the same would happen to any other Comanche who dared fight the bluecoat rule. But Quanah knew better, for Ecapusia and Tatsipï had ridden with him for as long as he could remember, and with Quanah's father before Quanah had even been born. So Quanah welcomed both men home. Quanah said the old buffalo they had brought with them was sacred, and must not be harmed, but allowed to live out his days in peace. For The People depended on the buffalo, and this was a sign of riches that would eventually return to them.

"Will they not notice," Flea asked, "that there are two new old men when we go for our rations, or when they come to visit us?"

Quanah said: "They are not good counters, but if they speak to you, just tell them you want to be a Christian. Always, that makes them happy."

Yet Ecapusia's wife spoke with concern, saying *taibos* were not all fools. That bluecoats would remember the names of Ecapusia and Tatsipï and they would learn that neither had been eaten by some monster that lived in the big water. That blue-coats would come into their lodges one night, with their long knives and curses, and return the two men back to the dark walls and dungeons in Flo-ri-da.

She was wise, this woman named Lavender Growing Under The Peach Trees, which is why Ecapusia had courted her. Lavender Growing Under The Peach Trees said that Ecapusia and Tatsipï must have new names to fool the bluecoats on the days when they brought the cattle outside the bluecoat fort called Sill and issued their rations. Quanah agreed.

As a holy man, Tatsipï also said that Lavender Growing Under The Peach Trees was right. So he and Ecapusia shared a pipe and thought of what new names they would take.

"We should," Tatsipï announced, "honor those who helped us on our journey home."

"Yes," Ecapusia agreed.

"From this day forward," Tatsipï said, "my name is Blind Man Who Brings Excrement And Urine With Him."

The laughter of The People was stilled by the shout from the holy man. "I do not joke," Tatsipï said. "We would be dead and buried in some sandy land not worth spitting on if not for a blind man who could not see with his eyes, just with his brain. And . . ." Tatsipï tapped his chest. "His heart." He nodded with finality.

Quanah called it a good name.

"Besides," Blind Man Who Brings Excrement And Urine With Him added with a smile and he waved his hands over his eyes. "My eyes will not see for much longer. Even though I am younger than Ecapusia. And feel younger than Lavender Growing Under The Peach Trees."

Now The People waited for Ecapusia, who shook his head. "The Colonel David Thomas Robert Kirk is not a fitting name for any one of The People, though we would not be here today if not for him." Grinning, he pointed at the ponies of The People. "Or his fine horses."

Those who heard the quiet-voiced old warrior laughed at his wisdom and humor. Ecapusia thought until his head hurt, but no fine name came to mind. He wanted to take the name of He Walks By The Light Of The Moon, for they would never have gotten off that sandy beach without the help of the young Cheyenne—or all of the Cheyennes—but Ecapusia could not take the name of a brave warrior who remained trapped in that dungeon of *coquina* walls. He would not do that. Never.

Blind Man Who Brings Excrement And Urine With Him said it was hard to come up with a name, a fitting name, and that perhaps they should smoke another pipe. Just when Ecapusia was about to agree, he looked into the crowd, and saw his wife, Lavender Growing Under The Peach Trees, but it was not her face that he saw.

Blind Man Who Brings Excrement And Urine With Him had seen a vision back when he was known as Tatsipï, and lay on his back in the dark cave of pine trees in the *taibo* land called Flori-da. Now, Ecapusia saw his first vision in the land of The People.

A strange man with the odd hat and a strange accent, the earring dangling from a lobe, the cross stuck in the thick briars of black hair that covered his chest. The man who spoke with the voice of a *taibo* who was not from this country. That face had replaced the face of Lavender Growing Under The Peach Trees, but just for a moment, which was good. Because Ecapusia was glad his wife did not resemble that *taibo*.

"I do not know his name," Ecapusia said at length, "but the last words he said to me ring in my ears. He said this with a smile, and it is true. This *taibo* could have sent us back to the dark place on the shores of the never-ending pond. His words must have been powerful, for they brought Blind Man Who Brings Excrement And Urine With Him and me home."

"Yes," Blind Man Who Brings Excrement And Urine With Him said. "I remember the man and his words."

Ecapusia smiled at his wife, nodded at his decision, and felt the joy of a new beginning in the home he had known all of his life, a home that had always welcomed him and a country that he had always loved, and would for the rest of his days. It was something to be thankful for, and he wished he knew the meaning of the strange *taibo* words. But it did not matter. For Blind Man Who Brings Excrement And Urine With Him and Flea had made it home.

"From this day forward," the old Comanche said, "I will be called *"Céad Míle Fáilte."*

ABOUT THE AUTHOR

Eight-time Spur Award winner **Johnny D. Boggs** is recipient of the Western Writers of America's 2020 Owen Wister Award for Lifetime Contributions to Western Literature. He thanks Comanche artist Nocona Burgess for help with this story.

★ ★ ★ ★ ★

Fire Mountain

by Michael Zimmer

★ ★ ★ ★ ★

CHAPTER ONE

Pineview was bustling.

Halting his mount at the head of the town's broad main street, Buck McCready eyed the scurrying townspeople with the same kind of wonder he'd once held for circus sideshows, where bearded women and tattooed men invited the guileless to step closer and not be afraid. He recalled that the paintings on the sideshow tent's wall had promised even more exciting oddities and frightening displays inside.

There wasn't much mystery about what had the citizens of Pineview worked up. If the smell of smoke and the gray pall mantling the valley weren't enough to convince a person there was something evil on the prowl, then surely the swirling bits of floating ash would. Destruction was on its way, and it was coming with a vengeance.

The last time Buck had ridden through Pineview, the place had been little more than a raw settlement scratched out along the bank of a swift-flowing stream of the same unimaginative name. Back then, Pineview Creek, with its lush spring grass, brilliant wildflowers, and towering ponderosa pines darkening the mountain slopes to either side, had seemed like a little chunk of paradise broken off and fallen to earth.

He'd been heading north then, bound for Oregon and Washington Territory. Now he was on his way back south, with no inclination to tarry longer than it would take to buy a few supplies to see him down the trail. After that, he'd be gone. Or at least that was his intention.

Sitting his mule at the head of the street, Buck contemplated the changes that had taken place since he'd last been through here. The street had lost its creekside meander and now ran in a straight shot south to north, and there was what looked like a thriving business district at its southern terminus. Buildings that had once been cramped and dark—solid log walls with sod roofs and dirt floors—had been replaced with more welcoming structures of planed lumber, glass windows, and roofs of tin and tar, while brightly colored signs advertised everything from beer to boots, cigars and stoves. Several of the larger establishments had second floors, and a few that didn't sported false fronts to perpetuate an appearance of size and prosperity.

There was a residential district now, too, with a scattering of flower beds, picket fences, and neat front porches. A few of those were also two-storied.

But of all the differences that had sprung up in Pineview since Buck's last visit, none stood out more prominently than what lay at the far end of the street, where a line of passenger cars and boxcars were queued up behind a panting locomotive that was adding its own black coil of smoke to an already badly smudged sky. The train's depot seemed to be the hub of most of the activity, although Buck couldn't tell whether the chaos there stemmed from arrivals or departures.

Beyond the depot and the mouth of Pineview Canyon, the broad Snake River Plain stretched like a tan blanket in the arid heat of late September, its sky the same leaden color as the town's.

Tapping heels to the ribs of the black mule he called Zeke, Buck rode into town. He dismounted at a mercantile on the west side of the street and looped his reins over the rail. The store's double front doors were propped open, and men and women were hustling through them in a near frenetic confusion. Some, upon exiting, headed for the depot with their purchases clutched tightly in their arms. Others tossed their goods into the backs of carriages, traps, and buckboards assembled in the street. One enterprising fellow left the store pushing a wheelbarrow piled high with merchandise and immediately turned south to make his wobbly trek toward the waiting train.

Catching the eye of a burly man in a corduroy cap leaving the store with a forty-pound sack of flour balanced over one shoulder, Buck said, "What's all the commotion about, friend?"

The guy stopped with an impatient scowl and looked him up and down, as if gauging his worth in time. Buck had a fair idea of the image he presented—a lean, weathered stranger in his early thirties, wearing wool trousers, low-heeled boots, and a faded blue shirt. Buck's hat was wide-brimmed and round-crowned, his revolver a converted Army Colt .44; he carried a heavy-bladed hunting knife on his left hip, and had a well-oiled bullwhip tied to his saddle. The coiled whip marked him as a muleskinner; the worn-down heels of his boots and sweat-stained hat spoke of a drifter. But drifting didn't stifle a man's curiosity. Motioning toward the mass of people clogging the boardwalk and spilling into the street, Buck repeated his question.

"What's it about?" the man in the cap echoed incredulously. "What do you think it's about?" He flung an arm behind him, toward the store, although Buck understood he meant what lay beyond the building, to the west. "Ain't you got eyes?"

"That fire is still a long ways off."

"The hell it is," the burly man retorted, and brushed past Buck to join the exodus in the street.

Standing next to the mercantile's door, a bald man wearing sleeve garters and a cotton apron reaching from shoulder to shinbone lowered a clipboard. "It's not as far away as you might think," he said, then cocked his head quizzically. "Don't I know you from somewhere?"

"I came through here a few years ago."

"No, it wouldn't have been that. I didn't show up myself until a year ago last spring, just before they opened the Crown."

"The Crown?"

The storekeeper pointed past him, and Buck followed the line of his finger to the mountain range that dominated the east side of the valley. Its slopes were dark with pines, its craggy peaks nearly lost in the smoky haze.

"The Crown Mine, up over the top of those mountains," the storekeeper elaborated, then shrugged and added, "You do remind me of someone, though. But what Fred said about the fire is true enough."

"Fred? That the guy with the sack of flour on his shoulder?"

"It is. The town's been in an uproar ever since the telegraph from Boise went dead last night, likely from the fire. Then the OSL . . ." he tipped his head toward the chuffing locomotive, the markings of the Oregon Short Line Railroad prominently displayed on the tender, ". . . barely made it through from the west this morning. The engineer said the fire's already scorched the bridge over Breakwater Canyon. The conductor says there won't be any more rail traffic until it's repaired."

"That could take a while."

"A couple of weeks," the storekeeper agreed. "Meanwhile, with the telegraph down and the last train leaving at sundown, folks have caught themselves a serious case of herd fever. It's like when a cow spooks at its own shadow, and the rest of the bunch takes off without knowing why they're running."

"I've seen it," Buck said.

"Folks want a seat on that train, especially those who don't own a business or have livestock to take care of. A lot of them are buying what they think they'll need to wait out the flames."

"Must be good for business."

"It is. I've got two clerks and my wife trying to keep up. If this continues, I'll be cleaned out by sundown."

"Are you planning on leaving with the others then?"

"No, although I bought tickets for my wife and kids to leave." He shrugged. "I might regret it, but I intend to stay and keep an eye on the store. Some folks are claiming all of western Idaho is burning, which isn't all that hard to believe with the amount of smoke that's been pouring through here the past week, but if the Breakwater Bridge is already torched, that means the fire could be moving well to the north of us."

"It's a gamble," Buck said, turning his face to the southerly breeze.

"So is opening a store in a mining town," the merchant replied. Then he turned away when someone from inside called: *Felix*. "I need to see what this is about," he said, and disappeared into the mercantile.

Buck followed more slowly, strolling through the market's narrow aisles to find what he thought he'd need to see him down the trail. He suffered only a single elbow to his ribs from an impatient shopper—a woman with gray hair and poorly fitted dentures—when they both reached for the last box of baking soda on a nearly empty shelf. Allowing her the purchase, he settled for some dried apples, two pounds of flour, another of coffee, and a quarter of a sugar-cured ham. He took his supplies to the counter, and while waiting for a clerk, noticed a jar of peppermint candy sitting on the counter. Succumbing to impulse, he added a pair of red and white sticks to his selection.

In time a sandy-haired clerk with a sullen curl to his lip arrived to accept Buck's money, then loosely wrap his purchases in a piece of brown butcher paper that he tied off with a cord and shoved back across the counter before moving on to the next customer. Buck put the kid's rudeness down to the tight press of demanding shoppers and took his package outside. He stowed everything except the peppermint in his saddlebags, then stuck one of the sticks in a corner of his mouth like a slim, colorful cigar, and broke the other into two pieces that he offered, one at a time, to his mule. Being a longtime fan of anything sweet, Zeke accepted the confectionery without hesitation. Buck was watching him chew the second piece when a voice rang out behind him.

"By damn, now I know who you are."

He turned to find the storekeeper—Felix—standing on the boardwalk with his clipboard still in hand. He came over with an expansive grin.

"Still riding that black mule, too."

"You say you know me?"

"Sure, I know you. Buck McCready, right?"

"That's what I've been told."

"I'm Felix Payne. I used to run a little grocery on Montana Street, down in Corinne."

Buck nodded and relaxed. Felix was talking about Corinne, Utah Territory, where freight used to be offloaded from the Transcontinental Railroad and shipped north into Montana by wagon. "Yeah, I remember your place. Payne's Groceries."

"And you worked for Jock Kavanaugh's Box-K. You were a wagon master, if I remember right."

"Toward the end," Buck acknowledged.

"They said you were one of the best mule men in the mountains."

"Well, I wouldn't believe everything I heard from that pack of horse thieves in Corinne. They were notorious truth stretchers, especially after a couple of beers."

"And if they're in town . . ."

". . . they've had a couple of beers," Buck finished for him, and they both laughed at the memory. Then Felix's expression sobered.

"What brings you to Pineview, Buck?"

"Just passing through."

"You wouldn't be looking for a job, would you?"

Buck's gaze shifted briefly to the store, then away. "I reckon not."

"I don't mean inside. The fact is, I need a good muleman, and they're scarce in these parts."

"What's the job?" Buck asked, interested now that Payne had mentioned working with mules.

"Come on inside. This isn't something I want the whole town to hear."

Intrigued, Buck bit off the end of his peppermint and handed what was left to Zeke. Then he followed Felix inside. They skirted the line of customers waiting at the counter and walked to the rear of the store. Buck ignored the surly clerk's puzzled stare as they passed. Felix led him to a small office with a desk and a couple of chairs, then on through that to a large storeroom. A heavy loading dock door on their left had been rolled open to allow some light inside, but save for a small mountain of oilcloth-covered goods stacked against the rear wall, the cavernous warehouse looked almost empty. An older man sat in a chair next to the supplies, a stubby clay pipe jutting from his nest of whiskers like a tobacco-stained hatchling. Felix's face darkened when he saw the pipe.

"Damnation, Wallis, get that pipe out of here!"

The older man eyed Felix for a moment, then stood and ambled outside.

Felix glanced at Buck and shook his head. "Damn fool," he muttered.

"Was that Cam Wallis?"

"You know him?"

"Used to. He was a good muleskinner in his day, until a wagon slipped off its jack while he was greasing the hub and pinned him against the side of a barn. I guess it busted him up pretty bad."

"That's more or less what he told me," Felix said. "He's handy around livestock, but a poor watchman."

"I haven't seen him in years. Last I heard, he was using whiskey to dull the pain."

"It's addled his thinking, if you ask me. He should know better than to smoke in a warehouse, especially one that's been used to store wheat and oats. It doesn't take but a spark to start a fire in grain dust."

Buck nodded, but his attention had already returned to the piles of merchandise Wallis had been guarding. "Is that why you brought me here?"

"It is." Felix walked over to the stacks and peeled back a ten-foot square of oilcloth. Underneath were several hundred pounds of flour and cornmeal in stenciled forty-pound sacks. "These are supplies I've contracted to deliver to the Crown Mine."

Recalling the storekeeper's earlier description, Buck hooked a thumb over his shoulder, in the direction of the mountains east of town.

Felix nodded. "They call it the Crown Range now, named after the mine."

"How far away is it?"

"Not too far as the crow flies."

"And with a pack mule?"

"Three days with normal loads and a full crew. It'll probably take you four, if you're interested."

Buck eyed the rows of supplies. "How much of this goes?"

"All of it. Right at two and a half tons."

"That's more than a one-man job, Mr. Payne."

"I can get you a couple of men, but I need a lead packer, someone who knows freight and mules, and how to get a job done. No one in Corinne has forgotten how you took Jock's freight wagons through to Virginia City, and won the old man his contract, too."

Buck was silent a moment, reliving the incident. His old mentor, Mason Campbell—the man who had rescued Buck from the Sioux, then raised him as his own—was supposed to lead that wagon train. But someone had gunned Mase down on a deserted Utah street just days before the outfit was scheduled to pull out for the Montana goldfields. With a lucrative freight-hauling contract riding on the Kavanaugh train reaching the rowdy mining camp of Virginia City before its competitor, Jock offered the position of wagon master to Buck. He'd almost turned it down in his determination to find Mase's killer. But he'd also made a commitment to Jock's Box-K, and in Mase's honor, he'd accepted the challenge. It wasn't until they were underway that Buck learned there was a saboteur among his crew, and that a gunman had been hired to stop him—the same gunman who had killed Mase in Corinne.*

"What about it, Buck?" Felix asked, pulling him out of his thoughts. "Are you interested?"

After a pause, Buck said, "What's the pay?"

"Two hundred dollars." Felix smiled at Buck's reaction. "It's a lot of money, I'll grant you, but there's a lot riding on it, too. The fact is, I've got a situation similar to what Jock had in Utah, although this isn't a race so much as a commitment."

"What kind of a commitment?"

"I guaranteed the Crown Mine that I could deliver their goods on a monthly basis. There were a couple of other outfits that wanted the contract, but I got it. So far, I've been able to

---

The Long Hitch, by Michael Zimmer

fulfill my end of the agreement, but with that damned wildfire burning so close, people are panicking. The men I'd normally use to haul these supplies to the Crown have left town. They said they didn't want to get caught up there if the fire burns that far."

"I can't say that I blame them."

"That may be, but it's my tail caught in a trap if I can't deliver these goods when promised."

"When are they due?"

"October first . . . six days from now."

"It puts you in a tight spot," Buck acknowledged.

"That's why it's worth two hundred dollars to me. It's not just these supplies that are at stake, but my contract with the Crown for next year if I don't meet my obligations this year. Sooner or later, if the mine keeps producing, they'll build a road up there, and then I'll be out of the picture. Like they say, Buck, you've got to make hay while the sun is shining."

"And they wouldn't care if the fire caught your mules and men on the trail."

It wasn't a question. Felix didn't take it as one. "All that matters to men like that is that their supplies are delivered on time."

"What about you, Mr. Payne?" Buck asked. "Would it matter to you?"

"Of course it'd matter. I wouldn't send men out if I didn't think they could make it. But if that fire has already burned along the Breakwater, then it could easily swing miles north of here."

"Or not?"

"Or not," he agreed. "If there weren't risks involved, Buck, I wouldn't be offering you two hundred dollars for half a week's labor."

"You said you could get me a couple of men?"

"I can get you two."

"Then I'll be leading a string myself. Six thousand pounds of cargo . . ." He did the calculations in his mind, then whistled softly. "Thirty mules, meaning ten pack animals apiece. That'd be a tough job in open country, let alone over mountain passes and through thick forests." He glanced to the loading dock, where a tendril of blue smoke from Cam Wallis's pipe curled past the door. "Is he one of the men you had in mind?"

"He is, and I'm afraid you won't have thirty head, either. Right now I've got twenty-two mules under contract, plus a couple of Indian ponies for my packers to ride. I might find a few more head from people wanting to leave on the evening train, but I wouldn't count on thirty."

"I know Cam's reputation. What about the other man? How much experience does he have?"

Felix seemed relieved by the question. "He's a good man. You won't have any trouble there." He paused for only a second. "Will you do it?"

"No, not for two hundred, but I'll do it for five."

"Five hun—!" Felix's head rocked back as if he'd been punched in the nose. "Damnation, Buck, that's . . ." His words trailed off. "Hell, I guess you've got my back to the wall. All right, five hundred dollars."

"And two hundred for each man."

Felix's lips thinned. For a moment, Buck thought he was going to refuse. He wasn't sure that wouldn't be the smarter move, all things considered. But Felix had pretty well summed up his situation when he acknowledged his back was to a wall. Besides, they both knew the money he'd spend on packers this trip would be more than offset by a new contract next summer.

"All right, it's a deal," he grated.

Buck nodded, but he didn't smile. Neither did Felix Payne. The two men shook hands solemnly, and Felix said, "Come into my office. I'll show you a map to the Crown."

CHAPTER TWO

Tentative knocking irritated Anton Luce. In his opinion, it reflected a timid character, and the distinct likelihood of unsatisfactory results. Unfortunately, Anton didn't always have the option of picking the best men for a job.

He gazed curiously at the door separating his office from the saloon's upstairs hallway, then resolutely went back to filling out his order for the upcoming winter. What he'd need most was whiskey and beer, but a couple of cases of cheap cigars and a few more of pickled eggs and jellied pigs' feet would help keep his customers salted down and thirsty once the deep snows of central Idaho put a stop to their restless search for gold.

Unlike most of the sheep fleeing town, Anton Luce had no intention of abandoning his livelihood. Basing his decision on what the engineer from the Oregon Short Line had reported earlier, he judged the odds were in favor of the forest fire going well to the north of Pineview, maybe even skirting the valley altogether.

His pen ceased its brittle scratching as a taut smile curled his lips upward. Although he was counting on the fire missing the town, he was equally certain there would be a few exceptions—little flare-ups here and there to conveniently eliminate some of the competition.

Leaning back in his chair, Anton had to marvel at the good luck some errant lightning strike or careless campfire had dropped in his lap. Pineview had four saloons. Taking out three of them would put his own High Dollar Emporium in the enviable position of supplying the alcohol and gambling needs for a sizable swath of Central Idaho for the rest of the winter. And on top of that, he'd made sure Felix Payne wouldn't find enough men to fulfill his obligation to the Crown Mine—which was going to leave Luce's Fast Freight and Express next in line for the following season's contract.

Just thinking about the possibilities made Anton want to laugh, but when the knock came again, even more diffident than before, his smile vanished. He'd forgotten for a moment that only fools placed their trust in luck, and that sooner or later good fortune always found a way to spin around and bite a man on the ass.

He eyed the closed door speculatively for a moment, then slid the top drawer of his desk partially open to expose the butt of a four-barreled Sharps pistol. Resting his hand on top of the drawer, fingers resting lightly on the pistol's walnut grips, he barked, "Come in, goddamnit!"

The door creaked open and a hank of sandy hair tipped into view. "Mr. Luce?"

Anton slapped the drawer closed with a curse. "Get in here, Foster, before someone sees you."

"Yes, sir," the kid replied, slipping sideways through the door and closing it behind him. He stopped, as he always did, to glance timidly around the office, then shuffled forward.

"What is it?" Anton demanded. He'd promised the churlish youth money for information—the amount dependent upon the value of the news—but didn't consider courtesy a part of their arrangement.

Foster had removed his hat upon entering. He held it in front of him now in an obvious gesture of servitude, clutched in both hands, knuckles pale against the darker fabric of the bowler.

"You said you wanted to know if Mr. Payne found a muleskinner."

Anton scowled. "That's right. Are you telling me he did?"

"Yes, sir, it appears that way."

"Who?"

"I don't know his full name. I heard Mr. Payne call him Buck."

"Buck? That doesn't tell me a damn thing," he replied. Then his brows furrowed at some distant memory, but the kid went on before he could sort it out.

"He just rode into town," Foster continued. "I think Mr. Payne must've known him from before, the way he acted."

Anton's scowl deepened. Some years back, both he and Felix Payne had operated businesses out of Corinne. In those days, before the ever-spreading tentacles of the railroad had diminished Utah's grip on the mining communities of Montana and Idaho, the big freight outfits—his own among them—had ruled the northwestern mountains. Although the two men had never been friends, their shared history was something Anton kept tucked away in the back of his mind.

"What does this new man look like?"

"I'd say he's around thirty, maybe six foot, brown hair." Foster shrugged. "That's about it."

"That's about nothing," Anton snarled, and the kid swayed back from the hot rush of the saloon owner's anger. "Brown hair? How's he wear it?"

"Kind of long in back, over his collar."

Anton's gaze narrowed. "What's he riding?"

"A mule."

"A black mule?"

"Yes, sir." Foster looked startled. "Do you know him?"

Anton nodded, more to himself than to the kid. "Go find Tom Burrows. Tell him I want to see him."

"I gotta get back to the store," Foster objected. "I told Mr. Payne I was going to the privy, but he'll start to wonder if I ain't back pretty quick."

"You find Burrows first, then go back to Payne's and start nosing around about this new man. Find out what you can, and as soon as you've got something I can actually use, haul your ass back here and tell me what it is."

Foster nodded and swallowed audibly, and Anton shook his head in disgust. He waited until the kid had left, then stood and walked to the window. He couldn't see Payne's store from here, it being on the same side of the street as the High Dollar, but the crowd in front of it looked as chaotic as it had ever since the OSL's conductor had announced his would be the last train from Pineview until the fires were out.

Staring into the street, Anton's view dissolved into an image of Buck McCready as he remembered him from Corinne. It was McCready who had been the cause of the Crowley and Luce Freight outfit going bankrupt, ruining him and sending Herb Crowley into the gutter with a bottle of cheap whiskey. A slow heat spread across the back of Anton's neck as the memory of the match between two of Utah's largest freight outfits played across his mind. McCready had not returned from Montana after the race, leaving any chance for retribution out of Anton's reach. But it appeared now that he was back, and once again sticking his nose into issues that were of no concern to him, but that could cost Anton Luce another fortune.

Well, by damn, he wasn't going to allow it to happen. Not again. The first time Buck McCready had stepped in his way, it had been a matter of chance and bad luck. This time it would be different. This time, it was personal.

CHAPTER THREE

"We're here," Felix Payne said, placing a finger on the lower portion of the map spread across the desk in his office. "This is Pineview, and this," he moved his finger a couple of inches, "is Pineview Creek. Half a day's ride upstream from here is a side canyon that comes in from the east."

"I saw it this morning," Buck confirmed. "Nice-sized stream with a big grove of cottonwood at its mouth."

"That's what I've heard, although I've never seen it personally. It's called Owl Creek Canyon, but don't ask me why."

"Who drew the map?"

"One of the Crown's managers. He gave me a copy after I signed their supply contract last spring."

"Then he knows the trail?"

"He'd probably been over it twenty times before he sketched the map." Felix's finger shifted sideways. "Another half day up the Owl will bring you to a narrow canyon called North Fork. Unless you have trouble along the way, you should reach it by the end of your first day. Just past it, but still on the Owl, is a decent place to camp with plenty of water, grass, and wood. That'll probably be your best bet for the night.

"Up to here, you'll have had it fairly easy, but once you start up North Fork it's going to get ornery. From everything I've heard, the trail is as crooked as a tinhorn. There'll also be rock slides and fallen trees you'll have to get your pack strings around. Then, toward the head of the canyon, it gets even worse." He traced a wiggling line that reminded Buck of a snake on hot sand. "This'll be the hardest part for the mules, sharp switchbacks and slick rock that'll make it difficult for them to keep their footing." He moved his finger once more. "After North Fork, you'll be above timberline. There's a glacier lake along the trail where they say the grass is good, although there probably won't be much wood for a fire. Chances are, you'll spend your second night there. It's not far in miles, but by the time you reach it, you'll be ready to stop. So will your mules."

Buck nodded that he understood, and Felix went on.

"After you leave the lake, you'll cross over to the eastern slope and drop down into some heavy timber, but the trail through here will be fairly straight, and there won't be any more steep grades. It'll still be another full day's travel to the mine, though." He looked up. "Any questions?"

Buck shook his head. It sounded like an arduous journey, but not an especially challenging one to follow. "What about the men?" he asked. "I already know Cam Wallis. Who's the second packer?"

"You've probably heard of him. China Jake."

"China Jake? Why are you asking me to lead your crew if you've got him?"

"Because no one will follow a Chinaman," Felix replied bluntly.

"Not even a man with his . . ." Buck's words trailed off, recognizing the truth of Felix's words. It might not be smart, and it sure as hell wasn't fair, but it was the way it was in that part of the world.

"China Jake will be your ace in the hole if you let him," Felix continued. "You're as solid a muleskinner as ever came down the pike, Buck, but your experience is mostly in hauling freight with wagons. Jake has been dragging pack mules through these mountains, hauling goods into camps too remote to reach by wheeled traffic, since the first big strikes in the Boise Basin in '62. And he knows the trail to the Crown."

"Where is he now?"

"Jake is watching my mules. I send them out to graze during the day, then he'll bring them in at night. Jake and Cam have already sorted the packs, so that's done. All you'll have to do tomorrow is saddle up and pull out."

Buck glanced out the small window above Felix's desk. The day was waning, the afternoon light grown dim behind the smoke. Picking his hat up off the chair at his side, he said, "I'm going to go take care of Zeke, then have a look around town."

"You can stable Zeke here," Felix offered. "I've got corrals for the pack mules, but there are a couple of individual stalls you can use, and some shelled corn in a grain bin next to the tack room."

"Obliged," Buck said. "I'll probably sleep out there with him, too, if you've no objection."

"You'll have company. Jake and Cam are both bunking down next to the stables where they can keep an eye on things."

Buck hesitated, recalling how Wallis had been guarding the Crown's supplies. Now he found out they were both staying close to the mules at night. He wondered if Payne was expecting trouble, then recalled the precautions Jock Kavanaugh used to take with his wagons and dismissed the concern. With a brief farewell, he put on his hat and left the office. As he walked back through the store, he spotted the sandy-haired clerk with the sullen expression ducking in through the front door. The clerk lurched to a halt when he saw Buck, then moved swiftly behind the counter, keeping his gaze averted. Buck's brow creased in puzzlement at the kid's odd behavior. Then he dismissed that, as well. He had 5,000 pounds of supplies to deliver to a remote, high-country mine, and an uneasy feeling that there wasn't going to be a lot of time to accomplish it.

CHAPTER FOUR

Buck liked China Jake from the start. He was a small man, slimly built but wiry and strong. Unlike most of the Chinese immigrants Buck had worked with over the years, Jake had been born in the United States. Orphaned before his second birthday, he had been raised by an orchardist near Stockton, California.

Jake had long ago shrugged off the tenets of a culture he no longer felt a part of. He kept his hair trimmed close, without the traditional queue of his countrymen, and wore the sturdy range clothes of his trade—canvas trousers, hobnail boots, a wool shirt under a dark vest, and a narrow-brimmed hat of a style once called a beehive, which made it easier for him to navigate the dense pine forests of central Idaho without having to worry about losing his headgear every time he passed under a low-hanging bough.

And he knew mules. That much was evident within the first twenty minutes of working together that evening. In a voice soft, eloquent, and devoid of accent, Jake informed Buck that the pack train was ready to pull out at first light.

Although Buck didn't doubt him, as head packer it was his responsibility to make sure the string was up to the task ahead. It was also important that he meet the stock. Mules had a different temperament from horses, and generally required a more personal touch. As Buck moved among them, talking to the individual animals, inspecting hooves and backs and leg muscles, he knew the long-eared mountain canaries were judging him—his skill, confidence, and authority—with the same critical eye he had for them. Experience had taught him that if the mules trusted and respected him, they would be more tractable in the days ahead. And Buck sensed that was going to be important. Felix Payne seemed certain the fire would burn well to the north of them. Cam and Jake weren't as confident.

" 'Sides, even if it do go north, ain't that the direction we're goin' in?" Cam had demanded, after Payne returned to his store following introductions. "Hell, we're liable to ride straight into the blasted thing, we ain't keerful!"

They ate supper together afterward, a simple meal of beans and side pork, eased down the throat by swallows of iron-strong coffee. It was Cam who prepared the rough feast, squatted over a small cook fire behind the store with his pipe cocked from his mouth at a jaunty angle, his eyes squinted against its smoke. Now and again a harsh, racking cough would tear through the man's slender frame, and his breath would catch, then wheeze dangerously before he pulled himself together again.

"It ain't nothin' for either of you two hounds to fret over," the older man had snapped the first time he went into a hacking fit. Worried, Buck had hurried over from inspecting the mules to make sure he was all right, but Cam waved him off.

"It's his lungs," China Jake confided after Buck returned to the corral. Having already been scolded by the old man, Jake had stayed with the mules. "He claims they were damaged when a wagon fell against him, but I don't believe it."

"What do you think it is?"

"I couldn't say for sure, but from the way it sounds, I'd guess his lungs are beginning to fail."

Buck studied the elderly man from between the corral rails. Felix had claimed Cam was in his mid-forties, but he looked at least twenty years older than that. He was as skinny as a starved rabbit, with straggly gray hair poking out from under a wilted

Stetson and clothes that were threadbare in spots.

It was obvious the smoke from the fires was playing havoc with the older man's lungs. During the meal and in the hour or so afterward, before they retired to their blankets, Cam acknowledged that a doctor at the time of the accident had suspected a punctured lung.

"It gives me fits, time to time," Cam admitted, stifling a cough.

"You figure you can make it to the Crown?" Buck asked. It was a blunt question, but an important one. They were already short-handed. If Cam couldn't keep up or pull his share of the load, they'd have to find someone to replace him or call off the trip.

"I'll be there right behind you, boy," Cam growled, and Buck nodded his approval for the man's adamancy. Then a fresh fit of coughing tore through the old man's chest, and Buck's doubts returned. It seemed a long time before Cam finally leaned to one side and spat into the weeds against the store's foundation. After wiping his lips with the back of his hand, he added hoarsely, "This damn smoke's as bothersome as a nit fly."

"That pipe that's always stuck in your mouth doesn't help," Jake said. "Why don't you give it up, at least until the fires are out?"

"You just mind your own damned string," Cam replied. "I ain't yet taken advice from a heathen. I don't aim to start tonight."

Jake's gaze narrowed and Buck stiffened, determined to step between them if he had to. But Cam lowered his eyes to the coals at the base of their coffee pot and kept them there, and after a minute Jake shoved to his feet and walked to the corral. Leaning forward, Cam casually pulled a twig from the fire and relit his pipe. Buck stared, waiting for him to speak or look up, to offer some kind of explanation, but the older man's expres-

sion remained inscrutable, and after a couple of minutes Buck
stood and stalked into the darkness.

CHAPTER FIVE

The evening light was fading rapidly now. From behind the window in his dusky office above the High Dollar Emporium, Anton Luce scowled down at Pineview's single thoroughfare. The OSL had pulled out just before sundown, its twin passenger cars packed like ammunition crates, the boxcars trailing behind them bristling with citizens too broke or too late to purchase tickets for a coach seat. Now, in the deepening twilight, the town looked almost deserted, its wide street empty of traffic, the boardwalk a plank highway leading nowhere.

Anton stood with his right hand held rigidly in front of the middle button of his brocaded red vest, a cigar clenched firmly between his fingers. On the desk behind him, the order he had been composing for winter supplies sat unfinished, the ink in the pen's nib dried to a black clog. He was staring south into the smoke-hazed distance, but it wasn't the vast grasslands of the Snake River Plain that filled his view. It was the look on his old partner's face when they learned of McCready's victory in securing the Montana mining contract for the Box-K.

Herb Crowley had known immediately what the loss meant for the company he and Anton had cobbled together through hard work and some less-than-honest business dealings. Anton had been a little slower to put all the pieces together, but when he did, his throat had turned instantly to dust. Buck McCready had ruined them both; maybe he hadn't meant to, but motive didn't change the outcome.

A heavy knock rattled the office door. Anton turned as it swung inward without invitation. A large man entered with a swagger that brought Anton a grim sense of satisfaction. Nobody had ever accused Tom Burrows of timidity.

"You're late," Anton said brusquely.

Burrows hesitated, and his expression momentarily darkened. Then, with a guffaw, he elbowed the door shut and crossed the room to Anton's desk. "There's maybe half a dozen people in this world I'd let talk to me that way," he said pleasantly; then his voice turned to stone. "After today, you ain't one of 'em."

"I'm paying you handsomely," Anton replied. "One of my requirements is that you show up when summoned."

"Luce, I don't summon worth a damn, and I ain't much concerned for other people's requirements, either." Halting in front of the desk, Burrows poured a shot of bourbon into a glass from a decanter sitting on one corner. Then he looked up with a taunting grin. "I'll tell you something else, anybody who does ain't fit for the kind of work you want done."

Anton bit off the retort that nearly slipped from his tongue. Burrows was right about the kind of men he'd need for a job like this. But there was a second truth to his hesitation, one that galled him deeper than he'd ever admit. The fact was, Burrows frightened him. The man's reputation as a killer was well-known throughout the Northwest, and his volatility was a part of his legend.

Changing the subject, Anton said, "Have you talked to Foster?"

"That the little runt who works for Felix Payne?"

"You know who he is."

Burrows shrugged. "Yeah, I talked to him."

"Then you know about the new man Payne hired. What have you found out about him?"

"I ain't found out nothing. The runt says his name is Buck

McCready. Some of the boys I talked to in the Little Ace says he used to work for a freighting company out of Corinne."

His lips settling into a hard line, Anton leaned forward to snuff his cigar in an iron ashtray. Noticing his impatience, Burrows grinned and took a long swallow of bourbon.

"And did any of those boys from the Little Ace Saloon say what McCready was doing in Pineview?" Anton asked.

"They didn't, although one of 'em mentioned he's been up Oregon way the last few years, skinning mules for an outfit out of The Dalles. They reckoned he was heading back to Utah. At least he was until Felix Payne offered him a job." His brows ridged in curiosity. "Just what is it you want done, Luce?"

"I want you to kill him."

Burrows had raised his glass for another drink. At Anton's words, he nearly choked on the liquor in his throat. "Payne?" he asked throatily.

"No, of course not," Anton replied, just barely refraining from adding: *you idiot.* "I want McCready dead." He paused, then clarified, "But not in town. Do it somewhere along the trail to the Crown."

"That makes more sense," Burrows allowed. "What about the others, the old man and the chink?"

Anton tapped a finger thoughtfully on top of his desk. In his single-minded fixation on McCready, he'd failed to consider the other two packers. After a moment's reflection, he shrugged. "That will be up to you. I want the pack train stopped and its supplies destroyed. And I want Buck McCready dead. Beyond that, just make sure nothing finds its way back to my door."

Burrows shrugged and set his empty glass down on the desk. "It's your money, Luce. If that's what you want, you'll have it."

171

CHAPTER SIX

They were up before dawn the next morning. Cam brought the mules in two at a time and saddled them, while China Jake and Buck hoisted the loads into place by lantern light. True to his word, Felix had rounded up two more mules, bringing the total to twenty-four. That was still less than the thirty animals Buck would have preferred, but it was nothing they couldn't work around.

In addition to the pack animals, they had Buck's mule Zeke and a trio of horses. Two of those were saddle mounts for Jake and Cam. The third was a zebra dun mare, too old to carry more than some basic camp supplies—skillet and coffee pot, some rice, hardtack, and side pork, plus their bedrolls. According to Jake, the zebra dun had been a member of Payne's pack string since the animals were purchased last winter, and had quickly assumed the position of bell mare.

For some reason Buck had never fully understood, mules would often develop a fondness bordering on devotion for a certain animal. In his experience, it was usually a mare, and more often than not a horse rather than one of its own kind. Smart muleskinners had learned to take advantage of that kinship, and would loop a bell over the horse's neck to allow its steady jingle to be heard by the rest of the string. No matter the situation or terrain, the sound of the mare's bell always seemed to reassure a long line of pack animals that she was still somewhere up front, and that there was nothing to fear as long as the older animal remained calm.

"A good bell mare is worth her weight in gold," Jake claimed as he buckled the leather strap around the dun's neck. Then he looked at Buck and grinned. "Well, maybe not gold, but we'll be glad we have her before we reach the Crown."

It didn't take long to get everything lined out. Although Cam Wallis was older than the others, and slower due to his injuries, he was still a good hand, and Buck had spent most of his life around mules, handling the big freight wagons and, more recently, packing into the mountainous country southwest of The Dalles. But it was China Jake who put them both in the dust with his skill and efficiency, lifting his packs effortlessly into place, then cinching them tight. In the lantern's yellow light, his diamond hitches looked as if they had been drawn onto the rough canvas covers, so perfectly were they aligned and knotted.

Felix Payne showed up just as Cam extinguished the lantern. He looked surprised to find them so far along. "I thought I'd come down and help, but it looks like you don't need it."

"I wanted to get an early start," Buck said. He tipped his head toward the western horizon, where twisted clouds of pale smoke snaked into the sky, their bellies tinged crimson from the inferno below. "I'm not sure that fire is going to go as far north as you'd hoped," he added.

Felix nodded solemnly. The southerly breeze from the past few days had died overnight, leaving the air still and heavy.

Stepping into the saddle, Buck took a loose hitch around his horn with the lead pack mule's rope and rode over to where Felix was unlatching the corral gate. Leaning down to shake the storekeeper's hand, he said, "We should be back by the end of the week if we don't run into any trouble."

"Let's hope you don't," Felix replied, but his grip lingered as if there was more he wanted to say. Finally, dropping Buck's hand, he got to it. "I had a man quit on me last night, one of my clerks. Do you remember Foster? I think he waited on you."

"The kid with the chip on his shoulder?"

"That's him. I figured he'd scooted to catch the Oregon Short Line out of the valley, like half the damn town did, but then I saw him this morning going into the High Dollar."

Buck recalled the saloon from his ride through town yesterday, a two-storied structure a block up the street from Payne's mercantile. "Maybe he wanted a drink," Buck said. "I know my throat feels about half raw from all the smoke I've swallowed the past couple of days."

"That's possible, but the first chance you get, ask Jake or Cam what they think about the High Dollar."

Buck hesitated. "That's an interesting suggestion, Mr. Payne. Any particular reason you're making it?"

Felix stared at him a moment, indecision like a flickering light in his eyes. Then he shook his head. "Just ask them," he said, and walked the gate open. "You might want to keep an eye on your back trail, too."

Buck didn't reply. It troubled him that there might be more to the job than Felix had originally let on, especially since he didn't want to share it. But with the light growing steadily, illuminating the towering columns of smoke in the west, Buck felt an urgency to get underway. He nodded for Jake to take the lead, the bell mare first in line, the rest of his mules strung out behind her tied tail-to-halter. Cam fell in on the heels of Jake's string with his own, and Buck brought up the rear where he could keep an eye on the entire outfit. Felix nodded a somber goodbye to each of them as they passed through the gate, but spoke to no one. Buck thought he looked worried, and that bothered him, too.

They followed the old road out of Pineview, hugging the creek's edge and avoiding the town's main thoroughfare, although Buck hadn't heard a wagon's rumble or a horse's whinny all morning. If they hadn't been in such a hurry, he probably would have opted to loose-herd the stock and keep just the dun bell mare on a lead while he and Cam brought up the rear, but there was no doubt, as the day brightened, that the smoke had grown heavier overnight, the fire drawn closer.

North of town they swung back onto what passed for a road in this direction, and by the time the sun pulled free of the mountains, they'd put a good five miles behind them. From time to time Buck would glance back the way they'd come, but Pineview was lost from sight in the haze, and above the eastern peaks the sun looked more like a small, faded peach than anything of significance.

They reached Owl Creek at midday. The leaves on the tall cottonwoods growing along its banks were already fading into brown after the hot, dry summer. In another couple of weeks they would begin their gentle drift to the ground—assuming they weren't turned to ash beforehand.

China Jake led them away from the main road, toward the mouth of Owl Canyon still a quarter of a mile away. As he did, he turned to casually look behind them. Even from the rear of the train, Buck could see the sudden alarm that flitted across the man's face. Twisting in his saddle, Buck stared back the way they'd come. Earlier, there had been nothing there except autumn grass and a gray pall of smoke. Now he spotted a trio of horsemen sitting their mounts atop a low rise near the valley's eastern rim, staring toward them.

Jake slowed his string crossing the valley; Buck hurried his, and they met at the canyon's mouth. Cam rode up to join them, the mules splayed out to the rear like strands of unraveled yarn.

"Who are they?" Cam demanded hoarsely, staring back to where the horsemen still calmly sat their mounts, watching and waiting.

175

Buck glanced at Jake, but the younger man shook his head.

"Well, whoever they be, you can bet they're bound for mischief," Cam declared.

"That sounds about right," Jake agreed softly.

"Just before we pulled out this morning, Felix told me to ask you two about the High Dollar Emporium," Buck said.

Jake darted a look at Cam, who rubbed thoughtfully at his lower lip with a knuckle. "That might could be," the older man allowed.

"What do you mean?" Buck asked.

"The guy who owns the Dollar also owns a small freight outfit," Jake explained. "He promised the Crown he'd build a wagon road from Pineview to the mine if they gave him the contract, but the Crown's owners didn't want to wait. They gave it to Payne, instead. Luce didn't take it well."

"Luce!" Buck's head came up. "Anton Luce?"

"You know him?"

"Yeah, I know him. Or I did back in Corinne."

"He came to Pineview after his Utah company went bankrupt."

"Bankrupt? I hadn't heard about that."

"Luce showed up here a few years back," Cam said. "Started hisself a saloon, but once they made that big strike at the Crown, he quick put together some wagons and harness stock and called it a freight company. It weren't much from the beginning and ain't gone far since, but I've heard ol' Anton can carry a grudge farther than any two mules put together."

"He was that way in Utah, too," Buck said. "Unless he's changed, he wouldn't be above trying to stop us."

"He hasn't changed," Jake replied, and Cam nodded sober confirmation.

"Anton has got hisself a streak of mean that runs from heel to topknot," the older man added.

"Then we're going to have to watch our backs from here on," Buck said.

He kept his tone even, but inside, he was seething. Now he knew what Felix hadn't wanted to tell him that morning at the corral. Payne had to realize how Luce would react if he found out Buck was leading his pack outfit, yet he'd deliberately withheld that information. Even though it was infuriating, Buck thought he understood the store owner's motives. Time was running out for Felix; he couldn't afford to lose his contract with the Crown, or risk having Buck back out of his commitment to haul his supplies to the mine. Freighting, no matter what the method used to transfer goods from one location to another, had always been a cutthroat business, and whether Buck agreed with him or not, Felix had only been playing the odds as he saw them—never mind that he'd been wagering Buck's life and the success of the haul on his bet.

Exhaling loudly, Buck looked at Cam, then Jake, and said, "Let's keep 'em moving."

CHAPTER SEVEN

Owl Creek was narrow and fast, but with a gentle flex that made it easy to follow. The trail clung to the left bank, well-marked and solidly packed from who knew how many others that had tramped this way before. The canyon's north-facing slope was steep and densely pined, but the other side of the gulch was more moderately sloped, with little groves of shimmying aspens scattered like discarded coins along the canyon floor.

Normally Buck would have ordered a noon break to rest the stock, but with the approaching maelstrom out of the west and a trio of men suspiciously dogging them from the south, he opted to keep the long string of mules moving forward at a brisk walk. As the afternoon waned, the Owl's walls began to pinch in on either side, and the trail became more sinuous. China Jake was lost from sight much of the time, and Cam's presence was marked largely by the increasing volume of his hacking coughs as the smoke intensified. Although Buck kept a close watch to the rear, he saw no sign of pursuit, but his gut told him the three horsemen were still following . . . biding their time.

An early dusk was closing in around them by the time they reached North Fork Canyon. They paused only briefly at its mouth to discuss their choices. Earlier that afternoon Buck had weighed the advantages of pushing on into the evening, but as he eyed the twisting creekside path disappearing into the canyon's interior, he realized they'd have to wait until morning if they didn't want to risk injuring the stock.

Jake led them to a long clearing another hundred yards up the Owl, where they dropped stiffly from their saddles and began off-loading the packs. They hobbled the mules but picketed their saddle stock and the bell mare, knowing that as long as the zebra dun was close, the rest of the herd wouldn't stray far.

With darkness closing in, Buck ordered Cam to start a fire and fix a meal, while Jake rubbed down the stock and checked for fresh cuts or sores. Meanwhile, he took his rifle and hiked back down the trail on foot. He probably covered a mile or so, taking his time and watching sharp for an ambush, before nightfall forced him to turn back. Although he hadn't spotted anything alarming, the uneasiness he'd felt all afternoon refused to lessen. They were out there. Damnit, he could *feel* them.

Cam had a meal waiting by the time he got back. Looking up as Buck stepped into the light of his small cook fire, he said, "Figured for a bit there you'd got yourself lost."

"No," Buck replied stoically, leaning his rifle against a nearby pack.

"Did you see anything?" Jake asked.

"Not a thing." He dug a plate and spoon from his saddlebags and scooped up a mess of rice and raisins—spotted pup, they called it—and some slices of beef cooked on a flat rock set close to the flame.

"Maybe they weren't following us, after all," Jake mused.

"That ain't likely," Cam replied dourly.

Recalling the hawk-eyed manner in which the horsemen had watched the pack string enter the canyon, Buck was inclined to agree with Cam. He took a bite of meat and chewed it down, and said, "I figure they'll jump us tonight, after we're bedded down. That wildfire's getting too close for them to want to stay out here any longer than they have to."

"What we oughter do is take the fight to 'em," Cam said.

"We don't know where they are," Buck replied. "And we'd have to leave the mules and packs unguarded to look for them. I won't do that."

"We could bundle some pine boughs in our blankets, then slip off and wait for them," Jake suggested.

"Oldest trick in the book," Cam said. "They'd never swallow it."

"Simple is best," Jake argued.

Cam snorted dismissively. "Chinaman's logic."

Jake's eyes narrowed. "There's a limit," he said quietly, "to how much bullshit I'll take from you."

"That's enough," Buck said, shooting Cam a warning look. "Besides, you're both right. We'll just change it up a little. We'll let the fire die to coals and rig a couple of bedrolls to look like some of us are asleep, then have a third one leaning against one of the packs so that they'll think there's a man keeping watch. We'll wrap that in a blanket, too, and I'll put my coat around it and my hat on top, but tipped forward so that it looks like I've dozed off. I can lay my rifle across what they'll think is my lap. Without a fire, they'll have to come in close enough for me to use my Colt."

"That sounds about right," Jake agreed after a moment's consideration.

"You damn right it's right," Cam added. "Long as they ain't out there now with their peepers peepin' on us."

"I doubt it," Buck said, then stood and dumped what was left of his coffee over the flames. "But let's kill the fire and get set up, anyway."

It took less than twenty minutes to set their trap. When they were finished, Buck sent Jake and Cam into the trees upstream, while he took a downstream position, the direction from which their ambushers would likely appear. He found a pine not too far away and scooted back under its low-hanging branches. From here the coals of their cook fire seemed to pulsate like a slowly beating heart, its faint glow the Owl's only illumination that evening.

Buck settled in cross-legged with his revolver in his right hand, its long barrel cradled in the crook of his left elbow. He didn't know if he was surprised or relieved when he heard a soft voice between him and the creek—close enough to make him flinch—whisper: "There they are."

Another replied in equally hushed tones: "Shut up, you damn fool."

Then the muzzle blast from a rifle speared the night, and Buck jumped and swore. The man who had breathed *Shut up, you damn fool* cursed loudly and shouted, "Lay into 'em, boys!"

Gunfire crackled from two sides, yellow lances splitting the darkness. Buck threw himself flat and thrust the Colt before him. Jake and Cam were returning fire, but they were farther away, and their shots were being deflected by the web of tree limbs separating them from their attackers.

Buck's view was less impeded. Targeting a muzzle flare barely ten yards away, he adjusted his aim and squeezed the trigger. He heard the man's grunt even above the report of his own weapon, but fired a second time for good measure, before rolling out from under the pine boughs. A frightened shout echoed from downstream. Buck rose and started in that direction but hadn't covered more than a few paces when a hulking figure appeared out of the shadows on his right.

"Tom!" the man called, and Buck said, "No," and pulled the trigger.

The man cried out and fell backward, and Buck resumed his downstream pursuit. He heard the shout again, though from farther away this time, and broke into an awkward run. But with the canyon's floor like pitch, he kept stumbling over the uneven ground, careening off pine boughs that tried to shove him first one way, then the other, until he finally gave up for fear he'd break a leg or knock himself senseless on a stout limb if he didn't.

Gasping in the smoky air, Buck dropped to one knee and waited with his revolver cocked, his finger taut on the trigger, but after several minutes with no sound other than the swift beating of his own heart, he stood and made his way back to the camp.

Pausing in the shadows outside the pale glow of their fire, he quietly hailed the camp. Jake and Cam answered immediately, and the three men stepped cautiously into the light. A couple of quick questions assured Buck that neither of them had been injured; other than for some pine-needle scratches across one cheek, he'd also escaped unhurt.

"I got one of 'em," Cam claimed excitedly, but Jake quickly refuted the claim.

"The only thing we shot were trees, although I think Buck might have hit one of them."

"I think I hit two of them," Buck corrected. "We'll have to wait until morning to know for sure, though." Glancing around the exposed campsite, he added, "At least one man got away, so we can't stay here."

"I know a place near the mules where we can hole up until dawn," Jake said, and Buck nodded stiffly.

"Lead the way."

CHAPTER EIGHT

The first gray blush of dawn had barely reached the canyon's floor when Buck and Jake walked out to examine the previous night's battleground. As Buck had feared, they found two men, both of them dead.

"It was either you or them," Jake said, noticing the expression on Buck's face.

"I know," Buck replied. He stood from where he'd knelt next to the larger-framed man. "Do you know them?"

"That's Tom Burrows at your feet."

The name jarred a recollection from Buck's years in Oregon. Burrows had killed a man for refusing to give up his seat in a poker game. It hadn't been a fair fight; Burrows had simply drawn and fired into the player's chest, killing him instantly. There had been no trial afterward because no one wanted to attempt to arrest him, least of all the town marshal.

The other man was a local tough called Salmon River Kelly. According to Jake, Kelly was a part-time horse thief who liked to ride with Burrows, as if hoping some of the gunman's reputation might rub off on him. Kelly had been shot in the side, and Burrows had taken a slug through his neck. Judging from the unbloodied ground around them, both men had died quickly. Buck was grateful for that.

They found the trail of a third man ending where the ambushers had left their horses. One mount was gone. The other two remained hitched to saplings along the trail. They freed both animals, dumping their tack on the ground, then walked back to where Burrows and Kelly lay. Buck wanted to bury them, but Jake pointed out that there wasn't time.

"That fire's getting closer, Buck. Besides, if it was Luce who sent these men, he'll send out even more as soon as he finds out what happened."

Grudgingly, Buck led the way back to camp, where they found Cam slumped against one of the packs, chin tucked to his chest.

"Hey," Jake cried in alarm, and hurried to the older man's side. "Are you all right?"

" 'Course I'm all right," Cam snarled, jerking his head up, but the words sounded phlegm-smothered, and there was a shine of spittle at the corners of his mouth.

"You don't look all right," Jake told him. "You don't sound like it, either. Fact is, you sound kind of wind-broke to me."

"That's 'cause your ears are filled with smoke," Cam replied. He struggled to his feet, swaying briefly until he caught his balance, then spat into the ashes of last night's supper fire. "Hell," he added indignantly, wiping his chin with the back of his hand, "I'll likely be carryin' you two hounds before we reach the top, puny as you both look."

"I'd rather we didn't have to carry anyone," Buck said, stepping forward to peer into Cam's eyes.

"You just worry about yourself, boy," Cam replied stonily. "I'll be there the same time you are, if not five minutes before."

Buck glanced at Jake, but the younger man refused to return the look. His expression was stoic, like a chunk of seasoned oak. "Don't worry about him," he said harshly. "He's just a stubborn old fool."

"That's right," Cam retorted. "And mule-headed enough to see a job through to its finish, too."

Buck had had enough. "Let's get this outfit moving," he said curtly. "Before Luce shows up with an army."

CHAPTER NINE

Leaning back in his chair, Anton regarded the battered figure standing before him. He wasn't sure how to take Foster's assertion that Buck McCready had killed two of his best men—including the gunman Tom Burrows. It didn't seem possible. Yet what other explanation could there be for the kid showing up with such a tale?

Nor could Anton dismiss the memory of McCready's intractable pertinacity in leading Jock Kavanaugh's wagon train of freight north from Corinne. Anton knew in his heart that the firm of Crowley and Luce should have won that race—they'd had the lead nearly the whole way, dammit, and a hired gun to stop the Box-K if the elements didn't—but Buck had kept his outfit in an unrelenting pursuit that had ultimately proved successful.

It had also impressed upon Anton that McCready wasn't a man to give up easily. Or to be dismissed.

His gaze came back to Foster. The kid stood shivering as if chilled. He was hatless and bloodied, and claimed he'd been shot in the cheek, although the angle of the wound spoke more of a heedless flight through the night and a stout branch than it did a bullet. But the youth's claim . . .

"You're sure they're dead?" he repeated.

Foster's head bobbed in accord. "Yes, sir, both of them."

Anton looked away, considering his options. He saw two immediately. One was to just let them go, lick his wounds and count his losses, then tip his hat to that son of a bitch Felix Payne the next time he saw the wretched little shopkeeper. Hell, if it had been anyone other than McCready, he might have done it. But not again. Not when there was a second option.

Standing, he strode to an accordion rack nailed to the wall next to the door. His hat and coat hung there, along with a nickel-plated Merwin Hulbert revolver in a belt of tooled leather. He strapped the gun belt on first.

"W . . . what are you doing?" Foster asked, looking as confused as he sounded.

Anton's reply was terse. "Go find Cunningham and Harlow and tell them to meet me downstairs at the bar, now. Then swing past the livery and saddle my horse." He slid the Merwin Hulbert from its holster, but paused before opening the gate to check its loads. "Get yourself a fresh mount, too. You're coming with us."

CHAPTER TEN

There had been no moon to light their trail the night before, and there was no hint of the sun that morning, despite its pearly suffusion by midday. They'd left the Owl shortly after dawn to start up the North Fork in the same order as the previous day, Jake leading with the bell mare, the rest of them strung out to the rear.

The trail proved as difficult as Felix had promised, with boulders from the cliffs above strewn everywhere, and downed timber that had to be jumped over or threaded past. They reached the head of the canyon just past noon and halted to check their loads—tightening where it was needed, making sure the packs were still evenly balanced. The trail left the creek soon after to begin its final ascent to the top, a narrow ribbon of switchbacks rising toward where eagles nested and vultures waited and watched.

It was here, too, not long after starting, that the mules began to grow restive, yanking back on their lead ropes and snorting at shadows and sticks like they were mountain lions and rattlesnakes. Buck knew it was the ever-thickening smoke that bothered them more than the steepening grade. That and the ash husks swirling past them like gray snowflakes. Even the zebra dun was becoming fractious, and from time to time as they climbed, Buck would glance above to see Jake struggling to keep the horse calm, his own pack string moving forward.

They were probably halfway up the worst stretch of it, Zeke's hooves clattering on hardpan and granite as he struggled to keep his footing, when Buck heard a roaring like a runaway train slamming through the canyon behind them. The flesh across the back of his neck crawled as he swiveled around to stare back the way they'd come. He wouldn't have been surprised to see a sloth of angry grizzlies charging up the trail after them, but the path was empty as far as he could see. Then the sound came again, and at the bottom of the canyon the tops of the pines began to whip back and forth as if writhing in pain. The smoke bucked and churned, and the bits of blackened twigs and fine ash that had so recently fallen past them now reversed direction to barrel up the canyon's wall on a powerful gust of wind.

The sound grew to a shriek, and the mules brayed and kicked and laid their ears back. From above, the bell mare's terrified whinny added to the chaos. Then the tempest struck them with a force Buck could hardly credit as natural. Like a giant hand, it shoved him back in his saddle, and he had to grab his hat to keep it from taking flight. Zeke snorted his displeasure, but otherwise held steady; so did the rest of Buck's string, the wind being a more familiar phenomenon than the screaming of an unseen assailant they'd imagined coming up behind them.

Squinting against dust and ash, Buck watched a piece of oilcloth off one of the packs from above soar past. Then Cam's battered old hat sailed after it, as if to round up the stray canvas and hie it back into the herd.

The pummeling blasts lasted only a few minutes, before the air grew calm again. Using his thumb and forefinger, Buck scraped the worst of the grit from the corners of his eyes before raising his head and looking around. At first everything appeared normal. The wildfire's detritus was floating down again, in a direction that made sense, and the pines along the canyon floor had ceased their frantic gyrations. It was when he glanced overhead that Buck felt a sinking in his breast. A heavy coil of black smoke was spilling over the canyon's rim and falling rapidly toward them. He shouted a warning to the others, but couldn't tell if they heard him. Then it no longer mattered as the smoke curled around them in a choking embrace.

Buck lowered his head and closed his eyes, and after a couple of minutes he raised his left arm to cover his face. Zeke hawed in protest, dancing near the edge of the drop-off, hooves clattering atop the hardpan. Behind them, the line of mules shifted restlessly, making a guttural braying sound Buck had heard only rarely in his life, and then only in moments of extreme peril. His pulse quickened at the thought of the whole string slipping off the narrow trail and plummeting to their deaths. After a moment's adjustment to the roiling fog, Buck lowered his arm and raised a bandanna over his mouth and nose. Then he resolutely tapped Zeke's ribs with his heels, the pack string buckling down and compliantly following.

It was another hour before they cleared the switchbacks. Although the trail continued its upward climb, it was no longer so narrow and dangerous. Jake brought his string to a stop about a hundred yards past the canyon's rim, and the others rode up to join him. Buck looked at Jake, but Jake was staring wordlessly past him. It didn't take long to figure out why. Dropping from his saddle, Buck walked over to place a hand gently on Cam's knee.

"You still with us?" he asked.

Glowering at him from reddened eyes, Cam croaked, "Where the hell else'd I be?" Then he leaned from his saddle and spat. Straightening with effort, he pushed a lank of greasy gray hair back off his forehead. "It ain't bad enough . . . the fire's taken away my breath, now the wind's . . . stole my hat."

"I saw it on its way back down the canyon," Buck confirmed. "I think it might have waved at me as it sailed past."

Cam gave him a condemning look, then shrugged indifferently. "Well, the damn thing never . . . waved to me, so I reckon it's better off on its own somewhere."

"The way it was flying, it's probably back in Pineview by now."

"You can buy another hat," Jake said impatiently, then turned to Buck, before Cam could respond. "The trail between here and the Crown is fairly open. We could probably loose-herd the mules the rest of the way if you wanted to." He glanced at Cam, then away.

"Don't you do me no favors, boy," Cam growled hoarsely. He looked at Buck. "You, neither.

"How much farther is it to the mine?" Buck asked Jake.

"Most of another day, I'd guess."

Buck looked west to where the glow of the approaching flames lit the horizon. From here it appeared as if the entire range west of Pineview Valley might be ablaze. Although he wasn't surprised that Felix had guessed wrong about the fire's direction, its speed was worrisome. In the canyons it had been impossible to tell from which direction the wind was coming, but there was no question of it now. It had changed course while they were climbing the switchbacks, and was sweeping in from the northwest with a chilled bite that had been absent earlier.

"It's going to blow in a storm," he predicted.

"Them's about the truest words I've heard all week," Cam said throatily. "But you'd best hope it blows in fast, else we're all gonna be as crisp as ma's biscuits before the next sunrise."

Facing the older man, Buck said, "You figure you've got enough sand to make it to the Crown if we kept riding?"

"Now, that there is probably the dumbest thing I've heard all week," Cam replied. Then he got a panicky look on his face as his lungs closed off in a rattling cough that nearly tumbled him from his seat. When it passed, he dragged a sleeve weakly across his lips; it came away streaked with blood and mucus. He stared numbly at his cuff for several seconds, then raised his eyes to Buck's. "Keep your trap shut, boy."

Nodding stiffly, Buck walked back to Zeke, gathered his reins, and stepped into the saddle. "Let's go," he told Jake. "We'll keep the mules on their leads for now and try to ride straight through." His gaze slewed west to where the mountain peaks glowed like stacks of rose-tinted gold on the horizon. "I figure we'll have enough light to see the trail," he added bleakly.

CHAPTER ELEVEN

Anton pushed his men hard, using quirt and spur to keep his bay gelding alternating between a lope and a jog for most of the day, and savagely rebuking anyone who started to fall behind. Without a cavvy of headstrong mules to slow them down, they were making good time, yet he chafed at every small delay.

The wind caught them shortly after entering North Fork Canyon. What had been calm only moments before turned suddenly as wild as a trapped catamount as it swept first one way, then the other. The unexpectedness of its gale-like force startled them all. Anton's bay was especially unnerved by its shrill arrival, switching ends to face the wind, then crow-hopping through a maze of boulders, brush, and scattered trees, while Anton cursed and sawed at the reins.

Most of the others—Burt and Chad McLaughlin, who tended bar evenings at the High Dollar; Sid Cunningham, Anton's last remaining hired hand at the now all-but-defunct Luce Fast Freight and Express; and Bob Harlow, who did odd jobs around the saloon and freight yard as needed—were having similar problems. Only the kid, Foster, managed to keep his horse under control, guiding it off the trail and turning his back to the black smoke pouring down the canyon like a chimney unscrewed from the bottom. It wasn't until those first rapid blasts of steadily colder air calmed to a hard blow that Anton was able to force his horse back onto the trail. The others joined him there. As the last man rode up, Anton snarled, "If you boys can't control your horses, then maybe you'd better get down and lead 'em."

Only Cunningham had enough backbone to stand up to the saloon owner's abuse. "It didn't look like you were faring a whole lot better than the rest of us."

"I'm here, ain't I? Here and waiting for you jokers when we should be riding." He darted a quick glance at Foster, but the youth knew better than to pipe in with an opinion, and kept his gaze averted. "Let's go," Anton snapped, yanking the bay around and giving it another quick dig with his spurs.

They started up North Fork at a trot, but the horses soon turned balky in the stifling smoke, tossing their heads and fighting the bit. With Anton's own mount the worst of the bunch, he had to swallow the razor-sharp barbs he wanted to fling at the others.

Anton knew his foul mood was the result of Burrows's and Kelly's failure to stop the muleskinners. It had deteriorated even further with his discovery of the two men along the trail, each of them killed by a single, well-placed shot—shootings that had taken place in near pitch darkness, if Foster was to be believed. Although someone had taken time to wrap the bodies in oilcloth to keep the weather off them and scavengers away, they hadn't buried them. Nor would Anton allow his men to scratch out even a shallow grave. Buck McCready and his crew had too much of a lead as it was; he'd be damned if he'd allow them even more.

The down canyon wind held steady. Although not as strong as those earlier gusts, it was constant, worming through their clothing like icy fingers. Buttoning his brown herringbone jacket as high as it would go, Anton wished he'd thought to bring along something heavier. But who could have predicted the temperature would turn so frosty when the whole damn country seemed to be aflame?

No one spoke as they made their way miserably up canyon. The only sounds were the moaning of the wind and the protesting creak of the tall pines, shoved back and forth like bullied kids. Even the clopping of their horses' hooves against the rocky trail seemed muted. There was a spookiness to the day, Anton thought, and an ominousness to the narrow canyon that chipped at his nerves until his whole body pringled with tension. Part of the trouble was that he couldn't get the vision of Burrows and Kelly out of his mind. They had both been tough men, neither fools nor reckless in their habits. Yet they both lay dead by McCready's hand. It made Anton question how he could expect to fare any better with only a pair of bartenders, a hard-nosed freighter, a hostler, and a fool kid to back him when they finally caught up with the mule train.

Anton was still lost in these musings when, coming past a bend in the trail, he saw a man standing half-hidden in the alders across the creek. With his heart slamming into his throat, he jerked his horse to a stop and palmed his revolver, firing two quick rounds through the man's chest. Then the wind brushed the gun smoke out of his line of sight and he saw the figure standing as before, immobile. As he watched, it gradually transformed itself into a sapling, a tattered old hat caught near its peak.

Slowly, Anton lowered his pistol. He was aware of the others halted behind him, watching . . . judging. After a minute, he took a deep breath and reined back to face his men. Thumbing the Merwin Hulbert's hammer to full cock, he raised it in a straight-armed aim to cover the silent crew, and said in a voice he barely recognized, "The first one of you sons of bitches says anything about this . . . ever, I'll put a bullet through your skull and cut your tongue out after you're dead. Anyone here doubt that?"

He waited, giving them time to mull it over, but no one spoke, and there was no dubiety in their eyes. Nodding, he returned the revolver to its holster. Then he pulled his horse around and started back up the trail.

CHAPTER TWELVE

Even after leaving the narrow switchbacks above North Fork, it was another two hours across a low, grassy saddle between the head of the canyon and the glacier lake Felix's map had indicated they would find there. The lake lay at the center of a shallow basin on the edge of the timberline, a deep blue oval surrounded by boulders and freeze-stunted evergreens. Old firepits along its near shore spoke of past camps, as did the close-cropped grass encircling it. The trail to the Crown spun off on their left, still climbing.

It was coming onto sundown as they led their mules to the lake and let them fan out to drink. Looping Zeke's reins around his saddle horn to keep them out of the water, Buck dismounted and walked over to where Cam Wallis was barely clinging to his seat. Cam's eyes had taken on a watery glaze, and his thin chest and ruined lungs heaved erratically. Gently prying the lead rope from the older man's hand, Buck tossed it over the mule's neck, then helped him dismount and led him to a cluster of boulders where there was some protection from the wind. Flecks of blood stippled the front of his shirt, and there was a bluish tinge to his lower lip.

Pulling his bandanna down, Buck said, "It's consumption, isn't it?"

Cam nodded weakly. " 'Pears like."

"How long have you known?"

"Knowed certain-sure, or just wondered? 'Cause, certain-sure, it was just today, when the blood started comin'." He gave Buck a plaintive look. "Lordy, boy, I can't get no wind in me. It's like tryin' to breathe underwater."

"It's the smoke making it worse," Buck said. "That and the thin air."

Cam slumped back against a boulder. "I ain't gonna ask for my pay, Buck."

"Nobody's talking—"

"Hush now, and listen," Cam interrupted thickly. "I don't curry favor from no man, and I pull my own weight or step outta the way of them that do. Only . . ." His gaze swept the basin. "They ain't no place up here to step to, is there?"

"We'll get you to the Crown. You'll feel better after you've rested a spell. It'll be easier after this smoke clears out, too."

"It'd better be, 'cause if it ain't, I don't think I'm gonna be leavin' these mountains."

Buck didn't have a reply for that. Not if he didn't want to lie. Rising, he said, "Stay here and rest. I'm going to help Jake with the mules."

"You ain't stoppin', are you?" Cam got a kind of stricken look to his face. "Not on my account."

"No, we aren't stopping." Buck raised his gaze to the eerie red glow climbing the mountain toward them, and thought that if they weren't careful, and maybe a little lucky, it was possible none of them would leave this mountain range alive.

CHAPTER THIRTEEN

The trail opened up after they left the lake. Although still a clearly defined path, there was enough room to either side that the mules were no longer forced to travel single file. China Jake continued up front with the zebra dun, but they turned the rest of the pack string loose—lead ropes hitched to their sawbucks—while Buck brought up the rear and watched for stragglers.

There weren't any, not really. The mules were staying close to the mare and the reassuring jingle of her bell, while the flames, quartering in from the northwest, kept the herd moving at a brisk, anxious walk. Hanging on gamely, Cam fell in behind Buck.

The sun went down and took its light with it, but the land remained bathed in a quivering, apricot radiance. Flitting embers drifted overhead. Now and again one of them would float down into the tree-line scrub, but very few caught, and then only briefly. Farther down the mountain they likely would have ignited instantly, but spring came late to the high country, and summers were usually cool and damp.

It was after midnight when Jake called another halt. The mules immediately crowded up around the bell mare, like frightened children seeking the protection of their mother. Buck forced Zeke through the mob, Cam close behind. They were among the highest peaks of the Crown Range here. The boulders were spotted with lichen, and the few spindly trees they'd passed had appeared wind-twisted and vaguely grotesque in the wildfire's light. But when Buck reined in at Jake's side, he saw that, going forward, the trail dropped swiftly back into heavy timber—close-growth forests of towering Ponderosa pine. They were on its southern fringe here. The fire was pushing in from the west, and for the first time, its flames were clearly visible to the weary muleskinners.

"That's our destination," Jake said, pointing northward.

Buck followed the line of his arm to a solitary mountain peak, probably another four or five hours away. From here its highest point looked like a—he smiled. From here it looked like a crown, the kind he'd seen in books and newspapers, worn by kings and queens.

"The mine is at its base," Jake added.

"What's the trail like?"

"It runs more or less in a straight line. I don't think we'll have to put our mules back on their lead ropes, not as long as they can hear the mare's bell."

Buck eyed the ragged line of flames gnawing into the belly of the forest from the west. Fueled by resin-heavy pines and fanned by strong winds, the fire was burning hotter and faster than he would have anticipated. Watching, he estimated it was moving at about the same rate of speed as a man walking over level ground. Every time a new tree caught, it did so with an explosive blast that sent pillars of flame into the sky, and spewed a fresh crop of cherry-red cinders forward. Buck could feel its heat even from here, tamping down the high-country chill, promising even worse to come.

A voice at his side wheezed, "It's too far, boy."

Buck turned angrily. Cam had pulled the bandanna down off his face. He was peering intently into Buck's eyes, his own gleaming unnaturally in the throbbing light.

"It's too far, and you know it. Same as Jake—" He broke off in a rattling cough, grasping his saddle horn with both hands.

Buck bit back the denial he wanted to throw in the old man's face. Turning to Jake, he demanded, "Is he right?"

"If he is, we'll all die," Jake replied simply. "It's too late to go back, and too far even if we tried. And if we got down in there," he tipped his head to the east, where the forest seemed to run on forever, "we'd never come out."

"You got any ideas?"

"If we can reach the Crown before the fire cuts us off, they'll have room for us and our stock inside the main shaft. I'm guessing that's where the miners are holed up now."

Buck looked north, although without much hope. Without much option, either, he reminded himself, and lifted Zeke's reins. "Move 'em out," he told Jake. "As soon as we get into the trees, put your horse into a hard trot. I'll keep the mules close behind you."

Cam hacked and spat, then lifted his ruddled gaze. "Leave the mules, boy. They'll only slow us down."

"No!" Buck shook his head. "I won't do it, not yet." He motioned Jake forward, then guided Zeke out of the way. Mumbling under his breath, Cam followed. "You can go your own way, if that's what you want," Buck told him as the pack mules flowed past. "You'd probably be smart if you did."

"Jus' shut your yapper, boy," the old man growled. "If you two hounds're too dumb to know when you're licked, then I reckon I'll have to hang on 'til you do."

CHAPTER FOURTEEN

It was after sundown when they reached the glacier lake. Despite his desire to push on, Anton allowed Sid Cunningham to talk him into stopping long enough to rest the horses.

"We've been pushing 'em hard all day," Cunningham warned. "If we keep on like this, they'll start to cave on us."

Anton had to grit his teeth to keep from spitting out that he didn't give a damn if he killed every last one of them, as long as McCready and his mules were brought to bay. But Cunningham wouldn't understand that—none of them would—so Anton kept his mouth shut and reluctantly conceded to a thirty-minute halt.

Dismounting, he slipped the bit from his horse's mouth, then made his way to the shelter of some rocks bordering the lake. The others moved off in the opposite direction, standing close and lighting their cigars and pipes as they saw fit; Bob Harlow used a jackknife to slice a thumb-sized piece of tobacco from a plug he kept in his shirt pocket, and stowed it in a rear corner of his mouth to soften. Anton considered lighting a cigar of his own—he'd brought a couple of them along—but decided against it. He didn't want anyone thinking his resolve to catch up with the pack train might be weakening.

Anton knew he was being a jackass. He supposed there were a lot of people around Pineview who'd say he always was. But in the past he'd tried to treat the men who worked for him, the competent ones anyway, with at least a degree of deference. It was a concession he'd learned to make years before, when a crew of muleskinners had quit *en masse* to protest his haranguing them to move faster. It galled him to do so—he paid his help well, dammit—but he'd discovered to his chagrin that there were things in life even money couldn't supply.

Anton anticipated a similar mutiny tonight. He'd been listening to his men grumbling ever since they topped out above the switchbacks and spotted the approaching flames, so much nearer than even the most pessimistic among them had expected. The McLaughlin brothers were doing most of the complaining, but he'd also heard Cunningham and Harlow chiming in from time to time. Only Foster seemed to hold his tongue, either that or he was keeping his voice low so that he wouldn't be overheard.

Despite his impatience with the men, Anton could understand their fear. Rising and stepping clear of the shoreline boulders, he gravely eyed the no-longer-distant inferno. The whole damn horizon seemed caught in the throes of its own *danse macabre,* a frighteningly primitive gambol that gave even his own determination pause.

Separating himself from the others, Sid Cunningham came over. "Looks like the fire's going to do the job for us, boss."

Bracing himself mentally, Anton turned to face his crew. "I figured it would've been one of the McLaughlins," he said.

"They're more talk than gumption. Fact is, if not for that—" Cunningham nodded toward the wildfire—"I'd be inclined to see it through. But it ain't worth risking our necks for."

"I hired you to do a job."

"You hired me to run a freight outfit, which I've tried to do to the best of my ability. This ain't part of that."

Anton studied the others a moment, then said loudly, "Sid isn't quitting. None of you are, not until I'm sure those mules are stopped and Buck McCready is dead. It's as simple as that, boys, and any man doubts me had best draw his piece now."

"No," Cunningham replied firmly, hooking his thumbs behind his gun belt. "I'm sorry Mr. Luce, but we're—"

The sound of Anton's revolver cleaved the smoky air between them. The men jumped, and Harlow choked as if he'd swallowed some of his wad. Sid Cunningham stumbled backward with a look of surprise on his face. Then his knees buckled and he crumpled to the ground.

"You boys listen up, now," Anton said, his voice shaky but resolute. "We're going forward, and we ain't stopping until I'm certain those mules are stopped. I asked before if any of you had doubts about my word. Nobody did then, and you'd damn well better not now."

No one spoke or moved, and after a moment Anton nodded and returned the Merwin Hulbert to its holster.

"All right, let's mount up and ride."

CHAPTER FIFTEEN

They did their best. China Jake kept his horse and the zebra dun moving at a swift trot, and the trail was wide enough that the mules could follow without losing sight or sound of the mare, or snagging their packs on trees.

But the fire was too quick. It caught them a couple of hours into the final leg of their journey, although in a way Buck hadn't expected. From a distance the blaze had looked like a solid wall of flames; up close, its front was more ragged than he'd expected, flaring up along both sides of the trail and burning wide swaths of timber, but bypassing others. Eventually, he knew, the fire would consume everything in its path, but for now the fluctuating winds were offering them a slim reprieve.

Although they kept their bandannas over their faces, the smoke wasn't as bad here as it had been farther back. As they passed through the spinning colonnade of flames, it rose above them in a writhing mantle that reflected the light back onto the land in what Buck imagined hell must look like. Embers darted like maddened hornets, and his sleeves and trousers were soon pocked with tiny, charred holes, the flesh underneath blistered red.

The stock suffered similarly, the mules braying and whinnying at the fiery prods, sometimes kicking out blindly to drive the hot coals away. Buck did what he could for Zeke, trying to swat the embers aside before they landed, or as soon as he saw them, but he couldn't reach them all, and there was nothing he could do for the pack animals.

Cam suffered in silence, but there was a spark in his eyes now that had been absent earlier, a rock-like resolve to see the job through to its finish. Buck didn't ask how he was faring; that was also visible in the older man's red, tearing eyes . . . along with the acceptance that his will was no guarantee he'd realize his goal.

Neither Felix nor his map had mentioned any kind of clearing, so Buck was surprised when they came to a long meadow with green grass and a creek running through its center. They stopped at its ford and the mules spread out eagerly to dip their heads to the purling water, but when they raised them again, their muzzles were dry; the stream looked almost syrupy from soot and half-burned debris.

Buck splashed Zeke across the fetlock-deep creek to where Jake waited on the other side. "How much farther?" he shouted above the crackling wail of the fire.

Jake pulled down his bandanna. "Maybe another hour."

Buck's gritted his teeth. It was too far. But they couldn't stop here, either. Eventually the flames would advance into the meadow. Or else the smoke would drop back down and engulf them. Either meant an agonizing death.

Looking west, past the sporadic flames to where the fire burned hottest, sending its sable plumes into the sky, Buck felt a sudden hopelessness.

"The worst of it isn't here yet," Jake shouted, as if reading his mind.

"It will be soon enough." He looked around as Cam rode up beside them. Cam didn't speak, but Buck recalled his earlier advice to abandon the mules. For a moment he actually considered it. Then he shook his head. It wasn't the supplies he refused to leave behind, but the livestock. "We're going to have to make a run for it," he told them. "We won't leave the mules, but we can't stop if we lose one or two of them, either. They'll have to keep up as best they can."

"At a hard run, we should reach the Crown in thirty minutes or less," Jake said, but his expression implied he wasn't sure if even that would be enough.

"We'll have to do the best—" Buck stopped talking when he noticed Jake's attention had shifted. He looked over his shoulder, following the direction of the younger man's gaze. About the last thing he would have expected to see at that moment was a group of horsemen emerging from the flame-lined southern trail. "Who the devil . . . ?"

"It's Anton Luce," Jake said tautly.

"Him and others that work for—" Cam's voice was severed by a restrained cough.

Jake took up the dropped thread of his explanation. "It's Luce and the McLaughlin brothers, and that's Bob Harlow behind them."

Luce and his men were still at least a hundred yards away. They were huddled close just inside the meadow, talking among themselves. Buck thought they appeared as surprised to see the pack train as he was to see them. Then he noticed a fifth rider, hanging back behind the others.

"Who's the kid?" he asked. "The one in the bowler hat?"

"That's Foster. He works for Felix Payne."

"Looks like he's working for Luce now."

Cam pulled his bandanna down and spat a wad of bloody phlegm into the grass. "Has been all along, I figure, the damn fool," he croaked.

"That sounds about right," Jake agreed grimly. "Luce is a son of a bitch, but he pays good wages . . . if you can stomach working for him. He offered me a job last spring, but I turned him down."

Buck didn't ask why. He knew Luce's reputation from Utah.

Nor did he have any doubts about what had prompted the saloon owner to follow them into this hellish morass of flames. There could be only one answer to that, and Buck's hand moved instinctively to the rifle booted under his right leg.

"Get 'em moving, Jake," he said tersely. "Keep the bell mare with you if you can, but keep her in a high lope and don't stop for anything until you reach the mine. Cam, you go with Jake."

"Like hell," the older man protested.

"You can't fight all of them," Jake added.

"I don't intend to fight them. I just want to slow 'em down a little."

"They'll kill you, boy," Cam rumbled.

"I figure Anton Luce has wanted to kill me for a long time," Buck replied. "He hasn't done it yet." He looked at Jake, then Cam. "Go on, you two. Get out of here."

Jake glanced at Cam, who jerked his head toward where the trail plunged back into the forest to the north. "Lead on, heathen," he said, drawing his revolver.

There was no animosity in Jake's reply. "Are you coming with me?"

"Just 'till we get 'em started, then I'll come back'n help Buck."

Jake cast an anxious glance toward Luce and his men, edging their horses deeper into the meadow. He nodded curtly. "All right, just don't get yourself shot, old man." Then he pulled his horse around and gave the zebra dun's rope a tug.

"Go on," Buck told Cam. "Stay with the mules. That's an order."

Jake kicked his horse into a lope, the pack mules automatically following the bell mare. Cam swung behind the loose stock, hazing the slower ones into a quicker gait. Buck drew his rifle and settled it across his saddlebows. Cam's return within a couple of minutes startled him.

"I told you to stay with the mules."

"Them mules don't need my help," Cam replied. Then he noticed Buck's rifle, and snorted with derision. "A damn single-shot Remington? Hell, boy, we ain't huntin' buffalo."

Buck glanced over his shoulder to where the last of the pack animals were funneling into the north trail. "Goddamnit, go help Jake."

"No, sir, I ain't. You can't—" He broke off in a wet, sputtering cough that bent him nearly double. The revolver slipped from his fingers, and one of his reins fell. His horse danced back a couple of paces and might have bolted if Buck hadn't grabbed the dangling rein and pulled the animal back.

Wheezing, Cam reached out clumsily for the rein. Buck placed it in his searching hand, then leaned from his saddle to pluck the fallen revolver out of the grass. He wedged it back in its holster, then circled Cam's horse and smacked it on the rump with his hat.

"Go on," he said kindly as the horse trotted off. "Help Jake with the mules. I'll be along directly."

Cam hung onto the saddle horn with both hands, his head bobbing. Buck waited until he was certain the horse would follow after the pack mules, then brought Zeke back around to face the southern side of the meadow. Luce and his men had advanced nearly a third of the way into the clearing while he was dealing with Cam, and Anton had drawn his own rifle. Buck's throat constricted when he realized Anton was already leveling his sights on him. He snapped the Remington to his shoulder and quickly pulled the trigger. With such a hurried shot, he wasn't expecting to hit anything. He only meant to give the saloon owner pause. So he was surprised when Luce tumbled from his saddle.

The others hauled up uncertainly, exchanging glances. Then the two brothers Jake had identified as the McLaughlins wheeled their mounts and raced back the way they'd come.

Buck would have preferred it if they all fled, but Harlow and Foster stayed. Foster dropped to the ground and rushed over to where Anton was rolling back and forth in the grass at his mount's side, while Harlow slid his own long gun from its scabbard.

Buck swiftly rolled his hammer to full cock and thumbed the block open to eject the spent cartridge. He dug a fresh round from his belt and inserted it into the chamber. Familiarity with the old weapon gave him speed, but not enough to beat a lever gun. Harlow's first bullet screamed past Buck's ear with an angry hiss; his second peeled a layer of flesh from the side of Buck's neck even as he closed the Remington's breech. He sucked his breath in at the bullet's sharp bite, but couldn't afford the time to even reach up and explore the wound's depth. He tried to shoulder the Remington, but Zeke was shifting nervously under him, more spooked by the gunfire than by the encircling flames.

Buck kept trying to steady the rifle against his shoulder, but the sights were jumping all over. Finally he swung down and dropped to one knee. Harlow fired his third round, the bullet burrowing into the dirt at Buck's side, peppering his thigh with clumps of sod. He raised his rifle and squeezed the trigger in a single fluid motion. The Remington's big .50 slug pushed back solidly against his shoulder. Across the clearing, Harlow cartwheeled off the back of his horse.

Buck lowered his weapon to reload. Luce was already back on his feet, one hand planted firmly to his side. He gripped his revolver in the other. Foster stood behind him, looking more confused than scared. Bellowing a curse that seemed to rival the roar of the flames, Luce started forward, and despite the distance between them, despite the eerily pulsating light, his bullets were coming alarmingly close. The first tugged at Buck's jacket; the second hit the ground less than a foot in front of him. Tight-lipped, he closed the Remington's breech and threw the rifle to his shoulder just as Luce fired his third round.

The Remington jerked violently upward, and Buck cried out at the snap of bones in his right hand as the rifle was torn from his grasp. It flipped to the side, its forearm shattered by Luce's bullet. Pain lanced through Buck's arm from fingertip to shoulder as he instinctively cradled his right hand to his chest. Luce continued to stagger toward him, a demonic grin splitting his soot-darkened face, his ribs glistening with blood.

Buck reached for his revolver with his left hand, but the Colt was holstered too far back on his right hip. He tried sliding the belt around, but it snagged on something and refused to budge. He looked up. Luce had closed the gap between them to less than twenty yards, and still had half a cylinder of live rounds left in his revolver. He stopped and raised the gun, and Buck muttered a quiet, "Aw, hell."

Then a ragged howl echoed across the clearing. Buck twisted partway around to see what he thought at first might be a phantom. In the next second he recognized Cam Wallis, spurring his horse across the meadow.

Luce paused and his grin slipped; his eyes widened in alarm. Cam was firing rapidly, his pistol thrust before him like a saber. Luce jerked and half spun, then came back around to return the older man's fire. Both were shooting as fast as they could thumb their hammers and pull the triggers. Buck couldn't have said who hit whom first, but it was Anton Luce who took a clumsy step backward, then abruptly collapsed.

Half a second later, Cam toppled from his mount, pitching face-first into the knee-high grass at the stream's edge.

CHAPTER SIXTEEN

Standing at the mouth of the Crown's main adit, Buck stared at a sparkling landscape that, only a couple of days before, he hadn't been sure he would ever see again. Half a foot of snow had fallen overnight, smothering whatever buried embers might have remained after yesterday's icy rains. The gusting winds that had kept the wildfire burning so hot and wicked were calm now, the sky a deep, brilliant blue.

At Buck's side was China Jake; around them nearly forty others, the miners and outside laborers who had taken refuge inside the mine's broad main entrance to escape the flames, gazed in wonder at the drifted snowbanks.

It was an unusually early storm according to the Crown's manager, a stumpy man with bushy side whiskers named Burdett, but he insisted he wasn't worried about its effect on the mine's operation.

"This won't last," he predicted, his breath creating a thin fog in the chilled air. "Even at this altitude, we won't have to shut down for another month at least."

Buck didn't know, nor did he care. It was enough for him that the fire was out. Still, the conflagration had left its mark on the land, a stark transformation of blackened tree trunks, scorched bushes, and an acidic odor that not even rain and snow had been able to erase. The Crown's buildings—storage sheds, bunkhouse, kitchen and mess hall, stables, and office—had all suffered to some degree from the fiery hell that had passed through the high-mountain valley less than forty-eight hours before.

Glancing at Jake, Buck said, "I think I'm about ready to pull out."

"What about Foster?"

Buck turned quiet as he considered the youth and what to do with him. There had been no fight left in the kid after Luce's death, and Buck was beginning to think there never had been. It had been Foster who helped get Cam's body loaded onto his horse, then rounded up Zeke and brought him back for Buck. Foster was somewhere behind him now, hanging back in the mine's wide drift as he had in the meadow, as if wanting only to fade into the shadows.

"Foster can do what he wants," Buck decided. "I'm not going to worry about him."

"If we leave now, we'll have to come back later to haul out the ore they've busted up for the panniers."

"Someone else can do that. My job was to get the supplies up here. As soon as I collect my money from Payne, I'm heading south again."

After a moment's reflection, Jake said, "I think I'll stay. Felix will need a packer."

"He'll need several packers."

"I'll find them."

The miners were shuffling past them now, into the light and snow to pick up where the fires had forced them to leave off. As if nothing had changed, Buck reflected, but he knew it had.

Staring at the small miners' cemetery behind the Crown's bunkhouse where he and Jake had buried Cam yesterday in a hard rain just shy of sleet, Buck said softly, "He was a son of a bitch, wasn't he?"

"Cam?"

"Yeah."

213

A wistful smile crossed Jake's face. "You didn't know him very well."

"I know he rode you pretty hard a time or two."

"How? By calling me a heathen? He called you a boy more than once, and he called both of us hounds. I'll tell you something I'll bet you haven't heard about Cam Wallis. Last spring a bunch of prospectors cornered me in a livery in Pineview. They were determined to pound some sense into my chink head, as they put it, and convince me to go back to China. They were doing a pretty fair job of it, too. Then Cam showed up with a singletree and laid into them like he was chopping firewood. If he didn't save my life that day, he sure saved me from a bad beating."

"I wondered why you put up with him."

"I put up with him because there was solid wood under that rough bark, and because he was a man to stand by your side, no matter the odds." He looked at Buck. "Like he did for you with Anton Luce."

"He saved my life, that's for damn certain."

"Don't ask me to explain it, but that's why I'm going to stay here and wait until the panniers are filled," Jake said quietly. "It shouldn't take more than a day or two, and that way I won't have to make a second trip."

"You're going to stand by Felix Payne's side the way Cam stood by yours that day in the livery, is that it?"

"More or less. Like I said, don't ask me to explain it, because I can't. It's just something I want to do."

"Even after Felix sent us up here knowing Luce would likely follow?"

"Even then," Jake replied.

Buck turned his gaze back to the snowy mountain range to the south. After a pause, he said, "And you figure you can handle twenty-four head of mules by yourself?"

"I can if I take my time. They should follow the dun without giving me any trouble."

"That's a lot of packs for one man to handle. Heavy ones, too."

"Maybe I can get Foster to help me."

Buck worked his shoulder experimentally. Harlow's bullet hadn't cut too deep of a trough through the flesh, but it was still sore, the muscles in that whole area as stiff as dried rawhide. Worse was the damage to his hand, when Luce's bullet had struck his rifle. The force of his bullet and the way the Remington had been twisted out of his grasp had broken three of his fingers and cut a deep gash in his wrist.

Jake said mildly, but with the hint of a smile, "The bigger question might be, can you saddle Zeke with only one hand and a bum shoulder?"

"Zeke won't be a problem, but maybe I'll hang around a few days, after all. That way I can follow you and Foster back to Pineview and help with the mules."

"I'd welcome it," Jake said.

"I'll want to take a shovel along, find those I couldn't bring out with me and give them a proper burial."

"Luce and Harlow?"

"And anyone else who didn't make it."

Jake nodded, and after a pause, he said, "That sounds about right."

ABOUT THE AUTHOR

Michael Zimmer is the author of eighteen novels, including *The Poacher's Daughter,* winner of the prestigious Wrangler Award from the National Cowboy and Western Heritage Museum. He is the winner of the Spur Award from the Western Writers of America for his short story, "The Medicine Robe," and his novel, *City of Rocks,* was chosen by Booklist as a Top Ten Western for 2012. Zimmer resides in Utah with his wife, Vanessa, and their two dogs. His website is www.michaelzimmer .com.

★ ★ ★ ★ ★

Bloodline

BY MATTHEW P. MAYO

★ ★ ★ ★ ★

CHAPTER ONE

The old man laid into me today with that bullwhip. It's something his son gave him a long time ago for the old man's birthday. I wish he'd given him a hat instead. I only ever seen him use the whip on the oxen. And once when he was drunk, he skinned strips of bark off a oak tree out back of the kitchen. There ain't a whole lot of trees by the house and now there's one less.

Mama says I should know better than to make the old man angry. She says I am a vexation to him. I take that to mean I cause him grief. If that is the case, then he is also a vexation to me, but I dare not say so.

Now that I think on it, Mama causes the old man grief, too. I guess that means we all have something in common. Besides being blood kin. The old man will not admit to that, though.

He calls me a " 'skin," but with other words before it. He spits them at me as if they are hot coals in his mouth. Mama says that's because he's envious of me, but I am twelve years old now and I know better. He calls me that because I am part Indian.

The old man, he's known as Bull. Bull Barr. He's a big man, red in and out with anger and blood. I know, for I have tasted his knuckles on my teeth. He is also my mother's father. I am forbidden to call him grandfather. I don't call him anything, in fact. I only nod and keep my eyes from meeting his.

When he catches me looking at him, he calls me to him and

clouts me on the ear, sometimes on both. I reckon I don't hear so well now, 'cause Mama or the old man are forever waving their hands at me as if to say hello in a crowd. Only there ain't no crowd here, just the old man, Mama, and me.

Used to be there was the old man's wife, Martha Anne. He talks to her when he's drinking, which is most every night. There was a boy, too, Mama's brother. His name was Richard. But they're both dead, been so since before I come along.

Late this afternoon, close to suppertime, I was in the barn when he laid into me. I never heard the whip until it whistled by my ear. First lashing caught me over the shoulder and snapped like a snakebite on my chest, then back across my wing bone. For a breath, it didn't hurt, then it blazed and crackled like a lightning strike.

I stuttered, couldn't pull air in nor push it out before the next blow landed on me, and I tell you, I howled then. I try never to make sounds when I'm working with the old man, which is most days, but a bullwhip peeling your hide apart like a poorly sewed seam will make most folks shout.

He liked hearing me because he laid in with vigor then, laughing that ragged, shouty sound he makes when he's happy and drunk, which is not always the same thing.

I hunched up and tried to run by him but he cornered me in Chaco's stall. Only thing I could do was make myself small. He shouted, " 'Skin! Foul 'skin—that's all you are, boy! Brought woe on the Barr clan!"

Same as always.

Later, while Mama dressed my back and I bit down hard as I could on a wad of flannel, she said I should not have done it, whatever it was. I nodded, but I don't know what it was I should not have done. It's always that way, though.

Every morning after I fill the wood box and before I go to the barn, she tells me the same thing: "Keep your head bent, don't look him in the eyes. Do what he says, and it will be all right. You'll see." Then she winks and smiles and kisses me on top of the head. Mostly on my hat because I always wear it. Covers the scars up there.

Mama says it looks like a blind man laid train track on my head. I never saw it, reckon I never will. How many of us can see the tops of our heads, anyway? You have to assume it's there. Anyway, I don't wear the hat in the house when the old man is around.

After the whupping, she finishes working in the salve—the old man calls it goose grease, and he may be right. It stinks about as bad as their slimy leavings all over the yard—then she turns me around and looks at me. She is crying, which isn't unusual, but there is something else. Her mouth is twitchy and she leans close and whispers, like we do when we're not sure if the old man is awake, "We're leaving tonight."

I must look like I don't believe her because she shakes her head and squeezes my shoulders tighter. "This time it is different."

I about cry, mostly because her squeezing hurts my lash cuts. Also, we've trotted down this path before and it always leads back here. But as I say, this time she surprises me. I don't smell the wilty-flower smell of her medicine on her breath. I think it's whiskey, same as the old man, but unless she gets it from his bottles, I don't know where she lays hold of it. We neither of us leave the farm.

She don't say much, but nods toward our room, which is also the woodshed off the kitchen. It's comfortable but not so good in winter when the snow dusts in through the gaps. When it's cold, we sneak back into the kitchen and sleep by the stove once the old man's drunk and snoring in his bedroom.

I stuff things into a seed sack that smells like corn. Mama's hairbrush and the nice socks she knitted for us, and a carved wooden soldier that used to belong to her brother, which makes him my dead uncle, and a few other things, too. She's busy snatching up clothes.

Pretty soon the bag's full, but not heavy, and Mama looks at it, then at the door to the kitchen. I know she's wondering if the old man's asleep yet. I don't hear him snoring, but it can't be much longer. He was drunk when he started in on me with the whip and that was near two hours ago.

"We'll take the buggy," she whispers. "You rig it up, I'll fetch food and meet you in front of the barn."

She hands me my old wool coat, which used to be the old man's. It gave up the ghost a long time since, but it's what I got. "Go now." She squeezes my shoulder and I shiver as a hot snake crawls over that whip trail.

"He won't follow, Mama," I whisper, mostly to make her feel better. "Not now."

Mama looks at me like I filched too much bread and lied about it. I expect we both know I'm wrong. She's told me before he is relentless. "That's the word for him," she has said more than once, often when she's had more medicine than she ought.

"Go now."

I nod and ease open the back door. It squawks unless one of us remembers to grease it up. It's greased this time. Mama must have done it.

It takes me longer than it should, but I get Chaco out of her stall and I'm telling Ned to calm down—he's an old plowhorse but he's sweet on Chaco—when I hear the old man.

It's cooled off, it being late October, but he sleeps with his window open. The barn's a ways from the house but I hear that growl he makes when he's drunk and too stubborn to give over to sleep. He'll either pass out or get up and stomp to the kitchen.

I don't know which to do first—get the horse rigged or run to the kitchen. If I do one, the other won't get done.

Then it's too late to decide because I hear him stomping. I ain't quick enough. By the time I get to the back door, I see him through the screening. He's snorting hard through his nose, snotting on himself like a hydrophoby dog. One of his big hands is snatched tight in Mama's hair, which is loose from her bun and sways like a horse's tail. He swings Mama back and forth like he's trying to shake something loose from her.

"Dare you!" he bellows.

I scratch for the rope loop handle and cannot seem to find it in the dark. When I do swing the door open, he shouts, "Gaah!" He adds a few words I never heard before, and he's called me a pile of odd ones. Then he lets go of Mama.

She spins from him like they are dancing, and I swear it's as if time has slowed. She falls into the black cookstove hard enough to shove it back and rattle the damper in the pipe.

I shout animal sounds and swing my arms wild and sloppy, wanting to lay into him good for hurting Mama. For a wink of time it feels good, like something I should have done long ago. Then he gives me a stunner with the back of his hand. I pile up against the dry sink and my head bounces. I hear wood crack and then I am dizzy, can't see right.

Mama looks at me. "Run!" she shouts, over and over, "Get out of here! Run! Go!" shaking her head and shouting and crying. But I can't. I won't leave her. I keep trying to get up, so help me I do, but it's like I am underwater and yet flying crazy like a blind bird, all at once.

"Quit that simpering!" The old man smacks her hard across the face. "Sound like your mother. Why'd it have to be my son who died?" His voice is blurry, thick like wool batting. "Should have been you! Not my boy . . . he died a hero, fighting the cursed redskins, my only solace."

Mama wipes her bleeding mouth with her sleeve. She is sitting back, her legs folded under her, one hand gripping the stove door's handle. Then she does something I never heard her do. She shouts at the old man.

"That's not true and you know it, Papa! He didn't die fighting Indians! He was drunk and fell off his horse! You don't want to hear the truth of it. You! You're the reason! You're the reason for all of it!"

"No!" he shouts so loud it shocks us all. Then he kicks.

I've never seen the old man so quick. His boot catches Mama on the side of the head, the same bloody cheek, and her head snaps to the side. She flops to the floor, her eyes wide and staring at me.

Then she changes from Mama to something not my mama. She looks at me but she ain't seeing a thing anymore. She is dead.

I am dizzied up, balanced on my knees, leaning against the dry sink. For a moment it's all quiet in the kitchen. The old man and me, we do the same thing, we stare down at Mama.

Then I crack open that silent moment like a dropped egg. Of all the sounds I make tonight, the one that claws up out of my throat is something from some animal that ain't yet been discovered, a beast birthed of death and such sadness and anger as I hope to never know again. But I expect I will.

The sounds take shape after a bit and come out as "Mama!" Over and over I shout her name as I shove myself to my feet. I hit the old man as hard as I ever hit them sacks of meal when no one's around. The whole time I growl and I shout.

He doesn't know I am hitting him until I land a slap that clips his ear. Then he looks at me, and it's the only time I ever see him look confused and sad. It don't last long. Those wet eyes narrow up and I see the man in there I know too well, all anger and hate.

"Filthy 'skin!" he bellows in my face. "You're the cause!"

Good, I think. That's who I want to see. Then I land one more wide clout to his jaw before he knocks me cold.

Good + this. That's what I want to say. Then I had to
who so that to his line hame he knows me call

CHAPTER TWO

I come to in stink and wet muck and something hot clouding in my face. Whoever's breathing on me smells like they've been feeding on fly-blown meat. It takes a few moments to come to my right mind and I almost wish I hadn't. That's when I recall everything that happened. Mama and the old man.

The lashes on my back begin to burn something awful. I'm on my side and my head thunders like a cannonade. With the whip strikes burning fire on my back and shoulders and the wet stink all over me, I don't know what to think.

Then something grunts in my face and I know. I'm in the sty. The old man, he must have dumped me in here. I have a memory, fanciful, but I think not, of him looking down at me and spitting on me. Could be it was the pig's drool.

My next thought, given the stink, is that I am dead or on my way there because other than the pig, the only things that end up in the sty are kitchen scraps and the dead calves and kittens and chickens the old man throws over the log walls. The hog, the old man calls him King, is an enormous boar, biggest animal outside of Ned I ever seen. And he eats everything tossed to him.

I recall thinking that if the old man ever took the notion to butcher that pig, though he never will as he likes him more than he likes about anything else, except whiskey, that would be meat I could never eat. It would be a mix of all the dead things the old man ever dumped in there, some of them carcasses greening with age.

I hardly dare move, though piled up on my left side in the muck it hurts like the devil himself is stabbing me with a glowing poker. That boar's big face, tusks yellow in the dark of night, hangs in the air before me. His flat snout snuffles and pulses as he sniffs me.

I try not to breathe, but it hurts too much to hold it in. My breath leaks out and I reckon that's why he squeals low, like a warning. He backs up a step, then two, and stares at me. I see his tiny, wet, pig eyes watching me. I bet he ain't used to anything living being dumped in here with him, not sure what he's supposed to make of me. I don't think he's smart enough to dwell on it for too long. He'd as soon commence to gashing and tearing at me.

I figure I have little time to surprise the big boar. I'll have to scramble to get out of here, but I don't count on being so stiff and sore and dizzy in the head. Seems to take an hour for me to push up onto my knees.

I sway on all fours like an animal myself, gagging at the stink of the muck. Some of it went in my mouth. I spit and gag some more and then I hear a noise outside of the sty and I stop breathing again. The pig steps toward me, his head low and grunting.

I have to get out of here. Surprise is the only thing I figure will help me. I growl low like a dog and I stand and flail my right arm at the runny muck. It spittles up and the pig sidesteps from me, but commences to grunt, angry-sounding again.

I move toward the log wall behind me. The pig moves toward me. I growl again and slap at the muck. In that manner, I am able to get to the wall. I bump into it—it's closer than I think. Then King rushes me. I growl and flail and it doesn't do anything but rile him more.

I turn my back on him once, and my legs make a sucking

sound in the muck as I lurch over to the log wall. His nose shoves at my trailing leg and then I feel teeth as his mouth closes on my leg. I jump for a higher handhold, the wall being near as tall as the old man, tugging my leg up with me, and that pig's nose rams the logs. He squeals and I am up, atop the wall.

I am a meal he will not be tucking into. I am also filthy and aching, but I am alive. So far the old man hasn't laid a big, bony hand on my shoulder and tossed me back in with King.

The sty sets a ways back behind the barn, where we keep the four cows and goats. Off that leans the chicken shack. As I walk to the barn, I notice the night has turned colder than I expected. It's October, so I should not be surprised. I see my breath and I am glad for it, for that means I have breath to see.

I walk to the water trough, grateful I filled it from the river only that morning, and dunk my head. It ain't big enough for me to crawl all the way in. Cold or not, I am mucky and stinking. I can at least get the filth off my face and out of my mouth and nose. I snot it out some, spit, trying to keep my sounds low, lest the old man be lurking.

As I wash, I wonder what to do next. I know what I want to do, what I should do. I have to do to the old man what he done to Mama. It's only right. It's my abiding thought as I wrap my fingers around the shaft of the hayfork. He might well kill me but he won't get far afterward, with that wagging from him.

If he hasn't heard me yet, he'll like as not hear my teeth rattling like stones in a tin can. I am that cold. I do my best to ignore the hot whip marks on my back and the thudding in my head. It thumps fresh with each step I take toward the kitchen.

The back door is part open and I listen but hear nothing. I am shaking as I nudge it. I know I'll see Mama laid out there, same as before, never to move again. I hold my breath and push in, no sound from the greased hinges.

She isn't there.

For a second I am certain I'd been wrong and she has gone off to doctor her cuts in quiet, like she always does after the old man beats on her. But I know otherwise. Don't mean I don't hope. I cross the room, looking in the dark toward the far end of the house but not seeing anything move.

I ease open the door to our room, the woodshed, and the weak light of the kitchen's oil lamp cuts in. There she is, on the bed, laid out as if she is sleeping. Her eyes are closed, and her hair is spread around her face like she is underwater and it's floating free. She looks stern, and the far side of her face is dark and lumped.

"Mama?" I whisper.

Her hands are crossed, laid atop her chest. I touch the back of her top hand with my grimy finger—pig muck don't wash off easy. Her hand is cold. She doesn't move, doesn't wake. I knew she wouldn't.

That means the old man dragged her in here. Least he felt bad enough to do that. Small comfort, as Mama used to say about near everything in a day's time, then she'd sigh. At least she wouldn't have to feel that way no more.

I am crying a little, my finger atop Mama's cold hand. I pull it back as if I've been bitten. Then I remember what I got to do. I grip the hayfork tighter and walk out, cross through the kitchen and the front room to the doorway of the old man's room. I hold there and listen.

I see from the moonglow through the open window that he is in there, on his back like Mama, but he is breathing. Hard and deep, I know the sound. Dead drunk, as Mama would say. One leg is bent at the knee, his boot on the floor as if he is about to shove upright and spring for the door. The arm on the same side, closest to me, is stretched out toward the floor and an empty bottle.

I walk over to him. That hand could easily snatch my trouser leg. I watch him a long time, the stink off me could wake the dead, but he doesn't move. He does keep snoring, though. His breath hitches up now and again and I think he might wake, but no. The whiskey holds him deep. I commence to trembling, grinding my teeth so tight I figure they'll powder.

I never feel so much as I do right then, more than I feel when Mama died in front of me. It's a powerful feeling of rage. I lift that fork, them three long, steel teeth aimed downward. I shake like a branch in a storm, and so help me the only thing that stays my hand is Mama's voice in my head, clear as a first snow, saying, "Promise me you'll never be like him. Don't bring yourself to his level, or you'll never be any better than that for all your days. You be a good man, you promise me, son?"

I would always nod and say, "Yes, ma'am." Then I'd say, "A good man like my father?"

She always looked startled, then she'd smile and say, "Yes, like your father."

Looking down at the old man, I do not want to be like my father then. But I do not want Mama to look down on me from on high in her seat of Glory and be disappointed. Though that thought burns in me, it takes a mighty effort to turn away from the old man. I leave his room without looking back, his stuttering, sawing breaths fading as I walk through the house.

It doesn't take me long to gather what I reckon I'll need. Much of it was already in a sack by the feet of the stove. It's a comfort knowing Mama had been the one to set it there, filling it before the old man had come in on her. I won't take the sack from our room, the one with clothes and trinkets. I will have to move fast and do not want to lug the extra weight.

She'd put in the last of the bread she baked, a full loaf and the nub off another, and a fist-size hunk of cheese wrapped in what Mama called her tea towel. We never drink tea, so I don't know why she named it such. She also put in a jar of her pickled cucumbers.

I see the carving knife in the block at the far end of the counter and I slide it out of its slot and hold it up. It is something I rarely ever touch, but it is a wide, keen blade and I grunt and slip it into the sack. I look around a last time and see the kitchen matches. Why I don't take the entire box, I do not know. I grab a handful of them and stuff them into my trouser pocket.

I visit Mama once more and tear up again looking at her. Before I lose my will and stay right there, I kiss her forehead and whisper, "Goodbye for now, Mama." I grab the pair of socks she knitted for me last Christmas. Then I leave, holding my breath until I am out past the barn once more.

Come morning, I'm certain he will check the sty and see I cheated King out of his dinner. I consider riding Chaco, or even Ned, but figure the old man would accuse me of horse theft and send the cavalry after me. This way, he might figure me a good riddance, since he never liked me anyway.

He always says I am to blame for everything foul that happened to his family. I never could understand that, as I am part of the same family. But with me gone, I figure he will finally have what he always wanted.

My breath feathers out silver against the purple night air. The moon is up, pinned high and about at half-face, as if that other old man, the one up there, is frowning down on what we did here tonight. I can't blame him. We are a pitiful sight, the Barr clan. Even if I am only half a Barr.

I take the hayfork with me, figuring it might make a useful walking staff. I am sore and the night is going away and I have much ground to tread. Doing it moving like an old-timer isn't going to get me far. I set off for the mountains I know are there, though I can only see them in the daylight.

But they are there, in the dark, and soon I will be, too.

CHAPTER THREE

There is one direction I have to go, the only one I ever considered venturing in all my life. It is northward, toward where I reckon my father is from. Mama always was tight-lipped about him, but I heard slips here and there from her. She said once that he was a man from the north. I asked her three, four times why he left, but she only said he had things he needed to attend to.

"But he's coming back to us, right Mama?"

She always smiled and nodded. "Someday we'll see him again, son."

As I walk, my whip wounds and my head paining me fierce, I pretend I am thinking about important things, trying not to think about Mama staring me down, telling me to run as she lay dying. Well, Mama, I am doing it. Not exactly running, but doing the thing you didn't do all those years. Maybe you couldn't do it, I don't know. I'll think about it some other time. Right now, I am going to find my father.

I walk steady for near an hour, and reach the farthest pasture I am familiar with. The stump fence proves an obstacle I had not thought would slow me. Sore as I am, I have to rove south along it to find a low break to climb through. Beyond that the trees thicken, but my luck holds and the moon stays bright enough that I can see trunks before I walk into them.

The walking is level and my steps make twigs crunch underfoot. I have to take care to keep the tines of the pitchfork pointed away from my face. I don't dare use the business end to plant and push off with, lest I stab my foot. Soon I feel my breathing coming harder and know I am walking upslope, not much but it heartens me, for that must mean mountains. My father and his people are mountain people, a tribe of the high places. I am certain of it.

Long have I dreamed of seeing such country. From books Mama read to me in a whisper at night tucked tight in our bed, I know that nested amongst the mountains there are rivers and valleys with big trees. In the highest places, there will be snow all year-round with blue ice capping the peaks. What makes it blue, I don't know, though I guess it has to do with the sky, the nearest blue thing up there.

I believe game is bountiful in the mountains, deer and rabbits and goats of some sort, and big birds such as eagles, too. Though I don't think my father's people tamper with eagles for food. Mama said they are a ceremonial bird.

I know bears like the high places. That gets me to thinking about the only bear I've ever seen. It's the one the old man uses in the cold months to cover himself. Calls it his war robe, then he looks at me and laughs, the sound you make before you spit on the ground. He spit on me plenty over the years, mostly at my feet. He is a powerful chewer of tobacco, is the old man. And he's a fair aim with it, too.

As to the bear, it's a skin he sleeps under. He says it is warmer than any woman he ever met and, once he killed the thing, quieter, too.

I know all about how he killed it because he told the story plenty of times when he was drunk and chatty in the barn. That was about the only time he seemed to want me around. Wouldn't brook no interruptions, though. I lost a tooth once when I was younger and asked him a question. It grew back. But he told the story of that cinnamon bear so much I felt like I was right there with him on the hunt for it.

It was before I was born, Mama's mama hadn't yet hanged herself in the haymow, and the boy, as the old man called him, that would be Richard, his son, brother to my Mama, was off fighting "your kind," as the old man always said, then he'd look at me and laugh and spit.

The old man had gone to town one day to sell the cream, butter, and eggs. Even when Mama's mama was alive, the old man never let anyone else go into town.

While he was at Allsop's Creamery, he overheard other farmers talking about a cinnamon bear that had come down out of the hills and terrorized the town. It killed three weanling piglets, somebody's yapping dog, and a sheep or two.

It rattled the door on the Schoenfeld's outhouse when Mrs. Schoenfeld was in there rattling the inside, as the old man said, then he'd laugh. Mama said he found that funny because Mrs. Schoenfeld is a large woman and prone to gassiness.

The gabbing men said they were fixing to go out after it, but when the old man commenced to unload his milk cans in the spring room, those men stopped talking.

"They were all afraid of me. More than they were of the bear!"

I'd nod and keep my mouth shut tight. I know how those men felt.

Then the old man drove the wagon home in high dudgeon. That's what Mama said her mama called it when the old man was worked up. He fetched out his shotgun and whiskey and food and saddled up old Ned, then lit out after that bear while, he said, "the men in town were deciding how many pairs of socks to pack!"

He was gone for three days, though he found the bear on the first day out. "I run it ragged," he'd say, nodding, then he'd swig from his bottle and rub his big red nose. "I let it hunch up and recover its senses, then I'd prod on it and pepper it to get it moving again. Set it to bawling over hill and beyond like a no-good child! It'd bleed and run, bleed and run, barking and carrying on. Then I'd give it another taste!"

He always found that funny. Me, I was thinking of that shot-up bear, no water nor food nor sleep to speak of. And the old man, drunk and in high dudgeon, close behind.

That's when I stop and lean on the hayfork. The new day's sunlight has been brightening my trail all the while I've been walking and thinking. My back is sizzling like fat on a fire, but that isn't what catches me up short. It's all this thinking about the bear.

After three days of pestering it and wounding it and laughing at it, he shot that bear dead and skinned it out and lugged it to town atop ol' Ned, who couldn't have been too happy with such freight.

"I brought shame on those soft-bellied men," the old man would say, then sneer and swig more on the bottle.

Mama said he was relentless. Long time ago I asked her what that meant. She said it's something that will not stop, cannot stop until it has done what it needs to do.

"What's it do after that?" I said.

She looked at me like I asked her for a slice of the moon for supper, then she shook her head. "He will never stop. It will never end."

Until now, I reckoned this whole time she'd been talking about the bear.

CHAPTER FOUR

By midday I am as tired as I've ever been and feeling more poorly with each step. I know I should have brought the goose grease with me, though how I was to spread it on my back I am unsure. My head is cracking apart from the inside and cooking on the outside.

My old green felt topper isn't of much use keeping the sun off as the rear of the brim's gone, chewed by moths before it was mine, back when the old man used it on a scarecrow in the garden. 'Bout cooks my neck. I hope I'm not coming down feverish. I'll find out.

I make it up into the hills where the trees thin and grow in clumps of six or a dozen, some of them sizable. Most are piney, with rough, red bark and bursts of needles with a cone nested in them like a jewel in an opening fist.

It is beneath one such tree, with a sweep of low branches, that I decide to rest. It grows downslope of me, so I slide off the scant path I've been following. I think it's a game trail, for I spy deer pellets once in a while. I barely know that I'm crawling beneath that tree's green skirt.

Though I'd sipped from streams all morning, I have no water with me and wish I had thought to take one of the old man's wooden canteens from the peg in the tack shed. They leak until they swell from the water inside, but they do the job in the end.

As I lose my fight with staying awake, I reason that as my father got along for twelve years without me, surely a few more days would matter little. In truth, I have no idea how long it will take me to reach him and his people. A week? Two? Back at the farm, the mountains never seemed far off. Now that I am making for them, they never seem to get closer.

Some time later, a smell comes to me. I feel I am asleep and having a poor dream, yet I open my eyes. It's going on toward full dark, but I see branches near my face. I fancy I smell the sweetness of pine pitch. I flex my nose and sniff again. It's faint, but it isn't pitch. My own stink? No, not mine.

The old man gives off a powerful reek, worse when he's been working setting posts or sawing lengths of stovewood. Might help if he bathed more than once a month. Mama always made certain I washed "tip to toes," as she said, at least once a week, more often in summer.

I hear his voice, grumbling downtrail of me.

My guts seize like stone, my eyes open wide as cups. He is following me. I expected he would be pleased I was gone and leave me be. Is he afraid I would tell someone how Mama died?

So the old man, Bull Barr, will take me back and make me do everything Mama always did. I would have to cook for him and milk the cows and fetch his bottle and sleep in the woodshed and . . . Mama.

Had he buried her before he lit out after me?

It got cold since I crawled under the tree. I see my breath, and shivers work me up and down. I stopper my mouth with my sleeve and shift forward away from the trunk to hear better. My back is wet and sticky, as if I grew into the tree while I was asleep.

His boots grind closer. They are his hobnail hunters. I hear the steel nibs on the soles biting into, then sliding off stone, shoving forward, upslope toward me. I hold my breath and near-close my eyes. My heart thumps like someone punching me steady. I feel it in my throat.

I know what he'll be wearing—his grimy longhandles, the pink ones that began life as bright red. His brown leather braces, the tall, lace-up boots, and his canvas rucksack on his back. There'll be a couple of bottles in there.

". . . bad seed, a devil child with no soul. He is soulless, Martha Anne . . . wonder he didn't kill us all in our sleep. Scalp the lot of us!" He moans and keeps walking, his voice louder, shouting. "Brought shame on our family!"

He stops again and I hear liquid slosh. "Should have fed him to the coyotes while his bones was soft. A wastrel . . ."

They are all things I've heard before, but that was back on the farm, in the barn or the pasture or the house. Now they are spoken in the hills that lead to the mountains that will lead me to my father. Now the old man is following me. I should have known better. I did know better, but I have been a fool.

His sloppy footsteps continue upslope, closer to me, then slowly past. I wait a long time and feel my face heat. I am feverish from the whipping. The wounds have gone too long without tending, but there's no time for thinking about that. There will be later.

I climb up out of the hole, on my knees, sliding and gripping the top of the feed sack closed. Something inside—I think it's the kitchen knife, clanks against something else. It's the loudest thing I ever heard.

I don't move a hair. I listen and listen. Then I feel something wet against my leg and a rank smell tickles my nose. Pickles. Mama's pickles. The jar broke.

Laughter, that raggedy shouting laugh that means nothing funny at all, a sound I've heard every day of my life, is close, not far upslope.

"You can't best the Bull, boy! Ain't nobody ever has! 'Specially not a cur of a 'skin!"

He is close, ten strides back to me? More? I don't know what

240

to do. Stay put? Climb higher, westward along the slope? The pickles decide it for me. If I can smell them, he can, too, and he'll use the vinegar stink to find me. I slide back down to my spot on the far side of the tree trunk, hoping the near-darkness will mask me.

I claw at the earth, scooping a hole, and shove the sack in it, covering as much of the wet patch as I can with pine duff and gravel. It helps, but Mama's pickles, tasty as they are, will leave your breath rank for a spell after a meal, so I know the old man will smell them. Likely already has.

That's about all the thinking I have time for because I hear his boots grinding on rock, scuffing back toward me. They're draggy and sound as though he's walked days without rest. That's because of the liquor. It slows a body down.

I hunch tighter behind the tree trunk and hold my breath. He stops on the thin game trail upslope of me, muttering and shifting his position every few seconds. He sniffs and sniffs, shifting around, sniffs some more. He grunts and I hear glugging. Then I hear that sighing sound he always makes after he finishes a drink.

He tosses the bottle and it rolls by me. Then he grunts and pees, the stream drizzling down at me. I don't move, though I want to get away from that. Presently I feel wetness from it on my backside and along my right leg. He must have had to go for ages, for he keeps on and on.

I bite the inside of my mouth and close my eyes tight. It will end and he will go back home to the farm. Go away, I wish in silence, not looking nor breathing. Go back the way you come.

Finally, he stops and I know he is fumbling with the buttons on his trousers. Often at the farm he will not bother.

"Too easy," he says then, and trudges on upslope, back the way he was headed before I broke the pickles.

I peek out from beneath my arms, but I don't see nor hear

anything. Same as before when I crawled up out of here.

I am little more than a frightened chipmunk down in my hole by the tree's roots, waiting for the coyote to sink his fangs into me and shake me to death. I am fevered, but my face feels hotter. Burning up with the shame of what I let him do to me. Today and all the days leading to it.

I know then I've not been thinking straight. I see it now. I hear Mama's words like I am hearing them for the first time, and she's right. He will never let me go. He will never stop hunting me. For now he has the one thing he always wanted, an excuse to kill me.

I am the cinnamon bear and the old man is playing with me.

CHAPTER FIVE

He'll camp soon and then I can leave this spot and climb higher into the mountains. Then I'll be safe. My father will be there and he will know how to stop the old man, how to send him back to the farm.

I have to get as far from here as I can.

I wait for much of an hour in case he's nearby. I don't think he can stay awake, as he's been drinking. While I wait, I roll down the top of the feed sack and pull out what I can without making the broken glass clink. Every time I make a noise I seize, but nothing moves near me in the night.

Pieces of the busted jar lift out easy enough, but the pickles, thin sliced with onions, make a soppy mess. I am tempted to eat some of them, but I can't see and I'm fearful I'll eat glass with them. I picture splinters sliding down my throat and into my belly and all the havoc they could cause down there. I feel rough enough, no need to add to the pile. The bread's not bad, though it got wet from the pickles, and I nibble on a corner of the cheese.

I ought to have put more thought into what I took from the kitchen. The matches in my pocket are damp from pickle juice, or the old man's pee, I don't know which, but I reckon they'll dry. The knife I wipe off on the sack, and after I wring that out, I slide everything back in, including the knife. There's nothing else in there for it to break.

Feeding myself once the bread and cheese are gone isn't

something I planned for. I vow to give it good thought come the morning. Right now I have to get away from this hillside and the old man. I do not want to go back to that farm.

As I shift to crawl my way to the trail, my left boot toes something that makes a clunking sound. It's the empty whiskey bottle the old man tossed at me. Since I forgot to take a canteen, the bottle could prove useful. I pat the ground and find it, unbroken. Them bottles are tough.

The mouth of it smells rank, but I am used to whiskey stink. I hold the bottle in one hand and the sack in the other and climb on out of there.

The moon isn't nearly so friendly as last night. Once I'm out from under the branches I see nary a star above. There is a glow from behind great quilts of clouds that helps me see edges of things, trees and boulders and such.

Aside from stumbling over the old man, drunk and sleeping, I fear walking off the edge of the trail. I passed steep drop-offs earlier, so I know the terrain is growing more dangerous the higher I climb into the hills.

These, I remember, are called foothills, because they are the feet of the big mountains. I picture the mountains as large men sitting with their knees pulled up. Right now I am climbing up along the feet. By tonight I will work my way up a leg and reach a knee. That is my aim.

In a day or two, I will scale the chest, cross over to a shoulder, and perhaps I will see to the other side. That will be where my father and his people live. I have put much thought into this over time, but never more since walking out here.

Seems to me living way up in the mountains is not nearly so practical as in a valley with grasses and trees and a river cutting through the middle of it. That's what I feel sure I will find once I make it up to the shoulder and look down the other side. There I will see teepees or log huts. I am not certain. But that's where they will be. Over the mountains.

I plan to make tracks through the night and take care to leave no trail. It feels good to know where I am bound. Finally, I am leaving the old man behind. And I did not break my promise to Mama. I did not do what the old man deserves. Some other person will do such. Or perhaps it will be time itself that will whittle him down to a useless nub. But it won't be me. I will be gone.

It isn't until the sun is up that I realize that though I gained something in the night, the bottle, I also lost something. The sack with food and the knife swings from my right hand, but the pitchfork, my walking staff, is gone.

I must be more tired than I think, for I look around at the rocks and scant trees, as if it will be there, fetched on a low branch, or sticking in the trail behind me. But no, I did not drag it out from under that tree where I hid from the old man.

I picture that fork with its smooth handle laying there to rot out its days, never to be found, and it makes me sad inside. I'd used that fork every day for more years than I can recall. I walk on, running a knuckle into my eyes and snuffling.

It's not the fork so much as it is Mama being gone. I walk and cry and after a spell it feels better, like something knotted in my chest worked itself loose. It's there, but not so tight.

I fill the bottle at a clear-running stream and glug down the whole thing, then fill it again and walk on.

As I walk I'm surprised to feel so odd. My eyes are funning me, for the glare of the sun is not near as bad as I expect it should be this time of the day. I walk beneath trees, then out from under them again, shade and sun, shade and sun. And those mountains before me never seem to get closer. I am fever-ish. I walk faster.

Later I feel a tapping against my leg and see that walking has worked the tip of the kitchen knife through the sack. The entire blade, about as long as a man's foot, sticks out. This keeps up, I'll lose it and won't know it, so after some fiddling, I figure a way to carry it on my waist, wedged beneath my rope belt.

The wood handle on the underside of my right forearm feels good, knowing Mama used that knife every day of her life, working in the kitchen. That little feeling sets me to thinking about my family.

That's what Mama said I should always think of them as. She told me about how her brother, Richard, when he was younger than me, always wanted to get away from the farm. He run off twice, but he was caught, once by the old man, the other he was dragged back by the law. The old man beat him plenty both times.

This was years before I was born. Mama was younger than I am now. But she said she remembered it like it all happened yesterday. That's how she would say it. Me, I do my best to forget the day before today. Only good time was at night when Mama would read to me.

One night the old man heard us. He must have been lurking in the kitchen when we thought he'd passed out in his bed. He kicked in the door of the woodshed and said, "Give it here." He stuck out his big hand.

Mama must have known what he meant because she closed the book and hugged it to her chest. It was a book about King Arthur by a fellow named Bulfinch. She pulled her knees up under the blanket and I know she was trying to sit in front of me, to protect me. She held the book close and said, "Papa, please. It's only a little reading."

"Ain't reading that's the problem, you stupid girl! That's your sainted mama's book and you been readin' it to that heathen!" He swatted her hard, and her lip opened again. The next day the side of her face was the color of a ripe blackberry.

After he took the book and left us, she rubbed my head and

said, "Don't worry, son, we'll not give up on books." Then she whispered. "I got others he don't know about." And she did, too. We were more careful, but it was never the same. And I never did find out what ol' King Arthur got up to in the end.

Anyway, her brother finally made it off the farm. Was near sixteen years old when he ran away in the night and joined up with the army. The old man lit out after him, searched for some time, but came home alone.

He didn't say anything about it, but Mama told me she overheard him telling her mama that the army sent him away, said the boy was their property now, not his. I can't imagine belonging to anyone, except that's what my life was like on the farm. I was his property. If that's so, I was property he never wanted.

Mama's brother was in the army for years and would write to his mama regular, telling her how they were clearing the land of the heathen savages.

Mama said the old man would have his wife read them letters to him over and over at the table at night, though they weren't never addressed to him. Never a mention of him in them. Then they got an official letter saying the boy was dead. Mama said that's when the old man got dark. She said he was not pleasant before that but after, he was mean, drinking more than ever.

One morning not but a week after they got the letter about the boy, Mama got up. The coffee pot was cold and the fire was out. She went out to the barn to gather eggs for breakfast, thinking her mother was feeling poorly or sad, and had stayed in bed. But when Mama got to the barn, there was her mama, in her old blue nightgown, blue as a pretty spring sky, Mama said. Her mama was dead, hanging from a rope around a beam in the barn.

She'd done it herself. Climbed up the ladder and tied it

around her neck and climbed partway down again, then kicked off. I know this because I studied on it some. I figure if she'd of jumped from the mow out into the air, that fall would have pulled her head clean off her body. What a terrible thing for Mama to find when all she was looking for was eggs.

Mama said once that happened, the old man was downright god-awful. She tried to leave a pile of times, but between him threatening her, and her own crying, first for her brother, then for her mama, she couldn't never bring herself to do it.

Once the pain hardened over like a scar, and she got used to the old man drinking and breaking things and telling her she couldn't do a thing right, then begging her not to leave him or he'd die, she said she had no choice but to stay.

"Stayed too long," she told me once, a long time ago when I was a child. Then she looked at me and smiled. "But that ain't right neither." She touched my face. "If I had left, I wouldn't have had you."

I recall thinking that was an odd thing for her to say. "No, Mama," I told her. "I'd have been where you were going."

She thought that was funny. Now I see why.

I asked her about my father a whole lot. For the longest time she told me the same thing, that he was a good man who had to go away, back to his people in the north, but that he'd return for us one day. For the longest time I believed that. Then I got older and one night I asked her more questions.

She stopped her knitting and sighed, then looked at me. "He was a man who come through these parts looking for work. Papa hired him on to help lay in firewood and fence in the far pasture. He was a good man. Just so happened he was an Indian. Come from a tribe up north, I am not certain of its name, but that's what he told me. Somewhere up in the mountains."

I pestered her something awful after that, but other than telling me I reminded her of him, she didn't say much more. Wouldn't tell me his name. I wonder now if she knew it. Could be they didn't speak the same tongue.

After a while I got the idea that thinking about him made her angry or sad. I know he never came for us. Might mean he up and died, but I kept thinking there had to be more to the man than that.

I imagine he'd been caught up fighting to keep his people free. Maybe they had been rounded up and carted off to a reservation somewhere. Mama said that was happening to all the Indians. I didn't think much of the notion, because that would mean he wasn't where I needed him to be. Somewhere north of the farm, up in the mountains.

In my head that's where he has been all this time, waiting for me. Has to be, so that's where he is.

CHAPTER SIX

It's late afternoon before I stop for a rest. The old man likely woke up surly and decided I was not worth the bother. I'd bet a whole one of Mama's canned peach pies that he gave up and went back to the farm. But I misjudged him once, and since I am making for the mountains anyway, I decide to hoof it steady while I have the daylight.

I am tempted to sit beneath another piney shade tree and rest my feet, but the only one I find is in the open, along the edge of a small meadow, gone brown and hot with hopper bugs bouncing in the autumn heat. Seems a waste of effort to live your life jumping up and down like that.

I move along until the land dips low once more and I am in the midst of waist-high rabbit brush. I reckon it will keep the sun off, so I ease myself down and groan like I've seen a whole lot more years than twelve. I set down the half-full bottle and my sack beside it.

I tell myself I'll not sleep, and only sit long enough to gnaw cheese and bread, and rub my feet. But if I tug off my boots, they'll stink worse than pickle juice ever thought of smelling, so I prop my boots on a rock and lean. My back won't put up with much poking, so it takes a bit before I find the right spot. I rub my face with the top of my hat and before I know it, I'm dozing. That's when the gunshots commence.

The first smashes apart my water bottle. Glass bits whip everywhere, some chunking into my arms and legs and face.

Another shot hits my food sack and kicks up a charge of dirt by my left leg. I think I scream, but the shots are so loud it's tough to tell what-all is happening.

It's like being woke by sudden thunder right over the farm, which happens sometimes in summer in the valley. It slams back and forth for what feels like hours. Mama always pats my head and tells me it's God playing games with the angels. I wished they'd play checkers instead.

I roll and try to find something to hide behind. There is nothing, so I keep rolling and crawling on my hands and knees like a child play-acting at being a dog. The shots stop and I hear the old man laughing.

I shout, surprising myself. "Leave me be! I don't want anything from you!"

His reply is quick, stomping on the end of my own words. "I want something from you! You owe me, boy! You took everything, left me with naught! I demand payment!"

I see the shot-up sack with what's left of the bread and cheese. Beside it stands the bottom half of the bottle, now a jagged stump of clear glass. I wonder if it's safe to nudge forward and grab that sack? That's all the food I have. I reach out and a bullet drives so close to my fingertips I think I've lost them. I yank my arm back and hold it close. All the fingers are there, but they're numb.

I hear him laughing again, then he shouts, "Ain't nobody don't pay Bull Barr!"

More bullets, so many so quick, fly at me like angry bees set on killing. They ping off rocks and zip into the dirt before me. I elbow my way backward, gravel working under my shirt, but I don't pay it mind. All I want is to get out of there.

After a spell, he commences with the bullets again. I gain my feet and run, keeping my head low. The old man must be up a tree or on a patch of high ground because he sends bullets my way, winging them at me from behind. They buzz close by, nicking trees or cracking off rocks to my right, so I run left, which is westward, good enough to get away from the old man.

After a spell the bullets stop, but I don't. My legs feel like logs, my fingers throb, and my back crawls with fire, but I don't dare stop. I have to get away from him this time. I cannot expect he'll leave me be. Mama was right.

It isn't until later I realize not only did I lose my water bottle and my food sack with Mama's tea towel, but my hat's back there, too. I have the knife, though, wedged under my rope belt and banging against my hip as I cut west along the valley floor at the base of the mountains.

At least there's trees. And as low as the land is, there must be water. If I keep the mountains to my right, I know where I am. I figure on hugging the trees until dark, then cutting northward once more. I make it high enough, I can get to where I need to be before he finds me again.

Dark catches me some hours later. I welcome it as I don't think I can lift another leg. I am that tired.

I hear a crushing, whacking sound and wonder if it's rock sliding off the stone face of the mountain across the way. I'm not certain what made me think that, but I'm wrong.

It's not rock sliding, but the old man, crashing through branches and shouting and laughing. I stop and look back and catch sight of a light, swinging wide, then disappearing, like an eye blinking. He must have brung the little blue chore lantern from the nail in the barn.

The night is clear and cold. I don't think he needs the lantern, as the moon's waxing and brighter than the night before. A chill breeze carries toward me and I pick out words from his shouts— " 'skin!" and "Martha Anne."

He's talking to his dead wife about me and I'm so tired all I want to do is sit down and wait for him and tell him I'll go back to the farm and work off whatever debt he says I owe.

Then I shake my head and blink hard. "No," I growl to myself. "No!"

Mama said he's relentless, so I got to be, too. I got to keep on and find my father. Then he will say, "Go back alone to your farm, old man! Leave my boy be."

I get walking again, warmed by these thoughts, swinging a leg forward, then the other. Soon, I leave the old man behind once more. I know it will not last, so I keep on, each step giving me more freedom.

I walk and walk, and it comes to me that the old man is asleep by now. I hope so, as I need rest as well. My back is paining me something fierce, my head is boiling hot again, and my teeth have gone back to chattering like river rocks.

What would Mama do? She'd smear goose grease on my back, make a poultice of comfrey and mustard for my chest, and set me up in bed. Now and again I'd take ill and couldn't hardly move. Mama said it's because I was a boy working like a man. Said the body needed time to catch up to such things. I don't know about all that, but I do know the old man didn't like it when I wasn't in the barn before him.

He'd stomp back to the house and break something in the kitchen. You'd think after all those years there wouldn't be much left to shatter into pieces, but he somehow found it.

I think about that and shiver more and tug my old coat tight about my throat. I am grateful to have it, even if it is more hole than coat in places, such as the elbows, which Mama was forever mending. "You are devilish on elbows. I never saw the like," she'd say.

I smile, and then I remember her face there in the kitchen, and I vow not to think about Mama just now.

The night is cool, and soon I'll smell snow on the breeze. Not yet, but soon. I have to get to my father and his people before that.

I keep moving and a minute later I hear water ahead, to my right. I follow the sound and splash into it before I know I am doing so. I back to the edge and get down on my hands and knees and drink deep.

Between the cool sips and my wet boots and the water I scoop over my face, I feel perked and decide to follow that river tight, keeping it close to my right. Noisy as it is, it might serve to keep my sounds hidden from the old man. Of course, that could work both ways. Come tomorrow, I'll wade across and climb north. I believe that will put me near a cleft in the mountains I saw before sunset.

Right now, I have a bigger problem than all that. I am as hungry as two dogs, and it's getting worse with each step.

I am used to feeling like I ain't had enough to eat. Seems it's always that way at the table, though Mama made certain I had bread or cheese or an apple once the old man was snoring his way through the night at the other end of the house.

But the feeling in my gut right now is the worst it's ever been. It's as if I've always been starving. I take to chewing on a nub of tree bark, then on a pine cone, but it's pitchy and gums up my teeth. It doesn't stop me from keeping an eye open for apples and late berries, though.

At least on the farm I had food, especially when the old man wasn't in earshot. Mama would fix me a bowl of hominy or slice up an apple from the keeper barrel and drip honey on it.

I take stock of my goods. I have two pairs of socks, one I use as mittens and one on my feet. Then I have the knife, and the matches in my pocket, though the heads got wet from the pickle juice and have mostly flaked off. But a fire isn't something I have time for right now.

I stumble on a root and that jerks me back to myself on the trail. I sure wish I could make a fire tonight. It's cold enough I can't go another step. Hopefully the old man will huddle up somewheres with his jacket pulled tight about his ears.

There's a patch of rabbit brush and I figure I might find some warmth down low. I see a darker spot and kick at it. Looks like a gap, so I jam my way in, crawling and patting the ground with the socks on my hands. It's bony and hard-packed. I scooch back out and crawl on my knees some feet away where I thought I'd trod on something soft. I was right.

I snatch up a handful and hold it to my face. It's dried

grasses, but it smells good. I pick as much as I can and gather it in my arms like I'm hugging it. It tickles my face and itches, but I don't care. It'll keep me warm where the fire failed me.

No, that's not right. The fire didn't fail me, I failed in building it. Turns out my matches are worthless and can't raise a whiff of smoke. It shows me how easy life at the farm was. I never gave much thought as I went about making a fire in the woodstove or eating a hunk of bread and a slice of cheese. Out here in the forest, it all comes hard. I have to give up on thoughts like that because they make me think of food.

The dry grass is the best thing I can find to keep me warm. There isn't much of it, but I stuff what I've gathered into the hole in the brush and when I crawl in this time, I notice the smell. It's musky like a billy goat, and makes my nose wrinkle, but it's too late to find a different spot.

I shove the wad of grass in as far as I can, six feet or so, then I burrow in with my head tucked down like a turtle in my old wool coat. The smell gets worse. It's an animal stink, wet and rank.

I should get out of here, but I am too cold. I don't get any sleep at all, so I sit with the grass pulled up around my chest and face like the worst blanket ever made. I start to fall asleep when a low noise wakes me. It's close, six or eight feet away. I hear it again and I know it for what it is—a growl. Then I hear more growls.

A long fingernail of ice drags up my backbone and my hair prickles all over my head. The smell, whatever is in this hole, gets a whole lot worse, too. By now I have a good idea of what it is. I hear growls all around me, and then howls.

They are range dogs, as I've heard the old man call them. Coyotes. I've seen what they do to chickens and rabbits, and even a skunk. And once, they fed on an old cow we had who was calving in the pasture.

I found her, thrashing and bawling, her back end all raw meat and chewed away. She couldn't get up, couldn't do nothing but look at me with big eyes and bawl, snot stringing out her nose and mouth. It was terrible. And no sign of her baby calf, neither.

I ran back to the farm and told the old man. He cursed me a blue streak and fetched his rifle. He shot that old cow in the head and we butchered her on the spot. We lugged the meat home in the work wagon behind Ned.

Then the old man beat me until he got tired. Said I was to blame.

Mama once told me if you hear coyotes outside your door, you are to stay in your house because they have a mystical eye that will enchant you. It's nothing they can control, but a power they're born with. Sort of like how I have skin that ain't like the old man's.

But she said their eyes will trap you if you look at them. Then they will eat you. One alone, a man might be able to fight him off, but a whole pack surrounds whatever it is they plan on eating and they dart in and tear at it, their black, wet noses all hunched up and their teeth wet and white, nipping and slashing. Before long their prey dies of a mess of bleeding bites and cuts it didn't know it had in the first place.

Tonight, the moon is not particularly bright, so I wonder how I'll see their eyes in the dark. The clouds will part at the worst moment, and I will see them staring me down, teeth bared and noses hunched, their hackles bristled. That's when they'll lunge.

My thinking goes on and on like this and I don't know what to do. I'm in the den of the range dogs, sitting right where they sleep or eat or mess, I don't know which. They are outside the brush, all around me. Their growls give sign to more of them, because I hear others, howling far off, yapping like they're trying to outdo each other, one talking over another.

Mama says that's a sign of low manners and that I should always let somebody else finish whatever it is they are saying before I commence to speak. Must be she learned that from her mama, because the old man don't care who's doing the talking. If it ain't him he'll start right up saying whatever it is he wants to.

As it was only ever Mama and me, we stopped talking and listened to what he was saying. It was always the same thing, though. How Mama couldn't cook anything like her mother and how I was less than useless. All things we heard every day anyway.

Serves me right for holing up near dark. If I'd stopped sooner, I would have seen what was in that hole in the brush, scat or bones. But tired as I am, once the growling and howling commence, I wake like I've been dunked in an icy pond. Funny thing what fear will do to a fellow.

I am going to have to fight my way out of here. I keep telling myself not to look the range dogs in the eyes, lest they put a spell on me and eat me where I stand.

I shove up to my knees and my right hand brushes something that makes me feel almighty good, considering the situation. It's the handle of Mama's kitchen knife wedged in my rope belt. I grip it through the sock covering my hand and slide it free.

I'll wave it like a big tooth, and slash right back at them when they try the same on me with their teeth. Might be I only have the one and they have mouths full, but this tooth is long and steel and sharp. I wish for a second I had the hayfork with its three steel tines. They'd be better teeth, but the knife is what I have, and that's no complaint.

For the moment my own teeth stop chattering. The howls, from what sounds like a dozen animals, are all around me, closing in and louder than a minute ago. I know if I stop to think, I will wither and miss my chance. That always ends with a beating by the old man.

This time I say no and I grit my teeth and shove my way back to the entrance of the hole quick as I can. If I come upon one of them beasts, I'll jam into it hard, knock it back some, gain enough time to get to my feet.

The thing with the fur I ram myself into is more surprised by me than I am of it. It's in mid howl and I slam right into it. I whip an arm up, and though it's dark, I see the animals clearly. They are all as skinny as I feel, and light colored enough that I see them hopping like they're dancing away from me.

Soon as I get out of there, I gain my feet and howl louder than any of these demons. I scare myself with the sounds I make, as I ain't never been one for shouting. Most noise I got up to was calling in the cows from the pasture or yelling at the goats once in a while when they were doing something I was sure to get blamed for.

I whip the knife side to side like I'm clearing tall grass with a hand sickle. It tastes fur at least twice, judging from the whimpers I hear. I almost feel bad, like I'm putting the hurt on a yard dog. Then I remember coyotes are wily creatures and will curse you with their eyes, then kill you with their teeth. The whole pack of them will set on me, so I aim to set on them first.

I keep up my wild slashing and run, waving the knife back and forth in front of me, partly so I won't run smack into a tree and knock myself cold. I don't want to wake up with a pack of angry, bleeding coyotes eating on me. I think I scare them so bad they don't know what to do. I also think there aren't as many of them as I guessed.

No matter, my legs keep moving and my arm keeps swinging that knife and I don't hear much behind me. Whimpers and squabbling sounds, and I get to thinking they are eating each other. As long as it ain't me.

Soon as daylight shows itself, I stop loping and listen and

look behind me for sign of beasts closing in. None. I also see no cuts nor bites on myself. I do see something dark spattered on my trouser legs and the same on the knife's blade. Coyote blood, has to be.

For a second or two there is a flame in me that wants that blood to be the old man's. I almost smile at the thought, then I shake my head and say, "I'm sorry, Mama." I slide the knife back into my rope belt and I commence to lope once more, because it's keeping me warm.

CHAPTER EIGHT

By the time full light comes, I look around and I get panicky. I am down in low country, can't see the mountains. Where had I run to in the night? I covered a fair bit of ground, but what if it was back toward the farm? A hard fist of fear and anger spins back and forth in my gut. I can't go back there. I won't go back there.

For a cool night last night, the day turns off hot. Hot as homemade sin, as Mama would say when she burned her arm on the stove door baking bread. I miss her something fierce. In time it might not be so bad, but all that is a long ways off. Right now I am hot and tired and sore from my hair to my crusty toes. I am also thirsty. That's why about midday, I hear something that makes me smile.

At first I think that low sound is a breeze passing through high-up leaves. But it keeps on, not tapering nor breaking up like wind will do. I sniff, close my eyes, and sniff again. Might be there's water up ahead. I sure could use it. And then, before I expect to, I come upon a full-bore gravel-bank river.

All I think about is how good that water is going to feel in my throat. "I could drink you dry, Mr. River. Dry. And I'd be thirsty yet." My voice is a raw whisper. Hearing myself is odd.

I wonder if I sound something like my father. I know once in a while Mama will say something that sounds like the old man, the way she'll round off a word like "barn" or snap "fool" at me for dropping a split of stovewood on the kitchen floor. Difference is she'll nearly cry and hug me and ask my forgiveness right off, whereas the old man will keep right on, then follow it with a clout to the ear.

I am feverish and dried out, but I reckon I could be worse off. I make for a grassy patch, more brown and nubby than green, but it looks softer than the rocks. I have a mind to drink, then bathe myself.

Since it is early enough in the day, by the sun it's midday, I consider washing my togs and stretching them on the boulders to dry. Between the sun baking them from above and the hot rocks cooking them from below, they should be dry pretty quick. I'll look in the river or on the bank for something to eat while they dry.

I shuck my coat, then my shirt, peeling it off my shoulders. The left one, in particular, is tricky, as the cloth has worked itself into the cut. I begin to tug it free, but it won't give in easy, so I stop and stuff the sleeve of my coat into my mouth and bite down hard.

The river's loud enough that it muffles my shouts. The whip marks are bleeding again, and when I look over my shoulder, I see they are red and angry like a slapped face. They are also oozing a yellow goop like what comes out of your nose when you have a winter sickness.

If I were tended by Mama, the goose grease would be an inch thick, and the bandages would be fresh every morning. But I am not, and I am feverish, and this river's looking mighty tempting. I strip off the rest of my clothes, one piece at a time, beginning with my boots.

The bottoms are near worn through, and the wadded news-paper mama put inside is about gone as well. I see my toenails have made hard work of the end of my right sock. The left is fine, which is curious. So far I have saved my extra pair of socks, except for wearing them on my hands. But I see that will have to change.

Finally, I have a pile of boots, socks, trousers, my rope belt and knife, the shirt, and my coat. Soon I am standing on bare rocks, wearing nothing more than my raggy undershorts.

I keep them in case some prospector and his family from back East should wander by. I have heard of stranger things happening in the hills. Or at least that's what my mind tells me. I pull my boots back on and clump down to the water's edge, then I step out of them and walk in.

Hot as I am, the chill of that water ripples through me. It's delicious, like the first lick of that vanilla ice cream Mama made two summers back, when the old man had gone to town. We got through a bowl each before he come back early.

Mama offered him a bowl of it and he smashed it on the floor, then took that old ice cream crank out to the dooryard and blew it to pieces with his shotgun. Never said a word, then commenced to drinking in the shade.

That nippy river won't let me mull sour thoughts of the old man for long. It's all I can do to hold onto my own breath. My chest works like a bellows and as I walk gingerly along, the water slowly rises up to my knees. I hold my right hand up under my rib cage and rub there where I know my lungs are hidden, hoping to calm them some. My breath slows as I grow used to the chill.

I chance a look down at myself. I am shocked, I don't mind saying it. I've never been much for carrying extra weight, but missing regular meals these past days shows on my body. I see bone points stretching skin where I'd not suspected I had much in the way of bones.

The river's loud, making splashing noises around big rocks, and does the same around my legs. It's tricky walking because the bottom is all rocks.

None of them are much smaller than my head, cobbles as the old man calls them. They wobble as I step on them. I lose my footing not paying attention and upend myself. I strike my back low down on a rock below the surface and wheeze my way to a sitting position.

When I stop sputtering and look back to shore, I see I've made it about halfway across the river. Before I fell in, the water was up to my knees. About six feet upstream of me is a boulder as big as a buggy, without the horse. I crawl and float over to it and see a sandy-bottom pool on the downstream side of it.

I rest there, my hands on the bottom, below my backside, and let the water come up around my head, under my chin. I close my eyes and enjoy the easier water, not quite so hard on my body, pounding downstream as it is. The big boulder gives me shade, and I sleep a little, napping like a cat will do in the sun.

After a fashion, I hear something other than the river bubbling by. It's a steady *crack crack crack*. I open my eyes and sit up enough so the water won't go in my mouth. The sun is bright and it takes me a moment to recall where I am and what I am up to.

The cracking sound keeps on. I look to my left, toward the riverbank from where I came. There, hunkered beside my clothes, is the old man. He's looking at me and grinning, whacking a rock as big as his hand against another on the ground between his boots. His rifle lays across his legs.

"You awake, 'skin?" His voice reaches me, though he has to work at it some.

I hold my hand up to my eyes and squint over at him. I don't say anything.

"Good!" he shouts and gives one of his snorting laughs. He drops the rock, then, mostly looking at me, except for glances now and again at what he is doing, he fluffs through my pile of clothes. I see my boots are up there next to him, too.

He says something, then I see his shoulders moving, so I know he is laughing. He pulls out his pipe from his left breast pocket, holds it betwixt his teeth, and lights a match. He looks at me and smiles behind the pipe. He almost touches the match to his pipe but then loses his smile and shakes his head slow-like, back and forth.

The old man moves the match down and lights something, twigs or grass, most likely, beneath the pile of my clothes. I feel my gut harden into a knot. I don't move. I keep my hand over my eyes, my eyes on him. Gray smoke boils up as my clothes give way to orange flames that jerk and quiver with the riverside breezes.

He stokes the fire and once the blaze is going well, he adds small hunks of wood from a pile beside him. Then he lifts one of my boots and turns it over and over as if he found something of magical use in a cave somewhere. He shakes his head and sets the boot on the fire. It burns up pretty quick. Second one does the same.

He holds his pipe in his teeth, but it only wags with words he's saying, more to himself than to me. "Martha Anne," I bet he's saying. "Martha Anne, that 'skin is no good."

Once it all burns up beyond use, he stands, cradling the rifle across his belly, and stares across the water at me. Quick as a fingersnap he hefts that rifle to his shoulder and points it at me. Jacks a shell and all.

I splash and thrash and get myself around the far side of the boulder.

I hear him snort and after a few moments I peek around the sunny side of that rock. He has the rifle cradled again and is laughing. It's the only time I ever seen him laugh that much. Almost looks like he's enjoying himself. Then I recall who it is I am seeing and I know that can't be the case. The old man never enjoys anything that much.

"We are coming to it now, boy!" he shouts and cracks off a shot.

I jerk back behind the rock.

"Nah . . . too easy," he shouts, then shakes his head. He turns away and walks up the riverbank, same way I came. I notice he has the kitchen knife wedged in his belt. That means he left me with nothing.

Then I think of two things. One is that I am wrong, because he actually has left me with something—my life. He could have shot me easy before I splashed my way around that rock. And the second thing I think is this: Mama was right. The old man will never stop. I should have known.

Thought I'd outsmarted him, but what makes me think I am smarter than that cinnamon bear? To live as it had, it had to have been a clever animal. But it still got itself killed by the old man.

One night some years back, me and Mama were in bed and I was telling her how the old man said the bear was big and scary, a "genuine man-killer," he'd said.

She looked at me and whispered. "It wasn't that big, you know."

"What wasn't?"

"That bear he shot."

I didn't know what to think of that, but Mama, she kept right on whispering. "I saw it when he brung the carcass home. It wasn't full grown yet, and did not look well. All thin and ganted up."

I thought on that, knowing Mama wouldn't lie to me. I'd not seen the bearskin but a few times in my life, as I was not allowed in that room. I do recall it didn't take up much of the top of the bed and its light-brown hair was tufty and patchy.

I think once more that he's pestering me, same as he did to

that bear. Poking and prodding me until I have less and less of myself left. He didn't let that bear sleep, didn't let it eat, nor rest up out of the sun. Kept dogging it, poking it where he wanted it to go. Then he shot that bear full of holes.

I realize I've been walking along the river, not deeper into the mountains. Like he wanted me to. Could be it's the same river that flows from the east to down below the farm.

How many days would it take for him to drive me all that way? Or would he kill me first and drape me over his shoulder and lug me home, to shame my dead mother like he shamed those men in town with that bear?

CHAPTER NINE

After a while, I stand, shivering, all the flavor of the hot afternoon gone. As I walk to the riverbank, I hug myself and prod among the smoking ashes. There isn't but a curl of boot left to me, of no use at all. I look up, but I know I won't see him. He's waiting me out, waiting for me to move along the river.

We are coming to some sort of end. He's going to shoot me and that will be that. I am the cinnamon bear, all but run out, near-pestered until I am done in.

I try to be happy I'm alive, but it's not easy, naked save for my underpants, and them not anything worth gazing on. They are ragged and grimy, cut-down winter long underwears that once belonged to the old man himself. Shouldn't matter, but a fellow without clothes is just another animal in the woods. I reckon that's me now.

I look at the river once more. What I am going to do I have no idea. The old man would rather die than give up a fight. He will not stop until I am dead.

But I ain't dead. Not yet. Tired as I am, I want to get up over those mountains and find my father. There has to be a way. "First off," I say to the bone-dry slope before me. "You got to get back across this river, away from where he wants you to walk."

So I do that, moving northward once more. I wait to hear a gunshot. If I do hear it, it'll be too late to run, as the bullet will be doing its job on me.

The further I walk without hearing his rifle crack the hot afternoon air, the more I wonder. The old man says I owe him, and I thought for sure it was my life he wanted as payment, but could be he's changing his tune and wants to drag me back. To that, I say no.

How I will do that, I don't know. But crossing the river means I have bested him at one thing, at least. He's been herding me like a stray calf, driving me back toward the farm. But no more.

I set foot on the far bank for the first time. I should have crossed before I stripped down. If I had, I'd have my boots and clothes and knife. I am a fool, a fool, a fool.

I hear no laughs, no rifle shots nip at my heels. I should run, but I am barefooted and sore and tired. I see rocks that lead up toward trees. Beyond that there's another stretch of gray rock, then above that, ledges of red rock that stick out.

My feet pain me so that I have to set down often and rest them. It's slow going and I'm not making much progress, so I shuck off my underwear and tear it in half. It don't take much effort. I wrap each of my feet and peel strips to tie them about my ankles. A couple of test steps and I see it's not much of an improvement, but it is something.

The rest of the afternoon passes like that, me stepping and stopping, knowing I should move faster but not able to. By the time dark finds me I have left behind trees of size and figure I best look for cover under the stunty pines. The low brush scares me off since I tangled with the coyotes.

I don't blame them for being ornery. They didn't invite me into their home. I don't think I landed any death blows, but I sure sliced up one or two. If I come across others, I am now out of luck. No knife, no clothes, only me and my half-Indian skin.

It was already browner than the old man's and Mama's, but now I've taken on a hot glow like a fierce sunset and my whip

welts throb as I walk. I select a little knot of pines that look to
share the same root and set down beneath them. Heat from my
burned skin and cold from the coming night air fight over me.
The cold starts to win. I'm so dog-tired I rest my arms on my
knees and my head on my arms and I close my eyes and try not
to think. It doesn't work.

A small stone ain't much comfort, but I suck on one and
pretend it's a flavorful hunk of beef. It doesn't work. I nibble on
a pine branch, then on twigs from a short bush, but they don't
work, neither. All they do is make me want real food.

I can't have it and I can't stop thinking about it. Mostly
Mama's hot biscuits and chicken with gravy. And beef stew
with them gummy dumplings bubbling on top. Or pie. Mama
makes the best pie. Made the best pie.

I will never again taste Mama's pie crust nor any other dish
she made. Of all the reasons to hate the old man, it's thoughts
of Mama's cooking that fill me up with so much hate I feel my
heart thump faster. Tired as I am I can't find sleep for the
longest time. So I sit tight beneath the little pines and I think of
Mama.

CHAPTER TEN

It's slow climbing to get up these hills, as they are rockier than I thought from a distance, but they'll lead me to the knees of the mountains. That's where I can lose him after all. I need a place to hole up and wait him out, a cave or some such.

I've been thinking about the cinnamon bear most of the morning, wondering if he lived in a cave, and I come to something. I believe I have outlasted that bear. The old man said he dogged it for three days and I am in my fourth since I walked off the farm.

I climb higher, switchbacking and sliding now and again on drifts of loose dirt. The slope levels off and the gray rocks grow bigger up here. As it's more open, the sun warms everything, including me, and I fight the thought that I should have stayed along the river. My tongue wants for water and feels like it's filling my mouth. I lick my lips but they're dry, and when I swallow, I wish I hadn't.

I am not certain what makes me look toward a particular rock downslope of me, but I do, and I see a big rattler sunning himself. He doesn't give a care about me and I feel the same about him. I do wonder how many others there are around me, though. I carry a rock for a time as a weapon, but it's too heavy, so I let it drop again. It clunks and rolls. I look upslope for other snakes and that's when I see it.

The first sign of people, other than me and the old man, since I left the farm. It's a rusty jut of steel. Then I see it's two rails, like a small train was here once, long ago. Though what a train would be doing up here I have no notion.

I stand swaying, staring at those bars of steel poking out of the dry gravel. One sticks straight out of the bottom of the slope, the other is curved upward. I lick my lips and look around. I don't want to meet up with whatever can bend such a thick rail.

I cough, and it feels like I been punched in the back between my wing bones. I'm about done in. I am tired and cold and sore. My feet bled right through the wraps of undershorts. Heck, that happened in the first minutes of tying them on.

Crazy thoughts pass through my mind, like using tree bark for shoes. Or rocks. I wonder if I find a couple of flat rocks and strap them on me somehow. It's a fool's thinking, but that's what I am at this point.

I don't want this anymore. I don't want to be naked and cold and hungry and thirsty and tired. I want to stop all this. But the old man won't listen to me, and he sure won't leave me alone.

He's running me down, killing me. I got nothing else to give but that one thing Mama said was the most valuable thing we all have. Surprised me when she said it ain't a gun nor land nor a bearskin blanket, but our life.

That's all I got now and since I keep going, trying to get away from him, I reckon that means my life is worth keeping. But a creature can only take so much prodding and being chased before it turns on whatever's chasing it and defends itself.

If this is the way it's going to be, then this old place is as good as any to end it. I know it can only end one way. He has a gun and clothes and food and water, and I have nothing but my last, most valuable thing. But I will try.

I poke around here most of the morning. It's midday and I can't help but think of those noon meals Mama used to make.

The old man, he could eat a heap of food.

I learned to only eat what Mama put on my plate before I set down at the table. I can't get enough, though, especially the last year or so. I'm always hungry. Mama said it's 'cause I'm growing. The old man ain't growing no more, I said, so why does he put away so much of it?

"To feed his mean," Mama had whispered and winked one day while I was helping clear off the table.

I eyeball this place. I guess it's an old mine, what with the tracks, and a caved-in entrance that's filled with more rocks than I can shift in a month of steady workdays. I wonder if it was for gold or silver? I'd rather have gold as it's worth more cash money. As I poke about the spot, I think of buttered beans and corn and pork roast and thick bread drizzled with molasses. That's when I find the hole.

I step right where I ought not to and my foot doesn't stop where the ground should be. It keeps going, and I almost fall in. I should have. I'd land on my head and it'd be all over with.

But I don't fall in. I slide to the edge and claw myself back out, facedown on the dirt. My boy parts drag something fierce on the pit's rim. That's a tender spot to be scraping along gravel like that. I'm afraid to look down at myself, sure I'm all bloody and raw. I peek and it's a little redder than before, but nothing worse.

Funny how we can be worn to a nub and thinking we can't go on another step, then we get scared by something, and quick as that we're worked up. It don't last long, though. Once I know I'm safe, I lay on the gravel and feel my heart *bump-bump-bumping* and my breath fetching up and the hot sun draining me out once more.

My right foot is lower than the rest of me along the slumpy edge of that hole and I know when I have my breath again, I want to look in there. Can't help it, I got to know such things.

That's when the thought comes to me—what if the old man fell in there? Would it slow him down enough that I could get away? There's no way he'd be as dumb as me, though, and let himself fall in. He's rested and older and smarter . . . but is he?

I edge to the rim. It's a hole like most others, as wide at the mouth as a man's arms stretched outward. It looks to narrow some, but I can't see all the way down. I shift to one side, blocking the sunlight, and there's the bottom, a fair bit down. Looks to me like a dry well, a deep hole with nothing to show for it but a hole.

Gets me thinking how a man could dig such a hole alone. I reckon it would take two men to do such a thing. Two men who felt sure there was gold down there. Why dig a hole straight down? Could be the mine entrance at the base of the rock face caved in and they thought they'd get at their gold another way?

I shrug and sit up. I don't care much, as I have no need for gold. I do have a need to stay alive, and the longer I stay out in the hot sun and do nothing, the more dead I will become.

The hole is about ten paces before the old mine entrance, and the mountain above is all rock. There's lumps of dirt hanging off it like crumbs on the old man's face when he eats while he's drunk. Neither me nor Mama ever told him he had smears of egg or breadcrumbs in his whiskers. I wanted to laugh at him, but I knew how that would end.

I have no notion of how long it will take the old man to find me. He will in the end, though, so I set to my task. The whole time I do it, I feel like I am going against Mama somehow, and it feels wrong, sour in my mouth. But I go at it all the same.

What gives me the idea is the bunch of dried-out bushes clogged at the top of the hole. The way they're wedged, they could be sitting on solid ground.

Since I can't get any further north because I'm out of strength, I decide this idea is the best one I have. But these dry plants won't do, so I search for something more to lay over the hole.

Along the west edge of the mine site, past a big pile of blasted, raw-edge, gray and pink rocks, sits a jumble of planks, what's left of the miner's shack. Hard to believe somebody lived in it. Then again, Mama and I lived in the woodshed, and that wasn't no fun in winter when the snow and wind whistled through the cracks. I hope the miner at least had a friend up here in these high rocks.

I make a deal with myself as I select boards. I will take whatever punishment comes of it. What I mean is this: If the boards I lay across don't break under him or if he don't walk across them, then I will give over to whatever the old man figures on dealing me. If they collapse under him, I will see what comes of it.

Near as I can tell the hole is four or five man-heights deep. That is to say it would take four or five of the old man standing on his own shoulders—now ain't that a picture—to reach the top. Might be there's handholds along the sides, or a ladder down there. I don't know. That's another part of the deal I make with myself.

If he can climb out of there, I will take whatever he chooses to do to me once he catches me, which he will do. By then he'll be more riled than a wet cat.

CHAPTER ELEVEN

It's near dark and colder by the second. Colder than last night under the little pines. At least I had those. Here, I have nothing but a tumble of rocks and sun-puckered boards from the wrecked shack.

I lean them against rocks and make myself a hidey spot at the base of the old mine entrance. Can't hardly tell it's there from outside, and now that it's dark I expect the old man will have a devil of a time seeing me. It's not like I have a campfire to light the way for him.

It might all mean nothing anyway if he's been spying on me, which he likely has. All afternoon I eyed downslope, but didn't see anything looking like him moving up on me.

I sit with my knees pulled up and try not to rub the whip scabs on my back against the rock. I figure if I can't eat and I can't drink, I can at least sleep. Takes a while, but I get there.

Morning comes early, as I'm on a slope that sort of faces the sunrise. A soft, orange light creeps in on me and I wake right up. I remember where I am and I don't move right off. Not that I can anyway. My legs are seized up, so while I try to stretch and limber them, I peek out between the boards. There in the purple morning shadows, I see the old man leaning against a rock across the way.

"I hear you moving in there, 'skin." He puffs on his pipe and shifts his rifle to his other arm. "Best come on out and take your medicine." He coughs, a wet sound, and I know he is

276

unwell, likely the ague has gripped him. He is prone to it in the autumn.

Mama always made him poultices for his chest and he always threw them on the floor. He'd wrap up in blankets and sit before the cookstove with the door open and drink whiskey. What will he do now?

He has me this time, as I have backed myself into a corner. Behind me sits a mountain of rock, to my sides more of the same, and before me stands the old man with his rifle.

I lick my split, shredded lips and shove out from under the boards. A couple of them slide down and clunk against each other. The sound is loud in this cold, rocky place. I lean forward onto my knees, then stand and face him.

I know what he sees. And I know for a moment he is shocked. His red, wet eyes widen. He licks his lips and rubs his mouth with the back of his left hand like he always does. Then he shakes his head and looks like he's smelling something off. "Look at you, a filthy, naked, savage 'skin, nothin' more."

This is the first time, maybe since I was a baby under his roof, that he has seen me naked. That's what I am now, a naked animal. My feet are bleeding again, I can feel them. My hair, which I expect Mama was going to cut short soon, as she does each season, is dusty and shaggy like a hummock of sheep grass at the end of summer. I am more bone-stretched skin than boy.

As I walked these last days, I took to holding my right hand cupped in that hollow in the center of my chest, where the bones rise up like in a grand cathedral, Notre Dame is the one I'm thinking of. Mama showed me an illustration of it in her book about Europe.

He shakes a finger at me. "I knew you reminded me of someone. I see it now. You look like your father. Yeah, he was a filthy Indian, no better'n an animal. Should have known. One day—One day!—I go to town for supplies and he and that trollop of a daughter of mine couple like beasts!"

He shakes his head and raises a tired hand in my direction, then lets it fall. "And there . . . There's what I get for my troubles. A creature the likes of which the world should not have to look upon."

He is talking of me, of course. And looking at me again, full on, something he's rarely done for more than a blink or two at a time. But he's not blinking now, he's staring at me. Shaking his head and staring.

For long moments we look on each other, me leaning against the boulder, my nakedness only covered by dirt and dust from these mountains that are not what I pictured they'd be.

For a man who looked my whole life as if he was made of tree and rock, boulders on boulders, with hands like stout oak branches, the old man doesn't look all that big anymore. He looks sickly and small, sort of caved in on himself, curling inward like a clawed hand closing up.

A breeze pesters around a rock upslope of us, coaxing a soft, whistling sound. It stops and the dust settles. The old man looks away, then back to me. "Okay, best get to it." He sighs. "You owe me and now it's time for you to pay. I am sick of this foolishness and I am out of whiskey. Now come on, get walking." He jerks his chin at me. "Get on down here."

I stare at him and it comes to me that the story of the bear as he always told it was not true. Or at least he'd not told all of it. He never said what happened before he shot the bear. Never said how it was at the end. I think at the end that bear turned on him. It had to.

You pester something enough and it will turn and fight. Any man who does not want that from a foe is no man, for though that means he will shoot that thing he's pestering, he will shoot it in the back, not the front. That means the old man never let that young, hungry, tired cinnamon bear turn around and face him. Fight him. Instead he shot it from behind as it ran from him, scared and crying.

I don't move. For the first time, I don't do as the old man says. His saggy face shakes and his wet eyes don't leave mine. I know he's going to shoot me.

"No," I say, and shake my head.

He looks tired and mean and I see his cheek muscles working beneath his gray, scraggly beard. Then he smiles.

"I expect you're heading north, eh? Let me guess, to your father's people." He spits and coughs. "Yeah, I thought so, I can see it in your soulless eyes, you redskin bastard. Well, I'll let you in on a little secret."

He leans forward and smiles again. "You want to meet your father, you come back to the ranch. That's right. Been there all along. I found out he was dallying with my own daughter and kin, my Mary, why, I laid him low. Didn't take much, invited him in the stable for a sip of firewater. I know how you 'skins like your liquor."

He shifts the rifle to his other arm. I watch him do it.

"I smiled and patted his shoulder and told him I knew how it was and that it was okay, see? Then I give him a drink and welcomed him to stay at the ranch as long as he liked. In fact, forever. Then I smiled and hit him on the head with a peening hammer."

He coughs again and spits a green wad, then wipes his mouth with his sleeve. He looks at me. "Then I chucked him in the sty. Been there since. So you come back to the ranch, I'll introduce you to him proper. You can stay there as long as you like. Forever, see?" He laughs again, and it ends in another cough.

Nothing he says surprises me. It all makes odd sense. Like when there's a buck at the edge of a meadow, and you can't see him, but you know he's there. Then he finally steps into view.

The old man has lost his smile once more and he walks

toward me, looking small and old. As if the weight of the rifle is almost too much for him to carry. He's looking at me, not where he is walking. For the first time in my life, he is doing what I want him to do.

He steps on the planking and for a moment it looks as if it will hold him up. It barely sags. But as with everything eventually, people and boards and rocks and animals, time has made it dry and brittle. With no warning, the planks crack, and he looks at me, the beginning of surprise on his face. Then he drops into the hole.

CHAPTER TWELVE

He makes a lot of noise on the way down. I think he hits the sides, bounces off rocks as he drops. It doesn't take him long to get there, then there's a quiet moment or two, long enough to draw a big breath. That's when he commences to screaming and howling.

"Both my legs are broke! I see the bone! I see the bone! Oh god, you help me, boy! Get my pack, you got to help me. Go fetch a rope or something. Help me, boy!"

I walk wide around the pit, and I do go to his pack. He left it leaning against a big rock. Inside I see a canteen and when I lift it out, I am pleased to feel it's mostly full.

There's food in there, too, some of that jerked meat he never lets me or Mama eat, and a hard crust of bread and a block of cheese he's likely been gnawing on as he walks. I sample it all, a little at a time, and sip that cool water from the canteen and listen to him carrying on.

"Make a rope, boy, use my clothes, my blanket! Hurry! It's unbearable, I tell you! I ain't got whiskey. Got to get home . . . Oh, Martha Anne, oh it hurts . . ."

There aren't any boots in the pack, but there is an old pair of socks Mama made him last Christmas. They smell foul but I tug them on over my raggy feet and pull out the blanket. It's wool and has some holes, but it's warmer than being naked. He's got other clothes in there, a shirt, drawers, but I don't worry about that just now.

281

I walk over to the pit and sit down, close, but not so close he can see me. He has that rifle.

"You up there, boy?" His voice trembles and I know he's crying.

"Yes," I say.

"Help me, boy!"

For the first time, I have things to say to him. So I do. "You know, I am the last of your line . . . old man. I carry your blood in my body. And now it's on my hands. We have a lot in common, old man."

"This ain't the way it should be," he says.

His voice is wet, raw.

"Boy, listen to me! All will be forgiven! I tell you true! Come home and we'll run that farm together, boy! You and me!"

I smile. I am relieved. "Good," I say. "I wanted to hear that."

"What?"

"You. Begging."

He screams then, and I imagine he shifted around some down there. Broken bones will play devil with you if you move too sudden.

"It doesn't have to be this way, boy!"

"You should have thought of that," I tell him. "A long, long time ago."

I sit quiet for a few minutes, my eyes closed, my face to the morning sun. I listen to the wind, to the old man whimpering like a dying dog.

Some time later, I lean forward and look down at him. I am careful because of the rifle.

"Too easy," I say. Then I stand and tug on his pack and walk away.

Down in the pit, the old man whimpers, sounds that soon only he can hear.

I reckon now I'll get to see what's beyond these mountains.

Already I have made it farther than the cinnamon bear ever got to.

After a while, I hear a rifle shot. I stop and listen. I do not hear another. I get back to walking north once more.

And once more I am followed, this time by ghosts.

ABOUT THE AUTHOR

Matthew P. Mayo is an award-winning author of novels and short stories. He and his wife, photographer Jennifer Smith-Mayo, along with their trusty pup, Miss Tess, rove the byways of North America in search of hot coffee and high adventure. For more information, visit MatthewMayo.com.

ABOUT THE EDITOR

Hazel Rumney has lived most of her life in Maine, although she also spent a number of years in Spain and California while her husband was in the military. She has worked in the publishing business for almost thirty years. Retiring in 2011, she and her husband traveled throughout the United States visiting many famous and not-so-famous western sites before returning to Thorndike, Maine, where they now live. In 2012, Hazel reentered the publishing world as an editor for Five Star Publishing, a part of Cengage Learning. During her tenure with Five Star, she has developed and delivered titles that have won Western Fictioneers Peacemaker Awards, Will Rogers Medallion Awards, and Western Writers of America Spur Awards, including the double Spur Award–winning novel *Wild Ran the Rivers* by James D. Crownover. Western fiction is Hazel's favorite genre to enjoy. She has been reading the genre for more than five decades.

The employees of Five Star Publishing hope you have enjoyed this book.

Our Five Star novels explore little-known chapters from America's history, stories told from unique perspectives that will entertain a broad range of readers.

Other Five Star books are available at your local library, bookstore, all major book distributors, and directly from Five Star/Gale.

Connect with Five Star Publishing

Visit us on Facebook:
 https://www.facebook.com/FiveStarCengage

Email:
 FiveStar@cengage.com

For information about titles and placing orders:
 (800) 223-1244
 gale.orders@cengage.com

To share your comments, write to us:
 Five Star Publishing
 Attn: Publisher
 10 Water St., Suite 310
 Waterville, ME 04901